A CAT'S GUIDE TO SAVING THE KINGDOM

Dragoncat Book 3

CHRIS BEHRSIN

Edited by
WAYNE M. SCACE

A Cat's Guide to Saving the Kingdom Copyright © 2021 by Chris Behrsin.
All Rights Reserved.

No part of this book may be reproduced in any form or by any electronic or mechanical means including information storage and retrieval systems, without permission in writing from the author. The only exception is by a reviewer, who may quote short excerpts in a review.

This book is a work of fiction. Names, characters, places, and incidents either are products of the author's imagination or are used fictitiously. Any resemblance to actual persons, living or dead, events, or locales is entirely coincidental.

Editing by Wayne M. Scace
Proofreading by Carol Brandon
Cover Design Layout by Chris Behrsin

To my brother Tim, and his two cats Raffy and Taffy – three incredibly generous individuals.

I

DRAGON EGG-AND-SPOON

Purple mist loomed on the horizon. It stretched out from expanse to expanse, and beyond it stood the warlocks and the threat of war. It whipped up a stench in the air, reminiscent of rotten vegetable juice. It brought with it a bitter wind that seeped right through my fur, washing away what should be the warmth of spring.

The warlocks weren't far from Dragonsbond Academy now, and beyond it – so all the Driars said – were thousands and thousands of magical creatures, an army growing by the day. But they would be no match for us, because we had dragons, and we had magic too, and we also had me.

To many, I was just a cat. But to the prophecies, I was a mighty Bengal, descendant of the great Asian leopard cat. The crystals foretold I would defeat the most powerful of warlocks, Astravar. Just as soon as I finally worked out how to get my staff, I could fly out there on Salanraja's back, nestled within her corridor of spikes that served as a natural saddle for cats. Then, with said staff clenched between my strong feline jaws, I would shoot a beam of energy at him. I'd knock him off his bone dragon, and I'd finally be able to rest.

I just wished I could fast forward to that point. Because, right this moment, I wasn't flying towards the mist with a staff in my mouth.

Instead, I had a spoon sticking out of it, with an egg balanced precariously on top of it, and I felt like an absolute fool.

"Can't I just drop the egg?" I asked inside my mind to my dragon, Salanraja. "*This is tremendously boring, and my mouth hurts...*"

"*Gracious demons, no,*" Salanraja said. "*We have a chance of winning this, and I want to show the other dragons how magnificent I can be, even with my 'unnatural' spikes.*"

"But what's the point of it all? Eggs are much better for eating than carrying in your mouth on a spoon."

"*Prestige,*" Salanraja said. "*And that is worth all the food in the world.*"

Really, there was no telling my dragon. No matter how much I argued with her, she kept telling me we had to win at least one event on 'Sports Day'. Or at least if we couldn't win, she thought we had to at least try.

It was ridiculous, really. I would much rather sit in Aleam's study by the fireplace, waiting for someone to bring me my staff until Astravar came, and then I could fly out and fulfil the prophecy. But every year there had to be a 'Sports Day', even if war was looming on the horizon. Especially if war is looming on the horizon, Driar Yila had told us one assembly. Because during such times we needed to keep our spirits up and it would help us stay fighting fit for when the warlocks actually marched in. We didn't know where they'd march yet. But we apparently had to be prepared.

So, they'd had me tied to Salanraja's leg, as we stumbled over to the finish line – last. Then they'd had us flying all kinds of stunts, making me dizzy. I felt like I was chasing my tail for ages once I finally returned to the ground. Now, it was the 'dragon egg-and-spoon race', the most pointless activity in the whole wide world. Our goal was to land on the top of the keep tower as fast as possible, making sure that we passed over the designated checkpoints as I, all the while, kept my egg precariously balanced on the spoon.

There came a cry from my right, and I nearly jumped. This almost sent the egg flying, and Salanraja sent out a desultory groan in response.

Rine flew past on his blue dragon, Ishtkar, or should I say they dived together towards the ground so fast that I thought they were going to bore a crater. But right at the last minute, Ishtkar pulled herself back up, and Rine shot back up, sending out a tail of ice behind him from his staff in his right hand. I wondered how he could keep the egg on his spoon in his left until I noticed the glistens in the ice crystals attached to it.

"He's cheating!" I said. "He's using his magic to keep the egg affixed to his spoon."

Salanraja chuckled for a moment, but then she cut off her laughter as if worried her rumbling belly might cause me to drop the egg. "*All's fair in the dragon egg-and-spoon. As long as the magic doesn't end up disrupting the flight of someone else.*"

"But it does disrupt. It's distracting. They should disqualify him..."

"It doesn't matter," Salanraja said. "*Because he's not going to win first place flying like that. He knows it though, and he's going for the stunt prize. Now shut up, because we're in the lead and I really need to focus.*"

She was right. I could see a few dragons behind us, but no one yet in front. We only had to fly between the westmost and eastmost towers of Dragonsbond Academy and then land on the keep tower. Then we'd win the race. So long as I didn't drop the egg or spoon, that was, which were together making my mouth feel really sore.

The wind whipped past me, and I could tell that we were going fast. But at least Salanraja was flying steady. After all, this was nowhere near as bad as the dragon stunt show.

"How long do we have to keep this up for?" I asked.

"*Just a few minutes. Now just focus. If we win this, we'll be the pride of all the dragons and students in the academy.*"

"Yeah, right." They'd probably tell me I'd cheated. Or that I wasn't a suitable competitor because I was a cat. Or some other nonsense that the humans here liked to spout.

There came a whoosh from beside me, and then a familiar giggling sound. "Here, kitty, kitty," someone called out, and I turned my head to see Ange. Usually, I was more than happy to see her. But this time, in the set of her narrowed eyes, I could tell she wasn't here to play fair.

Just like Rine, she ejected a stream of magic behind her. But instead of pretty patterns of ice, twisting branches shot out from the glowing green crystal on her staff, eventually dissipating into the sky metres behind. They gave her extra propulsion, which was how she had caught up so fast. With her other hand, she held her spoon without shaking it. It wasn't surprising, really, as she'd hardened the skin on her arm to the texture of wood. Green lithe branches sprouted out of her fingertips, twisting around the spoon and fixing the egg in place.

"They're all using magic. This isn't fair."

"Will you just shut up," Salanraja said. *"They're using the magic because they feel they need it. But don't forget, while the other dragons have been lazy because they thought they could rely on their riders' magic, we've trained for this for weeks."*

That was certainly true. Salanraja had taken me out on numerous flights, three times a day, saying that she was respecting my wishes by flying gently – but also at an incredible speed.

"Here kitty, kitty," Ange said again, and she edged her blue dragon, Quarl close enough that I could leap across. "Why don't you come over and sit on my lap?" She laughed.

The offer was tempting, admittedly. Quarl often seemed to me a much smoother flyer than Salanraja.

"Don't you dare," Salanraja said. *"If the rider leaves its mount, we'll be instantly disqualified."*

My dragon's rudeness and chagrin made it even more tempting for me to accept Ange's bait. But, in all honesty, I wanted to win. I'd had enough of the students here thinking that I couldn't do what they could because I was a cat. It didn't matter if I was destined to save the world from Astravar's wrath, everyone here in Dragonsbond Academy seemed to look down on me, as if a primal part of them couldn't quite fathom why I wasn't on permanent rat catching duty.

Even Ange, sometimes…

"I've had enough of this," Salanraja said. *"Hold on to yourself and hold on to that egg."*

"I've nothing to hold on w—"

I didn't have time to finish my thought, as Salanraja lurched to the side suddenly and bashed Quarl aside. The blue dragon let out a roar that cut through the air. I was disorientated for a moment – slightly dizzy – but I kept my focus on the egg and ducked to the side at the last minute to stop it falling off. I came to my senses and peered through a gap within Salanraja's corridor of spikes with one eye.

I mewled in satisfaction as I saw Ange's spoon plummeting to the ground, Quarl diving headlong right after it. Fortunately for her, the egg was still wrapped in the vines and didn't fall off the spoon. Ange and Quarl caught up with it and Ange clutched it within her grasp. But the manoeuvre had turned Quarl around, now flying away from us.

"Isn't that against the rules? Forget using magic, that's downright dirty of you, Salanraja."

"The rules say we can't use magic against other fliers. But there's nothing about not using pure muscle to bash them out of the way."

"It will certainly slow her," I said, and I looked back at Quarl and Ange, now becoming pinpricks on a low layer of grey floating cloud. "But it wouldn't have been my fault, you know, if you'd sent the egg off towards the ground. That was quite a risk you took, Salanraja."

"I thought you had perfect balance. The grace of the great Asian leopard cat, and all that..."

"I'm good at balancing myself, not at balancing things hanging out of my mouth."

"Well, you seem to be doing quite a good job at it," Salanraja said. "Now let me concentrate. I need to get ready for a perfect landing."

I wasn't listening to her, because I was focused on a small charcoal dragon gaining on us fast. Its rider was on top of it and hadn't even bothered to draw her staff, instead keeping her body tucked towards the dragon's neck to gain momentum. Her platinum blonde hair whipped back in the wind. Clearly, she didn't need magic, and she had her spoon tucked to her chest underneath her chin, using the dragon's head to shield it from the wind.

"I don't think we're going to win."

"What do you mean?" Salanraja asked. "I'm just about to come in to land on the tower."

"Seramina and Hallinar... They've saved all their energy until this last leg."

"Gracious demons," Salanraja said, and she hazarded a quick glance behind her. "I might have known. That mind-witch is a crafty one."

Fortunately, I knew what I had to do to stop her. I only needed to take a leaf out of Ange's book and distract her. If everyone else was allowed to use their magic, I thought I'd use mine too.

"Hang on, Salanraja. I've got this."

"What are you up to, Bengie?"

I didn't answer. Instead, I summoned the beast from within. I closed my eyes and tried to divert my focus away from the pain writhing in my transforming muscles. All the while, I focused on the spoon, on keeping it clenched within my strengthening but expanding jaw.

When I opened my eyes, I felt strong, and I felt complete. I'd only transformed into a chimera a few times since I gained the ability, and though I hated the act of transforming, it felt good to be this beast. I lifted my paw and extended my sharp claws, examining them. But I bit down the instinct to roar, as I wanted to keep that spoon clenched within my mouth. It now felt flimsy and fragile, as if part of a child's play set.

"You idiot, Bengie... Change back," Salanraja said.

"No... Get closer, and I'll scare her."

"You're making me sink, Bengie. You're far too heavy as a chimera."

"Just shut up and get close to her. I can scare her into dropping that spoon."

"It's too late, you moron. Oh, why, Bengie? We would have won. Why did you have to spoil this all now?"

Indeed, Hallinar seemed to be accelerating towards us. But what I didn't realise at the time was that we were actually slowing down. They passed overhead and to the right of us. I thought of turning back, but Hallinar already had her front claws raised, ready to land on the tower. She touched down with a perfectly graceful landing, and a bugle called out from somewhere within the academy walls below.

"We can take second place," I said to Salanraja.

"*There is no second place,*" Salanraja said, her spirits sounding ever so slightly dashed. "*After that, I'm not cooking for you tonight.*"

"Fine," I said. But I in all honesty wasn't too happy about it. I groaned softly.

Salanraja crooned beneath my feet sympathetically. She probably felt my intense disappointment about my food and didn't want to let it linger. We were bonded after all. "*Tell you what,*" she said. "*There's a second round of stunt flying coming up, more about choreography to music than sheer aerodynamics. If we can win that, then I'll reconsider letting you feast with me.*"

But it wasn't meant to be, because all of a sudden, a second call of bugles came from the wide stone towers of Dragonsbond Academy. On the top of them, prefects with their red cloaks craned their heads to look up at us. The sun glinted off the instruments pressed to their mouths. The tune they sounded had an essence of urgency in their notes. Though the bugles were loud, they were soon drowned out by a roar of dragons coming from those dragons who remained in the towers.

"What's that?" I asked Salanraja.

She growled. "*Sports Day is cancelled,*" she said, this time making it her turn to sound disappointed.

"What, why?"

"*I don't know,*" Salanraja said. "*But Olan just told me we're to return to Dragonsbond Academy at once.*"

2

PRIDE AND SUPERFICIALITY

Salanraja scudded down against the ground at the centre of the bailey. Given we would have taken second place if it weren't for the cancellation, we were the first to land on virtually empty ground.

Some guards milled around the closed portcullis though, and many of the serving staff had come out of the doors to the castle, as if waiting for something to happen. The bugle call that cancelled Sports Day had clearly been for something important. Meanwhile, dandelion puffs and grass seeds waltzed gently on the cooling breeze, and I wondered if they'd find any suitable ground to grow from with this whole place stinking of rotten vegetable juice.

"*Get off,*" Salanraja said, and I didn't hesitate to follow her orders. I'd been so long up in the air with her, I was feeling a little queasy. I sprinted down her tail, and she lifted into the air, leaving me standing alone there. She'd been ordered to make room for the other dragons to land, so as not to create any traffic problems. No one had yet told us what the urgency was, but I knew it was a matter of great importance.

I just hoped that the warlocks hadn't decided to march, because I didn't have my staff yet. In all honesty, I was looking forward to clutching it in my teeth and unleashing the power at Astravar. But it wasn't so much the battle itself I was looking forward to. Rather, I was looking forward to the praise and adulation I'd get after the battle.

King Garmin, I was certain, would offer me a grand gift for my efforts in defeating the most powerful warlock in the land. And I would ask for tithes of a house in the countryside outside Cimlean, with lots of room for me and Ta'ra – wherever she was right now – to run around in. I'd let Rine and Ange live with us as well, and Aleam could visit along with Seramina whenever they wanted.

I'd already thought of the problem of feeding our three dragons – Salanraja, Ishtkar, and Quarl – and I'd decided that I'd also ask for a cattle rancher, a shepherd, a fisherman, and a huntsman to be employed on our grounds. They could live in a separate house, of course, and they could each have a cat as long as they kept them away from mine and Ta'ra's territory and treated them well instead of employing them as rat catchers. Of course, the king would have to keep sending us tithes of sheep, chickens, and cattle, but that could be my reward for saving the kingdom. I could live, in other words, like a lord.

My mouth watered at the thought of all the nutritious food I could eat there – much of it roasted by not one, but three dragons. It was only natural, really – I'd had to accept that I probably now had no way of returning to my home in South Wales. Which meant that I had to find an alternative way to make life just as good as it used to be, if not better.

There came a cool gust from above, and the massive shadow of Quarl passed over me. Ange's dragon came into land, with Ishtkar and Rine flying only a short distance behind them. Ange paused a moment to watch Rine land, and then both riders scurried down the sides of their dragons to hit the floor at the same time.

Their dragons took off towards the East Tower. Rine and Ange looked just about to step up to each other, when another dragon blocked their path. A smallish citrine dragon flew right between them and landed, pushing Ange back as if in revolt. Bellari stood up in the dragon's saddle and scanned around her. Her eyes fell on me first, and she frowned. Then she turned to Ange and gave her an even more sour look. Finally, she scurried down her dragon on Rine's side and embraced him in her arms.

"Oh, you were such a fine stuntman up there," she said, brushing Rine's hair away from his cheek. Her dragon lifted off, as Rine planted a prolonged kiss on his girlfriend. I growled, liking this perhaps even less than Ange did. In many ways, Bellari was even more of an enemy to me than Astravar, and I had absolutely no idea of how to stop her from disrupting my plans.

Ange had turned her head away from them and instead was gazing up at her dragon turning in a circle to approach his chamber in the West Tower. I should have been angry with her, really, after how she'd played in the dragon egg-and-spoon.

"Of course you should be mad at her," Salanraja told me. *"For what she pulled, you shouldn't talk to her for at least a week."*

"Don't be stupid," I said. *"Ange is our friend."* I walked over to Ange, meowing.

She looked down at me, her eyes wide as if in surprise. "I would have thought you'd be angry at me," she said. "I'm sorry, I can get so competitive sometimes."

I rubbed myself against her bare calf. "All's fair in the dragon egg-and-spoon," I said, reciting Salanraja's exact words during the race.

At that, Ange laughed. "Oh, Ben," she said. "You're becoming more like us every day."

"I hope I'm still retaining my feline mannerisms. Because I'm a descendant of the great Asian Leopard cat, and if my ancestors can see me today from cat heaven, I want them to be proud."

"Don't worry, you're still as cat-like as cats come. Without the talking-like-humans part, of course. Come to think of it, I'd never imagined how a cat would hold an egg-and-spoon before now, but you held it exactly like I would have thought a cat would."

I mewled and rubbed up against her leg once again. Now, I was purring loudly. Ange reached down and picked me up in her warm arms. I looked up into her wide, bright eyes. Meanwhile, another dragon came down to land just a short distance away, and Ange turned her back to it as if to shield me from the stiff wind.

"What's all this commotion about?" I asked. "I thought we'd be flying all day."

"Yes," Ange said, and she glanced at the gates to the academy. "It's such a shame, isn't it?"

"I guess," I said, not quite meaning it. I'd much rather be curled up by Aleam's fireplace right now – even if Ta'ra wasn't here to provide extra warmth anymore. But then, to survive in this place and not be demoted to rat catching duty, I'd learned you needed to show at least a little enthusiasm.

"You don't sound like you mean it," Ange said. "But I understand. You weren't born into this life, after all."

"Neither were you," I pointed out.

"Ah, but I know that every day what I do helps my father, and I also know I'm providing a service to my kingdom."

I yawned and considered jumping back down and getting a drink from the fountain. But I remembered my question remained unanswered. "So, what's all this commotion about, then?"

Ange shook her head as she tickled me under the chin. "Haven't the faintest. But I'm guessing it's something important."

"You think the warlocks are finally going to march? I haven't even got my staff yet."

"I said I don't know, Ben," and she sounded ever so slightly huffy about it. "Why don't you ask Seramina? She has the gift of clairvoyance, right?"

"Sometimes," I said. "When she decides it's worthwhile to use it."

My words didn't quite seem to register with Ange as she was gazing over towards the door of the West Tower where Rine stood with one leg propped up against the stone. He had Bellari in his arms and was holding her very close as he stroked her hair and gazed longingly into her eyes. I smelled a slight whiff of stress coming out of Ange's glands, and I let out a softer meow this time to comfort her.

"Why don't you do something about that?" I asked.

"What?"

"Rine…"

Ange looked down as her grip on me loosened slightly. "Oh, not this again. When are you going to learn, Ben? Rine and I aren't meant to be."

"But you have feelings for him," I said. "And he has feelings for you."

"Do you know that for sure?" Ange said, raising an eyebrow.

"Of course," I said. "I can smell them."

"You can smell them... How do you know they're for me?"

"I just know, okay?"

Ange shook her head and that wistful look returned to her eyes. "Rine's always been so... You, know... Superficial. He's never really been in touch with his feelings, Ben. He doesn't really know what he wants, and I'm not sure he ever will."

"That's why you have to show him," I said. "When I want food, I don't just keep quiet about it. I meow and I meow, and I don't stop until I get what I want."

"Is that how you think love works, Ben?" Ange asks. "You just keep moaning about it until you get it?"

"Why not? It's how you get everything else in this world."

Ange sighed. "You still have a lot to learn about humans. Life is so much more complicated than that." She loosened her grip, so I jumped down before she dropped me on the hard cobblestones beneath.

Virtually as soon as I hit them, there came a roar from the sky. Ange and I both looked up at once, and even Rine and Bellari got a little distracted from their snuggles. At first, I thought it was another dragon coming in to land from the race, making everyone know it had at least got fifth place. But the roar wasn't coming from that direction, but from behind the gate.

A black dragon flew towards it. It wasn't a charcoal like Seramina's dragon, Hallinar, or Prefect Asinda's dragon, Shadorow. More, it was jet black and, I could swear, almost shiny. On it sat a man in a bright red robe, and an equally red, flat hat.

The mist had accumulated in the distance, and I didn't see the other five dragons until a moment later. But behind the jet dragon came a dozen other dragons – two ruby, two citrine, one stone grey, one charcoal, four emerald, and two sapphire blue. It appeared that this man, whoever he was, had decided to fly a little ahead of his flock.

"Well I never," Ange said.

"What?"

"That's Corralsa, Prince Arran's dragon."

"Prince who?"

"Does no one ever tell you anything, Ben? Prince Arran is King Garmin's nephew, and also the air marshal of all the dragon riders in Illumine. He's a very important man, and I've heard he's also incredibly handsome."

"Great," I said. "Another official."

Ange said nothing to that, but I could hear her heart thumping in her chest with my sensitive ears as she watched him with those wide eyes as he came in to land. His dragon thudded down just behind the gate, and Captain Onus of the guards went over to greet him.

"I knew it," Ange said. "So handsome…"

"Does that mean you're not interested in Rine, anymore?" I asked.

"I," Ange looked back at Rine and Bellari. "I never told you I was interested in Rine. But this man – I've heard so much about him…"

The prince clambered down from the saddle of his jet-black dragon, not even looking once at Captain Onus. He strolled in our direction, with his head held high and his hands clasped behind his back. He stopped a moment beside us, then turned to Ange, and gave her a look like she'd just burned his lunch. He then looked down at me without moving his head. "Why, pray tell me, student, is there a cat out from the cattery at this time? We don't fund this academy for raising pets."

Ange looked far too gobsmacked to answer, so I did so for her.

"I – pray tell you – am a Bengal, *direct* descendant of the great Asian leopard cat, and I'm of great importance to this academy. I don't belong, in other words, on rat catching duty."

"Oh, so you're the talking cat," the prince said. "I've heard a lot about your affairs."

"Then you must have heard—" I started.

"Oh, do shut up," the prince said. "I don't care whether you can talk or not. This kingdom will always be run by humans, and animals are meant to serve us, which means your opinion is not important to me. Only your servitude is."

"But he's much more than an animal," Ange said, her nostrils now flared.

"And students do not have a voice here until they're old enough to hold council," the prince said. "Now, if you excuse me, I have important issues to be seeing to." He spun around on his heel and strode off.

"So… You still like the handsome prince?" I asked Ange.

"Beauty is in the eye of the beholder," she replied.

"And why do you think he's here?"

"I don't know," Ange said. "But I'm sure it's the reason for Sports Day being cancelled."

"Then, maybe I'll find out if anyone knows anything," I said.

"Yeah, do that," Ange replied. She no longer seemed her usual buoyant self. Rine and Bellari had since vanished into the West Tower's corridors, probably out of sight of the prince. Ange looked once more over to where they had been, then she huffed, and she stormed off towards the fountain.

I decided it was probably a good idea to leave her alone. Besides, Ange was right. To learn more about this situation, I needed someone with the gift of clairvoyance. So I strolled towards Aleam's study, where Seramina had been staying for the last few months.

MEDITATION

Seramina sat on Aleam's mahogany bench with her eyes closed, her legs crossed with both feet resting on her thin thighs, and her hands resting lightly on her knees, palms facing upwards. Motes of dust danced around her like fairies, sparkling in the light coming through Aleam's gauze curtains. Seramina had removed the velvet cushions from the bench, and they instead stood propped up against the wall underneath the window.

Aleam's study always felt kind of empty nowadays, with Ta'ra – my old Cat Sidhe friend – no longer being there. She'd gone to look after the other Cat Sidhe's in the Caldmines Forest. I'd wanted to visit her, but before I'd even had time to do so the warlocks had set up camp outside the castle, and visits to and from Dragonsbond Academy became highly restricted. So, in other words, I hadn't seen her for quite a few months.

Now, only one bowl lay for food on the floor, and only one bowl for water. There was no cat there for me to snuggle against and get warm. But it was the lessons I missed the most. I'd taught Ta'ra a lot about what it's like to be a cat, and she'd taught me a lot about what it's like to be human too, even if she was a fairy.

I guess I had Salanraja, and I had people like Aleam, Ange, Rine, and even Seramina to keep me company. Yet none of them made a suitable replacement for Ta'ra.

I'd tried interacting with the other cats here, but they just didn't seem to understand me. For a long time, I'd felt a foreigner to the humans and had to learn to deal with it. What I hadn't considered so much was that now to my own brethren I was a foreigner too.

So, every time I saw Seramina occupying Ta'ra's spot, I just felt kind of odd. Still, she was a lot kinder than she used to be, and I didn't want to deal with her old, scary self again. So, I made sure to keep in her good graces. As she sat, she took deep breaths, and she didn't seem to notice anything around her at all.

I really didn't enjoy entering the room and not getting the attention I deserved. So, I went up to her and meowed. Seramina ignored me a moment until I jumped on the sofa and rubbed my nose into her belly.

She shuddered, backed up against the sofa, and then looked down at me with those scary fiery eyes that I'd learned to fear. This only lasted for a moment, before her gaze reverted to that usual shade of pale blue-grey.

"Oh, hello, Ben," she said softly. "I'm sorry, I'm trying to stay in control. You must be quiet, by the way. Aleam's sleeping in the next room."

I pushed my nose up to her again, and she raised her head and stroked me. But her movements didn't seem quite real, as if she wasn't completely there or didn't realise I was present. "What do you call this again? This thing that you do?"

"Meditation," Seramina said. "It's something that they taught us to do in mind-school, but I never took it seriously until now. I've heard rumours it didn't come from our world, but our sages actually learned it by studying yours from afar."

"And it calms the mind, soothes the soul, you say?"

"You should try it. I think it would do you good."

"I can't cross my legs like you can," I said. "And I can't sit for that long without sleeping or needing to groom myself."

"I'm sure if you learned to still your mind, you could do it too."

"No," I said. "It's impossible."

Seramina watched me passively. A long time ago, her stare had frightened me so much, I'd not wanted to go anywhere near her. But now – it's strange to say – but when she was calm, after doing this meditation thing, her gaze seemed the most natural in the world.

I pushed myself up against the crook of her elbow, and then I lay down on her lap, purring. She moved slowly to stroke me, and I rolled over on my back to let her rub my belly. It was so relaxing being there, in such calmness, that I almost fell asleep. Maybe I would have, if I hadn't remembered I needed information from Seramina.

"Say, have you heard about the prince's arrival?" I asked.

Seramina raised her eyebrows. "I haven't, no…"

"I just saw him arrive. I was with Ange, and you should have seen the way he treated her."

"And which prince do you mean?"

"Prince Arran, the air marshal. Apparently, I should know who he is."

"Oh," Seramina said, and she looked towards the door which was slightly ajar. Aleam's soft snores emanated from behind it. "I'm sure he has a good reason to be here."

"I'm sure he has, and I was hoping you'd be able to tell me what it is."

Seramina held her breath for a moment. "Ben, I don't do that anymore."

"What?"

"Use my magic willy-nilly. Now Astravar has met me, I'm at just as much risk of him finding his way into my mind as you are of him finding his way into yours. Or if not him, the dark magic… So, I must only use my gifts when absolutely necessary. Unless you have a good reason to need to know why the prince is here, I can't tell you. There's too much at stake."

Come to think of it, Astravar hadn't been visiting my dreams much lately either. It was as if, after defeating his demon chimera that he'd lost interest in me.

"I need to know," I said.

"Why?"

"Because he was rude to Ange and me, and I don't trust him."

"That's not a good enough reason," Seramina said. "You didn't use to trust me either, if you remember. But, with me, you had nothing to fear, and this is probably true with this prince too."

Suddenly, I caught a whiff of smoked trout coming from my bowl on the floor. I groaned, and I stood up shaking my legs, and dropped off the chair. The fish in the bowl was dry, and in another bowl the water was full of fur balls. This meditation thing might have been great for Seramina, but she wasn't doing her duty in replacing the food on time. She still, it seemed, had a lot to learn.

"If you're hungry, I've just roasted up a whole deer," Salanraja said in my mind. Really, I was incredibly glad to hear her voice.

"Great. Dinnertime," I said. *"But I thought you were angry with me and would not let me have any of your meal."*

I could have eaten in the dining hall. But the food had been pretty bad lately, apparently because of the warlocks cutting off supply routes.

"I changed my mind," Salanraja said. *"Unless you don't want it."*

"No, no, I'm on my way," I said. I thought about saying goodbye to Seramina, but she already had her eyes closed and was back in her trance, as if she had already forgotten about my visit. I groaned, deeply, and I left the room.

4

VENISON

As I climbed the spiral staircase up to Salanraja's tower, the sweet aroma of the different varieties of meats the dragons had procured and roasted with their own flames seeped out from the entranceways to their chambers. There were aromas of rabbit, mutton, various types of fish, and so many other delicious feasts all melded into one tantalising fragrance.

The dragons' towers were the place to be at dinner time. Due to what they called the 'pre-siege', the kitchens only served soup with a tiny bit of meat in there and lots of disgusting vegetables, and portions of inedible rice, potatoes and bread. Because of this, many riders had taken to eating with their dragons, who flew out specially to get the meat they needed.

When I complained about the poor nutritional quality of the food to Matron Canda, she said that she could serve me up 'cat food' if I wanted. But I knew what that meant. They'd put the worst meat processed in tiny chunks and serve it out to me all mashed up and yucky. My owners back in South Wales had never served me that processed stuff that I'd heard other cats had to endure, and I didn't intend to start eating it now either.

Thus, every time I climbed the spiral staircase of the East Tower, I was tempted to drop into another dragon's chamber and steal their food before I even reached Salanraja. But I also knew trying to take food off a dragon I wasn't bonded to would mean certain death.

I entered Salanraja's chamber soon enough, and the venison she'd promised me lay in the unexposed corner next to the opening to the wider wall. The meat was brown and had that smoky scent to it that I knew and loved all too well.

I chirped a thank you to Salanraja, who looked down at me with her massive yellow eyes, a slight grin stretched across her rubbery lips. Then, I rushed over to the venison and tore off a strip of meat, and I dropped it by the opening to the outer world from which came a nice cooling breeze.

The sun was now getting low in the sky, bringing a pleasant warmth that offset against the breeze. The air didn't smell as fresh as it should either. I couldn't see the purple mist from this side of the castle, but I could smell the rotten vegetable stench of dark magic. I had thought at first it was only Astravar that smelled like that, but it turned out that all warlocks and their creations did.

This is how this whole world would smell if the warlocks took over this world and continued their conquest into the other six dimensions, including my dear home.

Suddenly, a flash of light came from the crystal beside me – a massive, tall, multi-faceted thing that stood unnaturally on the cobblestone floor. It did that sometimes, often when it wanted to tell Salanraja and I something. But now I saw the same old vision of myself as the hero. In the vision, I held the staff in my mouth, with the crystal at the tip of it, glowing blue. I was atop Salanraja, and I knew Astravar was flying nearby on one of his terrifying bone dragons. I'd see him soon in the crystal's vision.

The visions seemed to have been getting more and more frequent lately, which annoyed me. I always saw myself with that staff in my mouth, battling my nemesis. But I had no idea how I was going to obtain that staff and, from what the Driars told us, time was running out.

Salanraja laughed as she saw me watching the crystal. *"It won't* change just by staring at it, you know. It's not going to reveal anything extra to you until it's ready to do so."

"And when will that be?" I asked. "I just want to get Astravar out of the way so I can get back to living a comfortable life."

Salanraja shook her head slowly. "*Life will never be comfortable. You're a dragon rider now, and you're meant to work for the kingdom.*"

"But can't I retire... Like Aleam? He doesn't go flying out on training drills every day and he doesn't have to sit in boring classrooms."

"*We'll retire when we're good and old.*"

I tried to imagine how many years I had left in my life but couldn't fathom it. The crystal had given me the gift of languages, but unfortunately it hadn't thrown in mathematics for good measure.

"The king will let me retire after I save his kingdom. Then we can do what we like."

"*Here we go again...*" Salanraja lifted one of her forelegs and examined her sharp, long talons.

"What?"

"*I'm getting a bit sick of hearing your 'retire in the countryside' fantasies. Have you ever thought about what I might want?*"

"I have. I decided to include a large garden in the plans where you, Quarl, and Ishtkar can have plenty of space to roam."

"*I'm a dragon, I don't roam in gardens. I roam in the sky.*"

"Well, you can fly out from there and there'll be ample space for your landings."

Salanraja growled, and for a split second I thought she was also going to breathe fire. "*When I grow old, I want to live in the Crystal Mountains with the other dragons. That's where most dragon riders end up, you know? We live like hermits up there. Just us and our riders...*"

"What? The mountains. Whiskers, no! It's too cold."

"*See what I mean?*" Salanraja said. "*You don't care do you?*"

Now, it was my turn to growl. I walked over to the venison and ripped off another chunk. The taste of it at least brought some solace to this terrible news. I knew from the start that bonding with Salanraja was a bad idea. Now it seemed my doing so had ruined my life. I took my venison back to my spot and chewed into it once again. As I did so, I couldn't help looking back up at the crystal, and the massive, winged creatures, which looked like a cross between a bat and buzzard that I tore out of the sky using magic from my staff.

Behind me, Salanraja let out a loud, breathy sigh. "You know, when I'd first seen that scene in the crystal, I couldn't quite believe it."

"Why not?" I asked.

"Well... A cat beating the most powerful warlock alive today. Who'd have thought it possible?"

"But we're mighty creatures... If only you'd seen one of my ancestors, the Great Asian leopard cat."

"Yes, I'm sure I'd be quaking in my skin. And I've still got to meet your mightily scary hippopotamus."

"There's nothing on earth scarier than a hippopotamus. Trust me, I've seen one."

"So you keep telling me," Salanraja said, and she opened her mouth in a wide yawn.

In the crystal, I'd now come face to face with Astravar. The view there had pulled back so I could see myself looking tiny on Salanraja's neck, the staff in my mouth and Astravar atop his bone dragon. A blue beam shot out from my staff, a red from his, and they fused at the centre creating a brilliant purple bulb of energy.

"How am I ever going to do that?" I asked Salanraja.

She turned to the crystal. "Exactly as you are doing there, I think. You'll hold the staff in your mouth, and you'll shoot out magical energy and defeat Astravar."

"That's not what I mean..."

"So what do you mean?"

"How am I going to get from this point, stuck here in Dragonsbond Academy, to where I battle Astravar with my staff so I can live in peace again?"

It was a really weird place to be in, this thing that humans called limbo. Cats were not meant to feel the frustration it caused. I mean, when we saw a mouse, or a butterfly, or something worth hunting, we would hunt it when it was there, and then forget about it if it fled out of sight. But this crystal kept reminding me that I had to find this staff. Really, part of me wanted to be out searching for it. But I didn't know where to look.

"Be patient," Salanraja said. "*The crystal will reveal the way when it's good and ready. It wouldn't still be showing this vision as a version of the future, if this possibility didn't exist.*"

"I hope you're right," I said.

Meanwhile, the crystal had now got to my favourite part. The purple bulb at the centre of mine and Astravar's beams had now crept even closer to the warlock, and it was about to knock him off its mount. Just before that happened, there came another roar of bugles that sounded more like hippopotami breaking wind than anything pleasant.

"What is that?" I asked. "*Please don't tell me we have to go back to Sports Day again.*"

"No," Salanraja replied. "*I believe it's the call for assembly.*"

"Why didn't they ring the bell?"

"*I guess they want to tell you this is more important than a regular assembly. This is a military matter.*"

"Prince Arran... I'd been so wrapped up in my meal, I forgot to ask you if you know why he's here."

"*I guess you're about to find out.*"

"Sounds like it..." I took another piece of venison in my mouth for good luck, then I scurried out of Salanraja's chamber and clambered down towards the bailey.

SCHOOL ASSEMBLY

I'd go as far to say that I was having a terrible day. First, I'd had to carry a spoon in my mouth whilst being tossed around on Salanraja's back for nothing. Then, Bellari had got on my nerves by nuzzling with Rine when he should be with Ange. After that, I'd had to deal with that rude prince, Seramina had ignored me, and that bugle had torn me away from my delicious meal. Now, the day would be topped off with having to listen to the Driars' boring voices in assembly as they waxed lyrical about the wonders of their school.

Hence, I wasn't in the best of moods.

I stormed through the bailey towards the assembly. The dragons that had accompanied Prince Arran on his journey were stationed around the castle – on the tops of the towers and strategic points along the *chemin de ronde*. Around me, students rushed to get to the Council Courtyard. It was so busy I could hardly see where I was going. Whenever a student looked at me, I growled back at them, and I could swear once or twice I even hissed. Still, I reached the courtyard pretty quickly, and passed underneath the archway into a sweaty throng of students.

Most of them were there before me, and I had to navigate through a massive crowd. It was hard to see what was happening on the dais, because so many legs blocked my view like boles in a forest.

No one was yet speaking at the front, and the loud chorus of students surrounded me as they collectively discussed their everyday affairs. I couldn't hear any of the conversation – their heads were too high, and I was too low for that. All I can say is that everyone was making an absolute racket.

Fortunately, being a cat, I didn't need to find my way by sight here. It made much more sense to navigate by smell, and I sought someone familiar. Soon enough, I detected the faint whiff of catnip scented perfume, which I tracked until I was right underneath Ange. I mewled, and I rubbed against her leg, looking up at her. She spotted me, smiled, and then lifted me up in her arms. Though Ange was short, she was close enough to the front of the assembly that I could now see the central stage.

Unusually, the three Driars stood at the back of the dais, rather than at their usual lecterns. The lectern at the centre – usually Driar Lonamm's – now had a red cloth placed over it with some kind of ornate silver statue on top – a white crystal balanced in an open hand.

I still felt a little edgy, but Ange held me tightly and stroked me gently to help calm my instinct to dart away. We were all waiting, I realised, for Prince Arran, and he was clearly late. I could see the annoyance on the tightened faces of each of the Driars. Now I was a little higher, I could also smell tension in the air – stress everywhere. I picked up a few words on the conversations. The students were uttering things like 'war is coming', 'there will be a siege', and 'they will charge'.

All this time, I still didn't have my staff, because if I did I was sure I could just vanquish Astravar and get this whole thing out of the way. Of course, I hadn't even considered the other warlocks as a danger. Part of me, I guess, felt that once Astravar was defeated, the other warlocks would flee from this mighty and dangerous Bengal.

"It will start soon," Ange said.

"It better," I said. "Because I need to get back to my meal."

Ange laughed. "Quarl told me that Salanraja caught a whole deer."

"As she had when I'd first met her," I said, purring.

"I'm envious. We only had fish."

"Nothing wrong with fish," I said, and I waited for Ange to say something else. Instead, the door opened to the keep behind the Driars. Driar Yila raised her staff up high, and the crystal on it glowed red as if to warn that if anyone else spoke, she'd bathe them in fire. The surrounding chattering quickly died down to a whisper, and then nothing.

As before, the prince wore his red robe and red cap, both looking as if made from some kind of velvet material – shiny and dirt-free. He carried a birch staff with a white crystal on it, just like Seramina's.

The prince took his place at Driar Lonamm's desk. He placed a palm on the crystal on the lectern, and both the crystal in his staff and the crystal on the desk glowed. He coughed once, and he held this posture as he addressed the silent courtyard.

"These are trying times, indeed," he said. "Not just for your beloved academy, but for the entire kingdom of Illumine. Unfortunately, it looks like Dragonsbond Academy will get hit first."

This caused a murmur to erupt from the students, and Prince Arran waited as if he had orchestrated this murmur. It didn't die down, and the volume raised in intensity.

"Silence," Driar Yila shouted out from her corner, and the red crystal on her staff let out another burning glow.

Prince Arran glanced at Driar Yila, and then he scanned the crowd with narrowed eyes. "I'm glad to see that your Driars have you well trained," he said after a moment. "Because you have to remember this. You are all servants of the king, and you must always remember your place, particularly in this time of war. If one of you breaks rank, or if one of you disturbs the order that we've built in this kingdom, then our entire operation might fall apart."

I caught sight of High Prefect Lars and Prefect Asinda at the front then. I could see the back of their heads – Lars standing perfectly straight, not moving one bit. Asinda was nodding slowly, one hand on her chin.

"Suffice to say," Arran continued, "time is also of the essence, and so I must keep this speech short. You are all probably wondering the reason for this visit. For days, my dragon riders and dragons have been scouting the land, as we tried to ascertain the exact location the warlocks are likely to target first."

"*What pomposity,*" Salanraja said in my mind. "*Trust that self-righteous fool to call them his dragons. Dragons belong to no one, and the only dominion humans can claim over dragons is that of the bond between rider and dragon. Even with that, no one is really in charge.*"

"Well, don't you serve his dragon, Corralsa?" I asked.

"*It's not servitude,*" Salanraja said, sounding slightly annoyed. "*It's a mutual respect whereby we decide to delegate specific decisions to her. If we ever wanted to do our own thing, nothing's stopping us. But dragons are wise enough to know that it's easier to work together sometimes than alone.*"

"Sounds like you're just using fancy wording to dress up the same idea."

"*Believe what you like. Just because you don't understand something, doesn't mean it isn't true.*"

While Salanraja had been explaining, Prince Arran had been telling us more about the importance of Dragonsbond Academy for training dragon riders to enter the king's Dragon Corps. This kind of spiel, we heard every week in droning voices from the Council of Three during our assemblies. But this time, Prince Arran also pointed out many times that he was in fact in charge of the corps. After a while, he paused, as if he was about to deliver an important point.

"War is coming," he said. "And the warlocks have chosen this as the target. They most likely think that striking at the very cradle, so to speak, of our corps will allow them to win, which is why we must fortify this location. We have already called for reinforcements and the White Mages are on their way, although you must understand it will take time for them to arrive. Meanwhile, some of the king's best riders and their dragons will be stationed here."

"The warlocks have strengthened their position over the last few years, and much faster than we expected they would. For a long time, we've feared this day, as we waited for you, students of Dragonsbond Academy, to complete your training before we sent you into battle. We do not know when the warlocks will charge, but our intelligence tells us they are likely to do so soon. When they do, everyone older than sixteen must fight."

He paused, clearly strategically, and another murmur erupted from the crowd, larger than last time. Everyone here knew that there were only two members of Dragonsbond Academy that were under sixteen – Seramina, and I. Both of us, I was sure, would still have to fight.

Driar Yila at the back banged her staff down at the back, screamed out, "Silence!" once again, and passed her basilisk gaze over the students beneath her.

"As I said," Prince Arran said, without looking back at Yila this time. "Order will be required and enforced in this academy. From now on, you are no longer students, but soldiers and you will behave like soldiers. After this meeting, each of you must report directly to your head prefect, who will act like sergeants reporting directly to my stationed officers. For now, this assembly is dismissed. Make sure you leave in an orderly fashion, and don't speak until you're in your private quarters. If anyone disobeys orders or breaks rank, there will be severe consequences."

The crystal on which Prince Arran had placed his hand glowed even brighter, and a stream of white light shot out of his staff towards the crystal above the dais. An eye with a deep blue iris appeared on the crystal of his staff, and the crystal on the ceiling displayed a view of us in the assembly. We were wracked with silence until one student sneezed. The view in the ceiling crystal immediately focused on that student. Then another student mumbled something, but only made it mid-sentence before the view focused on her, cutting off her words.

Then I growled, and I made to clamber down onto the floor, not wanting to be here any longer. But Ange tightened her grasp, and she gave me a chiding look. The view in the crystal immediately focused on me. On the stage, Driar Yila focused her harsh stare on me, and her crystal flared red.

"Shh," Ange said softly, and the crystals view focused on her soft lips. Both of us quietened down together. Meanwhile, at the front, Arran waited patiently, scanning each one of us until not a single whisper emanated from the crowd. All I could now hear was the sounds of birdsongs somewhere in the distance and, even fainter, the cawing of a crow.

"Very well," Arran said. "I see we have work to do. Now, you are dismissed. Except for that talking cat. I wish to see you at once."

Whiskers, I hadn't expected that. Probably he was going to enact one of his 'consequences', all because I'd growled louder than anyone else. Feet scuffed from the ground behind me, and the students started to file out. Still, Ange held me, as if she never wanted to let me go, and I felt safe there.

But I knew this feeling wouldn't last.

6

THE ISSUE AT HAND

Silence ensued, punctuated only by the soft voices of prefects giving orders. They arranged the students in neat rows and had them file into long trains leading into the bailey. A thick humidity hung in the air, bringing with it a coldness. It wasn't raining yet, but I could sense in my whiskers that it was coming.

Being the youngest class out of the three in Dragonsbond Academy, ours was the last to leave. Rine was there, and Bellari, as well as Seramina, and around one hundred other familiar students. Prefect Calin had been assigned to look after us, which suited me fine because I liked Calin.

He had short, cropped hair, a muscular stature, and he was one of the best sword fighters in Dragonsbond Academy. He arranged us in lines of five, then he walked up to Ange. "You should probably put him down now, Initiate Ange. He needs to stay behind to see the prince."

Ange sighed, then she started to lower me to the floor. But I shrieked, and I clambered further up her chest. I stretched out my claws to tell her that if she dropped me, then I'd tear her clothing.

"Ange is coming with me," I said.

The crystal on the ceiling above the dais focused on me. But the prince had now stopped watching us through it, and rather was talking to the other Driars at the back of the dais. Calin looked at me nervously. Ange smiled at him. Behind us, Bellari scoffed and turned towards the archway that led out of the courtyard. Rine stood close to his girlfriend, his cheeks looking slightly red. A crow flew overhead, cawing, and for a moment I wondered if it was Astravar. But it would have been stupid for him to come alone so close to where we had hundreds of dragons who could scorch him out of the sky.

After a moment, Calin nodded. "Fine," he said. "Everyone else move out."

He led the students towards the courtyard archway in a neat line, leaving Ange and I standing in an unnaturally chilly wind. On it, I caught that whiff of rotten vegetable juice again. I could swear it was getting stronger by the day.

"Can I put you down now?" Ange asked.

"No."

"Why?"

"Because you've proven in the dragon egg-and-spoon that you're not to be trusted. I have no idea if you'd run off as soon as you put me on the ground. As I said, you're coming with me."

Ange huffed, but it was a playful huff. I knew she was a little scared of having to deal with Prince Arran and the potential consequences. But I also remember her also saying that she thought the prince was attractive. I just hoped, at the back of my mind, that she wouldn't end up falling for him rather than Rine. That would be a disaster if I had to spend the rest of my nine lifetimes with this snobbish prince. Then, I would have to cast either Ange or Rine away, because there was no way I could handle both Arran and Bellari for life.

Ange carried me up to the foot of the dais and then stepped cautiously onto it. Usually, students weren't allowed up here, but Arran had called me forward after all. Prince Arran still had that weird-looking eye watching out from the crystal on his staff. As we approached, it looked at us, and then blinked slowly.

"Initiate Ange, I believe," Prince Arran said, without turning to Ange. "So, we meet again."

Ange lowered her head. "You know my name, sir?"

Arran looked back at Driar Yila. "Of course, I learn all the names of those who show signs of insolence. And here you are, disobeying my orders again."

"I didn't have a choice, sir," Ange said. "Ben… Initiate Ben, wouldn't go without me."

"Traitor," I said under my breath, growling. I knew she wasn't to be trusted.

Prince Arran looked down at me with narrowed eyes. I stared back at him, and I kept staring, waiting for him to blink and turn away. One thing these humans never learned is that you can't beat a cat in a staring competition.

"So, you take orders from a cat now, do you?" Prince Arran said. "I've never heard something so ridiculous. What is this establishment coming to?"

Ange looked at Driar Brigel, who shrugged his massive shoulders. Brigel then lowered his head as Prince Arran turned his hard gaze on him. Presently, Arran turned back to Ange.

"Answer me, girl," he said through clenched teeth. "I asked you a question."

Ange shook her head. "It's a fine academy, and I'm proud to be a part of it…. Sir."

"Then you'll do better refraining from molly-coddling this over-spoilt cat, and instead get back to your duties. Go and help the guards fortify our position or something. My dragon riders have been briefed and will have further orders for you soon. And remember, I'm keeping an eye on you."

"Yes, sir," Ange said, and this time she dropped me on the floor so fast I didn't have time to react. She nodded to the prince, curtsied slightly, turned on her heel, and marched off like a true soldier. I made to march after her, but the prince's voice boomed out so loud it caused me to freeze.

"What do you think you're doing, cat?"

I turned back to him. "Going to help the guards fortify your position, as you ordered."

"That order was meant for the girl, not you."

"You didn't specify, sir," I said.

Prince Arran put his hands on his hips and leaned forward until he loomed over me. "Are you really that stupid? I might have expected an inferior species wouldn't be able to understand orders."

"I'm not inferior. I'm a Bengal, descendant of the great Asian leopard cat."

"And I'm a prince, descendant of a long line of royals. I'm also air marshal of King Garmin's dragon riders, which consequently makes me overseer of this academy. Which means, little cat, that I'm your boss and you'll do exactly as you're told."

Behind me, the three Driars were exchanging glances with each other. It seemed that they thought this man as idiotic as I did. I'd seen apes on the television back home, and Prince Arran behaved just like one of those orange ones which swung around on the long arms. Orangutans, I believe they are called.

A roar came from one of the keep towers, and a bitter chill ran through my fur. Behind me, one of Arran's dragons took off from the top of the West Tower, and spiralled round, then landed in one of the chambers where a dragon lived. I guessed the dragons were also enforcing their disciplinary tactics. Salanraja, in particular, wouldn't like that.

Prince Arran snapped his fingers. "Stop dawdling, cat, and pay attention," he said.

"To what?"

He ignored my question. "How exactly are you planning to get the staff?" he asked. "The one that you're destined to use to defeat Astravar. I need timeframes, I need scoping estimates. Anything that I can use to plan our battle strategies moving forwards."

There it was – the question I'd been dreading all this time. "I haven't a clue," I said. "My crystal hasn't told me yet."

Prince Arran turned around to look at the three Driars. Without looking at me, he indicated a point on the ground next to him with a down-turned palm. "Stand here, cat, where I can see you."

I slinked over to the designated position and sat down. I started grooming myself, but the prince didn't seem to notice my intended insolence. Instead, he looked at the three Driars who had now formed a loose circle around him, each resting lightly on their staffs.

"What, pray tell me, is the meaning of this?" he asked them, with a tone as if he was scolding schoolchildren.

Driar Yila spoke out first. "Sir, the truth about the staff is known by Ben's and Salanraja's crystal, and we've been waiting until it's ready to reveal its position. We have the utmost faith that it will provide the answer when we are ready."

"Unacceptable," Prince Arran said.

I heard Driar Lonamm's voice catch in her throat. "Sir, we cannot go against the wishes of the crystal." Her cheeks wobbled as she talked. "That would be sacrilege."

"And that's the problem here…" Arran said, waving his hand. "This superstitious nonsense that you spout. We need to take action now, not to be waiting until we're magically provided a solution."

"But we've worked this way in the past, sir," Driar Brigel said. "Our reliance on the will of the crystals has served us well for many years."

"And never have we had warlocks encroaching on our doorsteps," Prince Arran said. "They've been gaining power for a reason. We need to identify inefficiencies in our system and stamp them out before it's too late."

I was getting sick of all this pointless talk. Really, we were just skirting around the issue.

"We have no idea where to find the staff," I said.

Prince Arran didn't even look down at me. "We have no idea to where to find it, sir. And who gave you permission to speak, cat?"

"Sir…" I said, and I said it as ironically as I could.

"Anyway, back to the issue at hand," Prince Arran said, clearly unaffected by my irony. Boring people are like that, unfortunately. "You could have extracted the information from the crystal using destiny magic. What happened to the mind-witch we sent you? The warlock's daughter?"

"Seramina is off duty for now," Driar Lonamm said. "She could be dangerous. If she uses her magic wrongly…"

Halfway through the sentence, Prince Arran had already turned around and was looking towards the East Tower, which housed Salanraja and about forty other dragons. "Forget this nonsense. I'll do it myself. Cat, lead me to your crystal."

Happily, I thought. I marched that way without permission. *"Kindly toast this arrogant prince for me as soon as we get to your chamber,"* I said to Salanraja in my mind as I went.

She said nothing in response as the five of us all marched together across the bailey to meet my dragon in the flesh.

7

FORCING DESTINY

Aleam was waiting for us in Salanraja's chamber. As he stood, he was hunched even further over his staff, and his face looked sallow and heavily wrinkled. Olan, after she'd heard about the prince's behaviour from the other dragons, had advised Aleam to attend the meeting. The great white dragon had apparently felt that the Council of Three might need his wisdom, or at least his diplomatic skills.

Meanwhile, a thick grey cloud had clustered over the fields outside, and I could taste the ozone in the air, which made a satisfying deviation from the normal sensation of rotten vegetable juice. There was also that thick humidity that told of a coming storm.

The crystal stood by the opening to the outer world, seemingly oblivious to this. It continued to display the same vision of me using my staff of destiny to knock Astravar off his bone dragon perch.

Salanraja had refused to toast Prince Arran. She argued that if she caused any physical damage to the man then Corralsa would cause equal if not greater damage to her. I could understand her fear, really. Corralsa was a big dragon after all.

This fear, however, didn't stop Salanraja growling at Prince Arran as he entered.

Arran looked at her and her mighty sharp teeth. He seemed

unfazed as he put his hands on his hips. "I see you're just as insolent as your cat. I guess you're suited for each other. But you still need to learn your place. If you're not careful, I'll get Corralsa to send you over to Bestian Academy."

Driar Yila also looked up at Salanraja, but instead of her usual harsh look, she shook her head as if to tell her not to test this man. Salanraja growled again, and then retreated to the corner where the venison had been before.

"What's Bestian Academy?" I asked her.

The words came out in my mind as if Salanraja didn't particularly want to speak them. "*It's where all of us dragons are trained,*" she replied. "*Every one of us hates it, particularly our trainer, the great grey Matharon. He worked us to exhaustion every day from when we were fledglings until we came of age.*"

"You've never talked about this before."

"*We dragons don't. We'd rather not remember.*"

Behind Prince Arran, Driars Yila, Lonamm, and Brigel filed through the entranceway to Salanraja's chamber exceedingly slowly. The three of them walked with their heads low against their chests and their hands folded beneath their waists. Prince Arran didn't pay any heed to their unnatural lethargy, however, for his focus was on the crystal.

He placed the base of his staff down on the ground and widened his legs as he stared at mine and Salanraja's crystal. The smaller crystal on his staff glowed white and a thin, wispy beam floated out of it towards the larger crystal. Static seemed to come off his staff, gently tugging at my fur.

"Prince Arran," Aleam said. "With all due respect, do you really think it's wise to force destiny? We're talking about the threads of the future. Your actions could result in unseen consequences, which might involve losing the war."

"I'm not going to alter anything," Arran said. "I'm simply going to ask it a question."

Aleam raised an eyebrow. "If the crystal had anything to say, it would have done so, don't you think?"

Arran strode over to him and leaned over the old man with his hands on his hips. "Look, Driar Aleam. You're one of the most respected figures in this kingdom, and the king has the dearest respect for you. However, need I remind you of my position? I've been appointed by King Garmin to fight this war using whatever means necessary."

"Including ignoring the counsel of others in knowledgeable positions?"

"That's enough! Silence now, all of you. I need to concentrate." Arran lowered his head and put his free hand on his chin.

"Be careful, Arran," Aleam said. "You must remember what happens if you try to manipulate the will of the crystals."

But Arran didn't seem to be listening. The crystal on his staff grew ever brighter and the wispy beam between it and mine and Salanraja's crystal gained substance. Soon, the images on the crystal grew towards a brilliant white. I had to close my eyelids a little – it was so intense.

A crash of thunder came from outside, accompanied by an icy and heavy wind that had no smell to it. The wind hit me, sending me sliding across the ground, and I had to dig my claws into a crack between the cobblestones to keep purchase. The four elder Driars present widened their stances so they wouldn't get blown over. Whatever this man was up to, the crystal clearly didn't like it.

Salanraja didn't seem to like it either, for she tossed her head upwards and cried out shrilly. Arran turned his head slightly. Then a second beam came from his staff, again white, and it hit the dragon on the bridge of her nose. Salanraja once again whimpered, and she slinked further into the corner.

"What was all that about?" I asked Salanraja.

"This prince is a pompous oaf," Salanraja said, growling quietly.

"I know that already. But what are you so upset about?"

"I'm upset because he really shouldn't be behaving like this, despite his title. Arran is the most powerful destiny mage in the kingdom. Even the king's White Mages cannot match his ability."

"So why don't you want him to cast that spell?"

"Because it was believed for a long time that you shouldn't interfere with the will of the crystals. It's complicated, Bengie, but let's say Olan doesn't like this either. She's had a word with Corralsa, much to the same effect."

"Then what's going to happen?"

"I don't know. None of us do. We've never tried this before. But this is how the warlocks got into trouble with dark magic originally. They tried to gain the power they wanted from the crystals, rather than allow the crystals to choose how they want to serve."

"I thought the crystals that the warlocks gained power from were dark crystals. Our crystal is different, surely?"

"No, Bengie. Dark crystals are just normal crystals that have been corrupted over the years through greed and other unfavourable human emotions. For years, the crystals were overused like this, until the warlocks came to power, and humans learned the error of their ways. No creature on this word truly understands the intricacies of these crystals. Gracious demons, I don't want to find out either. But with this pompous prince, we have no choice."

A roar came from outside, followed by a heavy beating of wings. Corralsa appeared at the opening to the outside world. The sun, still fighting to stay in front of the clouds, cast a sharp highlight onto Corralsa's black skin.

The light in the crystal faded back to a subdued grey. Every second or so, it pulsed slightly, and the ground underfoot shook as it did. The wind died down a little, but it still circled and howled around Salanraja's chamber like a yowling wolf.

Then came a familiar lilting voice, speaking out loud. It belonged to the crystal and always sounded to me like it had a Welsh accent. Except this time, this was more like a warrioress Boudica kind of accent – angry with a bite to it. The kind of voice a cat would hide from if it called him in for dinner.

"This is as improper as improper comes," my crystal said. "Who are you to disturb the natural order of magic?"

"I am Prince Arran, cousin of King Garmin IV and appointed air marshal of the Dragon Rider Corps of Illumine Kingdom."

"Your title means nothing in the order of affairs," the crystal said.

"But the situation does," Prince Arran said, "and we need your assistance."

"The situation bears no weight here. Dark ages come when men like you meddle in such unnatural ways. History has proven this time and time again."

"A dark age will come if I don't meddle. Your lack of communication with us leaves us with little choice."

"There is always choice!" the crystal boomed. "There is also patience, a virtue that has taken your people through the darkest times."

"There is no time for patience. We need your help in serving the kingdom. We need to locate the staff that belongs to the cat. And we need, as you well know, to change the future for the better. Tell me, oh crystal. Where can we find that staff?"

The glow from the crystal flickered stochastically. "I can tell you... But I warn you, prince. If you force something that's not due ahead of time, there will always be consequences."

"Our kingdom will pay those consequences united. If we can rid ourselves of the warlocks, there can't be too high a price to pay."

"You know so little, young prince, but you think you know the world through your gift. That is your weakness."

"Just show us where the staff is," Prince Arran said. "And let us be done with this conversation."

Outside, the sky darkened to near pitch. Then lightning cascaded out of the heavy clouds, flooding the landscape white. The crash from the sky was even louder than the last, and I half thought Corralsa would cower away, but she remained hovering in place, both majestic and terrifying.

"I will not be scared down," Prince Arran said. "Reveal the information I wish to know, and I need not disturb you again."

A torrent of rain poured outside, so thick it obscured the view between us and Corralsa. Now, the heavy wind brought upon it a yucky squall. I considered darting into the staircase for shelter, but something in me didn't want to move. If this prince could tell me where this staff was, then I could quest for it, obtain it, then use it to defeat Astravar. This nightmare might then be over sooner than I'd thought.

"Very well," the crystal said, "let your ambition and pride be your undoing."

The sky outside lightened to a sombre grey, whilst the view in the crystal returned to showing its scenes. But this time, underneath the facets, a new dream played out before me. A massive beast, as tall as the sky and wider than ten oak trees, stomped across a thick, dreamy looking wood. The ground looked wet and full of tall mushrooms. The beast's thick wooden legs crushed these under its stumpy feet as it made its way through the forest.

The hackles shot up on the back of my neck, as recognition dawned on me. Just last season, one of these creatures had almost sucked me into its insides and pancaked me to death. Spectral Manipulators and bone dragons surrounded the forest golem, guarding it. But both were dormant at this time.

"A forest golem," Aleam said. "But who..."

"It belongs to Astravar," the crystal said. "He has found and hidden the staff that only the cat can wield."

"That's the Aurorest Forest," Prince Arran said, and he turned to Aleam. "Am I right?"

Aleam nodded. "I know that place well. It's one of the best for gathering medicinal herbs."

"And poisons," Driar Brigel added.

Aleam had told me about this place before. It was so close to the Wastelands – a land full of magical creatures belonging to both the warlocks and the kingdom, that were in constant battle.

But since the warlocks had pushed their front forward, much of the Aurorest Forest now lay in the Wastelands, which had made it increasingly dangerous for Aleam to go there and forage for some of his more potent medicinal supplies.

"And this is where the staff is?" Prince Arran asked, turning back to the crystal. "The one that will save the world?"

"That is up to the decisions of your people," the crystal said. The vision flooded once again with light, which soon faded to a sombre and empty grey. Outside, the sun peeked through the clouds.

"I've seen enough," Prince Arran said, and he cut off the beam from his staff by twisting it sharply. "Driars, prepare the strategy room. We must discuss our plans at once."

He turned on his heel and strode out of the room.

8

DUST AND DISGUST

The strategy room was probably the dustiest room in the entire castle. It had a long oval mahogany table in the centre of it and thick red curtains in front of a single wall inset with full-height windows. Wolf spiders peered out from cracks in the skirting-board, and I couldn't stop sneezing.

Meanwhile, I sat on a velvet padded chair, wood carvings of dragons etched into the long beams across its high back. I had placed myself at one end of the table, licking my fur. Arran sat at the other end, and the three Driars of the Council of Three sat on my left just by the window. Aleam sat next to Arran on the other side, leaving only two chairs empty.

"I don't understand why they didn't hold the rest of the meeting in your chamber," I said to Salanraja. "It's horrible, and it's dusty, and it's not a good place to be."

"I'm guessing it's in case there are spies. We can't track every crow and sparrow that enters the castle."

"Or maybe it's because the prince didn't like you," I pointed out.

"I don't think he likes you particularly, either."

"Touché."

As I listened to Prince Arran drone on and on, my stomach started to rumble. It must have been ages since my last meal, and I considered mewling out for food, imagining the tantalising snacks I could be eating right now.

"We will send the cat out alone," Arran said, and hearing that caused the hackles to shoot up on the back of my neck.

Driar Lonamm glanced at me. "I wouldn't recommend that," she said. "Initiate Ben is still inexperienced. He's not fit to fight a forest golem alone."

"We can't spare the resources," Prince Arran said, lifting his head so I could see right up his nostrils.

"But he would probably never return," Driar Brigel said. "Then, we might not even have a staff to fight Astravar with. What will become of us then?"

"That cannot happen. The crystal has already foretold that he will survive getting the staff. He can't defeat Astravar otherwise."

"It's one possible thread of the future," Driar Yila said.

"And," Aleam said, raising his hand. "You've already changed fate by using your magic to alter the essence of time. The crystal told us that there will be consequences for this."

Prince Arran huffed and looked down at the table for a moment, examining it as if looking for flies. He drummed his fingers against the wood there, releasing some of the dust back into the air. "We haven't got time to deliberate... And I would have thought you'd have more faith in your air marshal. I'm the one that can use destiny magic here, and I've been using it for an awfully long time."

No one other than Prince Arran seemed very convinced about this from the look on the Driars' faces. Granted, he might have had powerful abilities to see the future. But something about his behaviour suggested he wasn't telling us everything we needed to know.

"And what does Initiate Ben think?" Driar Aleam asked, turning to me. Driar Yila coughed, Driar Lonamm mumbled something under her breath, and Driar Brigel shifted nervously. A moment of silence ensued.

"Go on then, cat," Prince Arran said. "Say something."

"I…" I stopped myself. I knew whatever I said would get ridiculed, and so I didn't feel like saying anything at all.

"Spit it out… We haven't got all day."

I looked straight at the prince. "I tried to face off against one of those things before, and I have no chance of defeating it. I have no magic, other than the ability to turn into a chimera."

"You'll have your dragon," Prince Arran said.

"A dragon isn't enough to defeat a forest golem," Driar Yila pointed out. "Unless we're very lucky."

"And Ben's crystal has foretold that he will be," Arran said. "We must fortify this castle for the safety of everyone involved. We can't spare a single soul on this quest."

Aleam lowered his head and cupped it in his hands. He shook it slowly and then stood up. "If you'll excuse me, my prince, I've got my own business to be dealing with."

He looked at Driar Yila, gave her a nod, and then walked out of the room. He didn't close the door on the way out. A breeze filtered through, which cleansed the air a little.

I couldn't believe my ears, really. They were going to send me out alone against a forest golem. It would knock Salanraja out of the sky, and then it would crush me under its massive weight. It wouldn't matter then whether the warlocks took the kingdom or not, because I'd be dead. I'd never taste a good meal again.

"What are we going to do?" I asked Salanraja. "We can't head out there on our own because we'll be killed."

"We have no choice," Salanraja said. "We can't break the chain of command, and so we need to do what Prince Arran and Corralsa say."

But I wasn't going to listen to this. No one was sticking up for me where they should. Aleam was letting this go ahead. The Council of Three was letting this go ahead. All of them were meant to protect me. I wasn't going to let some stupid prince, whom I had never sworn allegiance to, and had no intention of doing so in the future, dictate when I would die. Death was the greatest threat to my plans of retirement. But this decision would protect nothing but Prince Arran's inflated ego.

So, I made a decision, and I took the opportunity to act on it. I jumped off the chair and I sprinted out the door.

"Stop!" Arran shouted behind me. "That's an order!"

His shouts did nothing to slow me down. In fact, they probably made my legs pump faster. Last time I'd run away from an important meeting like this, Driar Brigel had used his leaf magic to slam the door in front of me. I half expected this to happen again, or for Driar Yila to shoot a fireball in front of me blocking my path, or for Driar Lonamm to freeze me in place with an ice spell.

None of this happened, and I was soon back in the open world. It seemed to stink even more of rotten vegetable juice, but I didn't care as anything was better than that disgusting, dusty room.

9

TANTALISING TEMPTATIONS

Outside, it had got suddenly balmy – the kind of weather you want to be out sleeping in, not dying in an unfair fight against a forest golem. But I didn't have time to think about the weather. Rather, I needed to find a place to hide, and I had little time.

The Council Courtyard wouldn't provide much cover, and so I sprinted across the yard and through the archway into the main bailey.

I considered trying to escape the castle. But everywhere I looked, Prince Arran had posted his dragons. I had no chance of getting past the wall uncharred. Given how nasty this Prince Arran was, I doubted that he'd go easy on me with the punishments. Besides, last time I'd tried to run away, it had resulted in me almost getting eaten by serkets and a giant spider.

With Prince Arran's dragons posted everywhere – on the *chemin de ronde*, by every door, by the portcullis, and atop the towers, I had no option other than to use my favourite hiding place – underneath the stone fountain where Rine and Bellari liked to sit and kiss. I kept myself low, edging as far as I could underneath. From my safehold, I watched feet pass by as prefects shouted out orders, and students filed into neat positions.

"*Bengie, Bengie, what are you doing now?*" Salanraja said in my mind.

"*I'm hiding from the prince. We cannot go over to fight that forest golem alone. It will kill us, and you know it.*"

"*Even if we've never seen such a future happen in the crystal?*"

"*But you heard it yourself, Salanraja. Prince Arran changed the future when he meddled with the affairs of the crystal.*"

"*And you think hiding is going to fix this?*"

"*I don't see any other choice. Just leave me alone, Salanraja.*" She tried to chide me more, but I'd had enough of listening to humans and dragons for one day. So, I mentally refused to translate her words, which became babble at the back of my mind.

I don't know for how long I stayed under the fountain. The very act of zoning out from Salanraja's thoughts made them sound like dream-speak, which probably sent me to sleep. The next thing I knew, a rich clucking sound jostled me awake. Seramina's voice floated down beneath the fountain.

"Oh, Ben," she said. "You do have a habit of getting yourself into a fix, don't you? Why don't you just learn to trust your elders for a change? All the Driars, including Aleam, at least have your best interest at heart."

I growled at her dainty feet, and the tiny toes pointing out of her sandals. Part of me wanted to reach out and scratch them as if they were mice. But I was admittedly still afraid of Seramina and what she might do if I caused her pain. Despite her apparent and recent niceness, she was Astravar's daughter after all.

"I'm not coming out," I said. "I'm going to stay under here forever."

"I don't doubt you might. Unless, of course, I provide a good reason for you not to."

Something small hit the floor, bouncing twice. The sweet aroma of roasted duck assaulted my nostrils. I stared at it, and it seemed to look back at me as if it had eyes. My mouth watered, and I felt the invisible pull towards the appetising food.

"I know what will happen if I come out," I said. "You'll pick me up, then I'll have no choice but to scratch you and hide under here again."

"But it's delicious and tantalising duck. Hallinar caught and roasted this only half an hour ago. Salanraja tells him you've not had duck for an awfully long time. Am I right?"

I knew it – Seramina hadn't changed. Despite her apparent niceness, she was still so cruel. Another morsel of duck fell onto cobblestones, this time less of a chunk and more of a strip. "Just think of all the delicious food you're missing out on, Ben. If you don't come out, you might never have roast duck again." She threw another chunk down on the floor, this time with a delicious amount of skin trailing off of it. I could smell the fat oozing out from the meat, and I wanted it so much.

Whiskers, I had to resist. My life and plans for retirement depended on it. But despite me knowing this, inch by inch I edged towards the base of the fountain. I didn't run for the duck yet, though. Instead, I stood there, staring up at Seramina. She looked back down at me with her pale gaze. She had no staff, no way of using magic. I was safe.

"Here's another one," Seramina said. "Look how delicious it is." Another chunk hit the floor. Whiskers, this was absolute torture. Then I realised. I was a cat, and I would be much faster than her. I only needed to grab a chunk, then I could retreat to safety and munch to my heart's content.

"Put your hands behind your back," I said. "And take two steps back."

"Very well," Seramina said, and she followed my instructions with a faint smile.

I edged forward, watching her every move. Seramina didn't even flinch, and the food drew me towards it. I quickly pounced forward and took the piece with extra skin on it inside my mouth.

It was only at the last minute that I realised something smelled wrong. It wasn't so much the duck, but the surrounding air. The sensation of snowdrop perfume wasn't coming from where I saw Seramina, but to my right.

As the image of Seramina in front of me dissipated, I screeched and turned back towards the fountain. But the real Seramina was too fast. A white beam hit me on the side of the head, tickling only slightly as a warming sensation washed over my skull. I felt suddenly sluggish, frozen in place. Seramina floated over from the right, and she scooped me up in one arm, while she kept the hand of the other wrapped around her staff.

I couldn't move my legs easily. They felt numb, but I could still speak and yowl. "What are you doing?" I asked. "You're such a cruel mind-witch." I screeched out, and I tried to draw attention to myself, hoping that a dragon would stop her long enough that I could return to my hiding place.

The dragon standing on the East Tower turned its head towards us. But before it could spot us, Seramina pointed her staff upwards. It cast a fountain of energy over us. Seramina's arms, and her face, and my paws, and everything else about us vanished from view.

The dragon on the tower roared, and other dragons around it joined in the chorus.

"Will you stop causing such a commotion, Ben?" Seramina asked. "We're on your side."

I wasn't listening. I was growling and screeching at the top of my voice. Even so, I couldn't move my legs to scamper. I couldn't see Seramina beneath me, but I felt her hurrying her pace towards the open door of Aleam's study. Aleam waited there by the doorway, looking from side to side nervously.

Seramina waltzed me inside, and then said, "We're in."

"Good," Aleam said, and he shut the door behind him and bolted it twice.

10

PLANS ARE BORING

Rine and Ange were sitting on the bench where Ta'ra should have been, when I entered Aleam's study. There was too much room between them and too much tension as well, hanging there like an approaching storm. But at that moment, I didn't care too much about my distant retirement plans with Ange and Rine. I had to preserve my near future first.

I scanned the room for a place to hide. The door to Aleam's bedroom was shut, so I couldn't retreat under his bed. That left under the sofa, or under the desk – both of which were too accessible by human hands. The window was also closed, so there was no way out that way.

Seramina gazed at me passively – her eyes looking relaxed, very unlike they'd been when I first met her. She stood next to Aleam by the door, with her staff pointed at me, the crystal on it glowing white. The original paralysis spell she'd cast had worn off. I could move my legs normally, although they ached a little, as if I'd just been chasing butterflies for hours. But if I tried any sudden movements, I had no doubt she'd paralyse me again.

"Gracious demons, sit down, will you, Ben?" Aleam said, a slight whisper in his voice. "Prince Arran is out searching for you. We have little time before they decide to search my quarters too."

Because of Seramina's trickery before, part of me didn't want to trust them. It wasn't just that they'd whisked me here against my will, but Seramina also hadn't given me an adequate portion of roast duck. But I realised that if Prince Arran found me, he'd banish Salanraja and I from Dragonsbond Academy altogether, and only let us back in if I returned with a staff in my mouth and the knowledge of how to use it to defeat Astravar.

Groaning, I made my way over to the sofa and sat between Rine and Ange. Ange put out her hand to stroke me, but I hissed at her and raised a paw with bared claws, so she jerked away quickly. Rine looked at her, then at me, and snorted.

I took a little time to scan the room, and the only thing that was different was a wooden easel against the far wall with a rolled-up scroll affixed to the top of it.

"Now, Ben," Aleam said, sounding slightly annoyed. "Stop blocking off your dragon and reach out to her. She can explain things through thought much faster than we can through words."

I hadn't even realised. That mental shift I'd made before had kept Salanraja still babbling at the back of my mind.

I focused on the words again. *"I'm here,"* I told her.

"Bengie, never, ever do that again!" She didn't sound happy.

"What?"

"You blocked me off, which is one of the worst things you can do to a dragon. Not only is it rude, but if you hold it long enough, you could kill our bond completely."

That sounded, admittedly, ever so slightly appealing. *"Aleam told me you need to explain promptly what's going on. So instead of giving me a lecture, maybe you should do so?"*

I felt Salanraja's frustration boiling in my own chest for a moment before she found the will to suppress it. *"We're going to escape,"* she said. *"The whole of Dragonsbond Academy – including the Council of Three – really doesn't like Prince Arran's idea to send us off into the fray like he discussed, and so we've gathered your most loyal friends to come on* the mission with you. There's no way we'll survive facing a forest golem alone."

"Even if destiny says we must get that staff?"

"Destiny probably dictated Aleam, Seramina, Rine, Ange, and their dragons would go along with you in the first place. The Driars here have always held that you shouldn't treat a crystal's reading as a given, reducing those resources that seem sensible for the mission at hand. That, they believe, is tempting fate. But Prince Arran is young, arrogant and doesn't believe in old wisdom. Hence, we've had to take matters into our own hands."

"So basically no one likes him. Why don't we just tie him up and lock him in the dungeon?"

"Don't be stupid, Bengie. Arran's dragons and dragon riders are completely on his side. He's also a member of the royal family, and so the only person who can give the edict to lock him up is the king."

"Why do we need an edict? We've got enough students and dragons here to overpower him and his forces."

"And with war on the horizon, how do you think the warlocks would react if one of their spies sees mutiny in our ranks?"

"I don't know..."

"Well, I do. They'd use the chaos as an opportunity to charge in and take Dragonsbond Academy as their own. I hope they never ever decide to make you a leader, Bengie. You're clearly a poor strategist."

She was wrong, of course. I was as good a strategist as I needed to be. I knew how to look endearing to people, for example, to get myself a good meal. "From what you're telling me, it doesn't seem a brilliant strategy to disobey this prince air marshal guy either. We'll just come back, he'll clip your wings and lock me in the cattery or something."

"We'll sort that out when we return with the staff, after we've defeated the forest golem." Salanraja said.

"If we defeat the forest golem," I pointed out.

"Let's take it one step at a time, shall we..."

While Salanraja and I had been conversing telepathically, Aleam had used his alembic to brew an aromatic cup of tea. The apparatus whistled, shrilly and painfully. Aleam turned off the burner underneath the bulb and then poured out four delicate teacups' worth.

Seramina took two of these over to Ange and Rine, and then she went back to grab a cup for herself.

Aleam turned to me. "Well, Olan tells me you've been fully briefed," he said.

"I wouldn't say fully," I said. "But I've learned enough. And I forgive you, Seramina. Next time, if you try using the food-bait and mind-magic trick on me, I won't fall for it."

"I'm sure you won't," Aleam said with a chuckle, while Seramina shook her head incredulously.

Aleam walked up to the easel on the other side of the room. He unrolled the scroll on it from the top to reveal a hand-drawn map of Dragonsbond Academy, with circles and crosses and other symbols scrawled across it. "Time then for our escape plan," he said. "Is everyone listening?"

Rine, Ange, and Seramina mumbled their agreement, and I groaned. Listening to him would probably send me to sleep, despite the imminent danger. I hated lectures. Plus, there was something about the flowery aroma of that tea that was making me extra tired. I yawned, then I noticed a piece of string dangling from a book on Aleam's high bookshelf. I went over to it, tried to swipe at it, but it was too high up. Instead, I chirped, hoping someone would lower the string so I could use it to keep awake.

"Ben, are you listening?" Aleam asked.

"Of course I'm listening. And I shall do so while focusing intently on this piece of string."

Aleam sighed, then he turned back to his scroll. He droned on and on about an escape plan and something about Seramina using her glamour magic, and for Ange and Rine to get ready to provide support, just in case her concentration lapsed.

"I can help too," I said.

Aleam's jaw dropped, and Rine turned back to me, goggle-eyed. "Whatever you do, don't turn into a chimera," he said. "This is meant to be a stealth operation."

"Fine," I said, and I went to lick the last morsels of smoked trout from the bowl on the floor.

Aleam was tapping nervously on the floor, glancing to the window every now and again. "We better be making a move then. There's no telling when Prince Arran will send his dragon riders to investigate here." He walked up to the door and glanced back at Seramina. "Are you sure you can handle this?"

"I don't think we have a choice," Seramina said, and she took her staff in her hands and walked out the door.

11

WHEN PLANS GO WRONG

I tried to follow Seramina. But Rine's heavy hands grasped me at the back of my belly and jerked me to a halt.

"Don't you dare, Ben," he said. "I thought you'd said you had listened to the plan?"

"I did," I lied. "I just thought it better to follow Seramina, as she has the glamour magic."

Aleam stood shaking his head. "It's going to take a while for her to cause a disruption. She needs time to distract Prince Arran's dragon riders."

"Right," I said, and I jumped up on Rine's legs, purring. Ange reached over to stroke me, and this time I let her. I had a feeling we wouldn't have any moments of comfort like this for a while, and besides, doing this brought Ange closer to Rine. Now, all I had to do was get Rine to hold Ange's hand. I tried to nudge Ange over towards him, but instead he lifted his hand and stroked me on the tail. I growled at him – it wasn't me that needed stroking, it was Ange. But he just didn't seem to get it.

"What?" he asked, shrugging slightly.

I stared at him a moment and then blinked off my frustration. "Have you told Bellari you're going away?"

He snorted. "Bellari? Gracious demons, no. If she knows where I am, then Prince Arran would get the information out of her pretty quickly."

"You don't have to tell her where you've gone."

"Oh, I do. I won't get to tell her I'm going away without telling her where I'm going."

I purred, approving very much of this situation. It meant that when Rine got back, Bellari would be angry with him, consequently increasing the chances that they'd break up and then I could work on getting Rine and Ange together. The only problem was Prince Arran might separate them permanently, and so I'd have to deal with that potential problem too. But, as Salanraja had so succinctly put it, I needed to take things one step at a time.

Aleam now stood at the doorway. After a moment, he turned to the three of us on the sofa, looking alarmed. "It didn't work. We've got Prince Arran with two of his guards coming our way." He closed the door and latched it. Then he backed away and paused, breathing heavily.

A knock came soon after – a heavy rap-rap-rap that sounded like it was produced by metal, not flesh. Either whoever was on the other side had a metal gauntlet, or they were pounding with the haft of a sword.

Aleam glanced over at the cupboard, as if wondering if he could hide me there, then he shook his head and glanced towards the window. "Check no one's outside," he whispered. "Not you, Ben. You stay there."

Ange and Rine stood up together, looked at each other, then Rine moved towards the window. He slid it open from the bottom, and peeked out. "Can't Seramina do—"

"Shh!" Aleam interrupted.

He glanced at the door again, then back to me and shook his head. I turned back to Rine, who signalled a circle with his thumb and forefinger. The wind from the window whipped his long hair into his face, and he brushed it away.

The knocking came from the door again, this time louder. "Driar

Aleam," Prince Arran said from outside. "Open up. This is the only place left that the cat can be."

"One moment," Aleam called out. Then he turned and whispered, "Go. Now!"

"But Driar Aleam…" Ange whispered, now standing up.

"Escape with Seramina, then we'll work the rest out. She knows to go ahead without me if needs be."

The banging came from the door a third time, this time so loud it shook the shelf and the equipment on the desk. "Driar Aleam. I will not ask a third time. Open the door, or I'll order it broken down."

I didn't need to be prompted further. I stood up on the bench, and I ran the short length between there and the window, then I leaped outside, scratching my hind paws against the window frame as I went. I had been in such a rush, that I hadn't really been watching where I'd been going, because I almost stumbled right into the armoured leg of one of Prince Arran's guards.

I stopped myself and dashed back into a bush underneath Aleam's window. It was rife with brambles, which scratched and stung, but I was so afraid of what might happen next, I didn't care. That was when I realised the guard hadn't even noticed me. He stood staring right at the window with glazed eyes. Meanwhile, Rine, then Ange clambered out of it right under his nose. A door creaked behind me, and I heard Aleam saying something softly.

A white light shone from my side, and I turned to see Seramina's staff, and the girl's platinum blonde hair flailing in the wind. Multiple white beams streaked like continuous bolts of lightning out of this staff, dancing in a zig-zag fashion. Some of these shot out towards the guards that Arran had arranged outside Aleam's abode. An even larger one was focused on the emerald dragon that sat atop the East Tower where Salanraja lived. The dragon faced the courtyard fountain, and it was so still it looked like a statue, or perhaps one of those hideous gargoyle things I once saw when out exploring some church grounds in South Wales.

Seramina looked down at me, this time with her fiery eyes. I backed away slightly.

"I can't hold this forever," she said. "Get over to Salanraja's."

"Salanraja's?"

"Yes, you moron," my dragon said in my mind. *"If you'd been listening, then you'd have realised that we were always going to use this place as the rendezvous."*

"I—"

"Just get going," Salanraja said. *"As the girl said, you don't have much time."*

Rine had moved closer to the bush, and he had drawn his foot back as if about to kick me. Just as his foot started to swing, I scurried out and towards the tower. I didn't look back at the two guards' legs I passed between, and they didn't seem to notice me either. Rine's and Ange's footsteps pounded behind. As I went, I saw the white light from Seramina's staff dancing around me, casting ethereal glows into the gaps between the cobblestones.

There was something off about that light. It didn't seem as strong as it should be. It wasn't steady, but guttering like candlelight. But I didn't let my fears slow me, and I didn't have time to worry about getting caught.

Dragons roared out all around me, and Seramina cried out. Next there came several shouts from the guards, and a deep rumbling growl of thunder emerged from a suddenly darkening sky. Even brighter flashes crashed around me, shooting into the ground from the gravid clouds above. The stones beneath shook, almost tripping me up.

"Aleam! The traitor..." Prince Arran's voice called out from behind me. "Seize him!"

Presumably with the entire castle focused on Aleam, I reached the East Tower's spiral staircase safely. I sprinted up it so fast that I was out of breath at the top. My burning legs carried me into Salanraja's chamber. She already had her tail lowered, and I rushed onto her, and then nestled myself in a safe place on her back within her corridor of spikes.

She took off, and I peered out from behind to see Rine, Ange, and Seramina standing at the opening of Salanraja's chamber. Their dragons came swooping around from the side of the academy in single file. Quarl came first, and Ange dropped onto him, landing with such grace in the saddle that she could have been a cat herself. Ishtkar followed, and Rine jumped down onto her, a little more clumsily, but he managed to stop himself falling off once he caught the pommel with both hands. Seramina jumped last onto Hallinar so lightly she almost seemed to float.

More flashes of lightning came from the academy, and I saw Aleam standing in the bailey at the centre of a group of Arran's guards, their staffs raised high, the crystals on them glowing in different colours. All the dragons in the castle now had their heads turned to him, and I'm not sure we even needed the cloak of invisibility that Seramina cast around our tight formation.

The prince's dragon riders surrounded Aleam with their crystals glowing on their staffs, and I thought that was it, then. They'd toast Aleam with their magic. But instead, Arran stepped forward, his red cloak trailing behind him. A bright white beam shot out from his staff, and it hit Aleam right on the forehead.

I couldn't see much now from this distance – us cats don't have great eyesight. But Rine later told me that Aleam's legs went wobbly before he collapsed to the ground in a heap.

Another crash of thunder came from the sky, and I took shelter behind Salanraja's neck. Soon, the heavens opened and, oh, did it pour.

12

FLIGHT TO AUROREST

Though the clouds cleared, trepidation still hung in the air. No one hollered a word from their mounts. No dragons roared into the sky. Even Salanraja remained silent inside my mind. We all flew onwards – Rine, Ange, and Seramina hunched in their saddles. The dragons' wings beat in a slow and steady rhythm, as if part of a rehearsed dance choreographed to help push the clouds and the looming darkness away. Only Seramina cast magic from her staff – a near transparent dome that engulfed our close formation, presumably containing a type of glamour spell to prevent any guard or dragon spotting us from afar. A bitter trailing wind had washed away the scent of ozone and rain.

The castle was now a tiny pinprick, almost invisible behind the low, thin layer of clouds. If Prince Arran and his lackeys could see us at all from there, they'd probably think we were geese or some other large bird. I wondered how long it would be until he noticed we'd left.

All this was my fault. I shouldn't have run away from that pompous idiot, Prince Arran. I should have made it look like I was going along with his plans, stupid as they were. If he'd had nothing to suspect, then the Council of Three would have found a way to sneak out some allies with me. Then, Aleam would be a part of our party.

I now had Ange, Rine, and Seramina with me to protect me against any traps Astravar might have deployed en route. But compared to Aleam, they were nothing. The old man would probably be arrested and thrown in the smelly dungeon that allegedly lay below Dragonsbond Academy and hadn't been used in years.

"We've got to stop," I said to Salanraja.

"Really, Bengie," she replied. "This isn't a good time for a toilet break."

"I don't need to go," I said. "But we can't face the forest golem without Aleam. We need to go back and rescue him. I can become a chimera, and Seramina can cast her magic, and then Ange can entangle them all in vines while Rine freezes them all to the spot."

"We've already been through this once. I'm not going to repeat it."

"But how can we get the staff without Aleam? And what will they do to him, Salanraja? He might have to go without food for days." A deep groan emanated from the pit of my stomach, as I thought about Aleam's potential suffering. Salanraja and I remained silent for a short while.

Soon enough, there came a deep rumbling sound from the direction of the castle. It was the dragons there, roaring, sounding now like distant thunder. Salanraja turned her head back, just as a faint sound of bugles called, sounding like cheap toy horns from this distance.

"Well, they've probably finally noticed that I and the other dragons are missing," Salanraja said.

"Won't they know where you are automatically? Like when you knew where I was when I ran away and got captured by serkets?"

"No, because I and the other dragons aren't bonded. Only with you do I always know of your location."

"But I thought you dragons can communicate long distance…"

"The other dragons can call out and we can answer if we choose. Even if we do, they'll have no way of knowing where we are unless we choose to tell them."

"That's a relief," I said, and I flattened myself on Salanraja's back, as I watched the sun set behind the distant castle, casting an amber light into the wispy clouds that lingered after the storm.

Uncharacteristically, her flying was so smooth, and the commotion must have made me so tired that I drifted off to sleep. I dreamt of open cans of tuna floating through the clouds, lit by warm sunlight. My reverie made for a satisfying diversion from this cruel and dark world.

What felt like moments later, the shrill cry of a seagull woke me. I'd learned back home to listen out for those vicious birds. They were one of the few dangers to cats in South Wales – a land that had been rid of horrors such as hippopotami and hyenas. The bird flew really close to Salanraja's tail, and I hissed at it, ready to swipe if it tried landing here. It wasn't until the seagull had flown away that I'd noticed what had been odd about it. Its feathers had a faint green glow to them and smelled of the kind of putrid lake where mosquitoes thrived, as if the bird had just been bathing in algae.

Salanraja laughed inside my mind. *"What are you so scared of, Ben?"*

"Birds," I said.

"I thought you hunted birds?"

"Not the big ones... Besides, this one glows in the dark."

"You really are a scaredy-cat, aren't you, Bengie? Despite being a descendant of the great Asian leopard cat and all that." She certainly sounded in better spirits than before, and admittedly after a little sleep, I felt less gloomy too.

"You still haven't told me much about where we're heading," I said. "What is the Aurorest Forest, anyway?"

"It's a forest. You know, a natural habitat with trees arranged close together?"

"I know that... But is it like the Willowed Woods? Do those horrible wargs live there?"

"No. No warg would dare to step into this forest."

I shuddered. "Why not?"

Salanraja's body rumbled underfoot, and I don't know if it was because she was laughing or sighing. *"There are things in the Aurorest Forest much worse than wargs. Life there grew so close to the warlocks' magic coming from the Wastelands that this life eventually adapted to contain magic itself. The mushrooms there will send you into a sleep you'll never wake up from, and the warlocks know how to track those spores. I'm sure Astravar will hunt you down pretty quickly if you get left there alone."*

"But would they send you to sleep too? Otherwise, you could just fly me away to safety."

"They would. Just because dragons are magical, it doesn't mean we're immune to magic. But it's not just the mushrooms we need fear. There are vines that will grow around you and entangle you faster than a mouse can move. Once they have you secured tight, only then do they unleash their thorns. Then there are small creatures that live underground and that nothing alive has ever seen, because rumour has it that when you see them, you're already dead."

Another shudder went down my spine, this time almost a spasm. "Do we have to go?"

"Of course. Astravar might have hidden your staff in a dangerous place on purpose, but we can't let that stop us. Once we retrieve it, you can fulfil the crystal's prophecy, and then hopefully this will all be over."

"But if Astravar had the staff, why didn't he hold it in the Wastelands?"

"Firstly, the Aurorest Forest is now in the Wastelands. The warlocks have pushed the border forward, remember? As for your question, I don't know the answer to it. But you shouldn't underestimate the forest. No doubt, Astravar's forest golem will be constructed from parts of the forest. And anything that came from the forest, the forest will try to prevent from leaving. It's as if it has its own soul, you see, albeit a very dark one. The forest will fight to protect the forest golem, and so we need to be very careful indeed."

"So it doesn't belong to the warlocks?"

"That's what the Wastelands is, remember? A no-man's-land, where battles rage between the magical creatures of King Garmin's White Mages and the dark magical creations of the warlocks."

"But that means we'll have allies in there too."

"I don't think so," Salanraja said.

"Why not?"

"It's as I said. The forest is a magical creation of itself. Most creatures that either we or the warlocks send in there won't survive very long. A forest golem is different, because it's made of the forest. As for the Manipulators and bone dragons there that we saw in the crystal, Astravar must have worked some powerful sorcery to keep them there."

Salanraja was scaring me so much I wanted to throw up that roast duck Seramina had fed me before. *"I don't want to go there anymore. Let's turn back..."*

"Nonsense. We're not even going to land in the Aurorest Forest. We'll fight the forest golem from the air. Burn it down until only your staff remains – because magical staffs cannot be burned by dragon fire – then we'll all go home and do what we have to do."

"I'm never going back to my true home," I said. Then Salanraja growled, because she didn't like to be reminded I wasn't from her world.

The sun was now hidden behind a looming green mist. This didn't smell of rotten vegetable juice like Astravar and the other warlocks. It smelled instead of mould and algae – another scent I wasn't too partial to. I imagined the mushrooms on the ground, and I wondered if they were making me sleepy or if it was just my imagination. There had to be a positive way of looking at this, surely. In the distance I thought I heard running water, and that got me thinking.

"What about food?" I asked. *"Perhaps if the forest has magical qualities, there are good things to eat there as well. Maybe we should at least try to hunt for something. Perhaps, magically, some salmon has found its way into the streams."*

"There's no salmon there," Salanraja said. *"And if it were there, I wouldn't know what it looked like."*

"But it's worth looking for, isn't it? Salanraja, I haven't had salmon in ages."

"Gracious demons, will you just shut up for one moment!" Salanraja snapped.

"Why? What's wrong with salmon?"

"Because we're about to land."

The dragons loosened their formation, and they lowered towards the ground. I could see the mist clearly now behind the darkness, for it glowed like there was a green moon hidden behind it. I imagined I could make out shapes shifting around there – some of them wavering from their roots, others stalking the territory like wargs.

We were heading right for the glowing mist that presumably marked the borders of the forest. The dragons were getting so close to it that if what Salanraja said was true, those things moving inside would eat us alive. A sound emanated out from the forest that at first sounded like a scream. But then, when I listened longer, I noticed the yowling of sad creatures, the hissing of a wind that doesn't want water to stay still, and all the other kinds of sounds I might hear in my nightmares, all singing in a chorus that seemed to say, *stay well away.*

I clambered up Salanraja's neck onto her head, to get as far away from that mist as possible. "*I thought you said we weren't going to land,*" I said.

"*Not in the forest, no,*" Salanraja said. "*The mist marks where it's safe and where it's not.*"

"But why do we need to sleep at all?"

"*Trust me, you don't want to send four tired dragons up against a forest golem. So long as no one lights a fire, we'll be fine.*"

Salanraja thudded against the ground, and she bucked her head so hard that she almost sent me tumbling off it. The other three dragons landed around her, and Ange, Rine, and Seramina launched themselves off from their saddles. Rine and Ange then produced two cotton bundles from Ishtkar's and Quarl's panniers. These turned out to be tents.

It took Rine and Ange several minutes to put these up. Soon after, Rine walked over to me and said, "I guess you're sleeping with me tonight, Ben. Without Aleam, we don't need the third tent."

"What, you're not sleeping with—" I almost said it, then I remembered how Seramina had gone back to her old scary self. No, Rine was right. It was better if I left her with Ange.

"Come on," Rine said, "let's get some sleep." He crawled into his tent, and I followed him. I doubted somehow that a thin layer of cotton would protect us from what horrors lay behind that luminous mist. But it was all we had.

13

A COLD NIGHT

It was much colder than I'd expected in the tent – even with Rine there to provide extra warmth. There was something about this place that leached all the warmth out of the night. Maybe the forest sapped it away, feeding on it and casting a green spooky translucent glow through the tent fabric, the way that sunlight suffuses through skin.

I tried snuggling up as close as possible to Rine. First, I sat in front of his face where his breath could keep me warm, until he pushed me away, mumbling that I stank of fish. Then I stretched outwards towards his belly, stretching out to find the room that a mighty cat like me deserves. But unlike most humans, Rine wouldn't budge when I tried to push him away.

I mean, it was okay for Rine – he had a sleeping bag to keep him warm. All I had was my fur, and a frigid draught crept underneath the tent flap, then stirred around me until finally lurching in to cut through that fur.

It was too much for me. I had to go outside and keep moving. I lifted myself up on my paws and shook off the stiffness in my muscles from the flight. Then I flattened my body and edged underneath the tent flap.

The first thing I smelled when I stepped outside wasn't the rotten vegetable juice that I'd expected, given the Aurorest Forest was now reputedly part of the Wastelands, or that equally putrid algae smell that came from the forest proper. Instead, I smelled snowdrop perfume, and I turned to see Seramina standing in front of her tent, staring out at the green mist. She held her staff horizontally against her thighs. She didn't seem to notice me there until I rubbed up against her calf, purring.

The snores from the dragons and the sounds from the forest seemed to riff off of each other as if part of a performance piece. The noise was even louder than those nights I'd accidentally slept outside in Wales, to be surrounded by crickets. It was no wonder I couldn't get any sleep.

Seramina looked down at me, a glint of green mist catching in her eye. "Oh, Ben... What are you doing here? Shouldn't you be sleeping?"

"Couldn't sleep. But I am nocturnal after all... What about you?"

"Someone has to keep guard," she said with a slight smile, again seeming a little forced.

"I thought that the dangerous creatures that lived in the forest could never leave it." I said. "Don't they need the mist to survive?"

"Oh, but there are also things that live around the forest. This is the wilderness after all, and the fringes of the kingdom also house bandits. You should never assume you're safe." She turned her gaze back from me towards the mist. "You know, it's strange. But it's somewhat beautiful. I'd never have thought that a place like this... It doesn't matter."

I examined the mist, trying to work out what she was talking about. Given humans have inferior hearing to cats, perhaps she couldn't hear the screeches and yowls and sounds of nightmares that came from behind that glowing screen. "I don't know what you're talking about. It smells funny, and it sounds wrong, and I really don't want to go in there tomorrow."

"I guess you've seen the faery realm," Seramina said. "Because in the books, they say it's the most beautiful of the Seven Dimensions."

"Is it really the beauty you're attracted to?" I asked. "Or is it the power contained within the forest?"

"What do you mean?" For a moment, I could swear, some fire sparked in Seramina's eyes. But as soon as it was there, it vanished. "No, I don't want the magic. It's not good for me. I've learned that. I must only use my magic when I need it, and I mustn't embrace anything else. My father... I mean, Astravar, once was good, they say, until dark magic twisted his soul... I could never let that happen to me."

One of the dragons snorted from the darkness, briefly interrupting the harmony of snores. Then there came a rustling from our side and Ange crawled out of the tent flap. She sauntered over to us, stretching and yawning as she moved. "Seramina... You should have woken me. It's surely my turn to keep watch."

Seramina shook her head. "It's okay, you can sleep more. I'm not tired."

"Seramina, really. You can't stay up all night. You've got to sleep sometimes."

"I'm fine," she snapped, her voice raised and the tone of it biting against the wind. She raised her staff, and it started to glow. Fire momentarily burned at the back of her eyes.

Ange took a step back, her arms outstretched. She looked back at her tent, probably at the staff that lay there on the floor next to her fleece sleeping bag. "Seramina... Remember what Aleam told you. Calm your mind."

"I—" Seramina lowered her staff. "I'm sorry. I didn't mean any harm." Though her staff had stopped feeding the night with light, it still emitted a slight afterglow.

"You just thought you'd hypnotise me back to sleep?" Ange had her hands on her hips and her eyebrows raised. "You can't solve your problems with magic, Seramina. But you often can with a good night's rest." She glanced back at her tent.

"I know... But really, I'm not tired."

More rustling came, this time louder and from the other tent.

"What's going on here, then?" Rine said, as he peered out from the tent flap, resting on his elbows and not bothering to lift himself up. He had his staff grasped in his hands, raised at an angle, but it wasn't aglow.

"Nothing," Ange said. "I'm just replacing Seramina on the watch. Unless you've decided to be a gentleman and fill in for me?" She cocked her head like a pretty bird.

Rine shook his head. "I don't know what woke me, the sudden commotion out here or the fact it's so cold. It's freezing, in fact. That magical mist must suck all the heat out of the atmosphere or something. Ben, why did you leave? I was relying on you for warmth."

"I needed to get moving. You weren't warm enough for me, Rine. Look, why don't we light a fire?"

"With what?" Ange asked.

"We have four dragons over there."

Rine snorted. "And you plan to wake them, Ben?"

"Uh, no, I thought one of you might. You're better experienced with these things."

"We're not lighting a fire," Ange said. "It's too dangerous. There's no telling what might be on the surrounding roads."

"Oh, and who put you in charge?" Rine asked.

"I'm the oldest…"

"But not necessarily the wisest."

Ange scowled at Rine. Really, this man wasn't doing himself any favours with the lady he truly loved. I made a mental note to have a word with him about that later.

"I think you'll find she's much wiser than you," Seramina said.

"Well, I don't think it's particularly wise to freeze to death," Rine said. "Come on, we've got three magic users and a cat that can turn into a chimera, as well as four dragons. What can possibly hurt us?"

"Bandits if we're sleeping. Or worse, they could steal our staffs, then what will we fight the forest golem with?" Ange asked.

"Plus, a fire will make it harder for us to see them, and easier for them to see us," Seramina said – trust the girls to stick together.

"So will lighting the place up with that," Rine said, pointing to the crystal on top of Seramina's staff. He pulled in his legs to his chest and then leapt to his feet. "I'll go and get firewood. You want to come, Ben?"

"You mean into the forest?" I asked, and I growled a protest for effect.

Rine laughed. "No, we're not entering the Aurorest until morning. But there's plenty of trees outside the forest. There should be some decent firewood, and you could turn into a chimera to help keep guard against the *bandits*." He put an extra dry undertone on the last words, as if to communicate he didn't believe in such bandits.

"He shouldn't turn into a chimera, Rine," Ange said.

"Why not? We could all do with his strength."

"Because the more he does, the more he risks becoming one for life."

"And wouldn't that be cool?" Rine reached down to stroke me under the chin. "Our own personal chimera."

"Didn't you hear her?" Seramina asked. Her staff was back in her hands, glowing white, and her eyes were afire again. "We're not lighting a fire…"

"Whoa," Rine said.

"Seramina…" Ange said. "Control, remember?"

The mind-witch lowered her head, and the light on her staff guttered out. "I'm sorry… It's just… Aleam. I'm worried. Will he be okay? If my magic was stronger, he would be with us right now."

Ange sidled over to her and put her arm over her shoulder. "He's a tough old man. He'll wriggle his way out of this somehow."

"But what do you think Prince Arran will do to him?"

"I don't know," Ange said. "But it can't be anything too horrible. Prince Arran might be royalty, but he's still subject to the king's law. I'm sure the Council of Three will find a way to release Aleam, and then he'll fly right back out here to help us."

"Right…"

"You should get some sleep, really."

"But you seem so tired as well. I'll be okay," Seramina said through clenched teeth.

"Maybe," Ange yawned and turned to Rine. "I guess if our man here seems awake enough to get firewood, then he'll be well enough also to stand guard."

"No way," Rine said. "I'm getting under the sleeping bag again."

"So, I'll stand guard then," Ange said. "If Rine's too selfish to do so."

"No," Seramina said. "Really, you look exhausted, and I can function without sleep."

"Why don't I keep watch?" I suggested.

Rine guffawed, and Ange turned to me and stared, wide-eyed. "You can't do this, Ben," she said.

"Why not?"

"Because you'll just doze off. Besides, anyone who might have the eye on this camp isn't going to let themselves be deterred by a cat."

"Then I should become a chimera," I said.

"I thought we said that you weren't to become a chimera," Ange said.

But I wasn't listening. The power just felt so good. As I sucked it in, I could swear some thin tendrils of that glowing mist swept towards me, infusing me with the magic of the Aurorest Forest. My muscles writhed and twisted, and I mewled, and then growled and then roared out in pain. Two other heads emerged out of my neck and tail, and I had that sensation of being three animals again, with access to all their sights and hearings, and the ability to taste the world on my snake head's forked tongue.

"There," I said. "Two parts of me can sleep while the other one stays awake. Problem solved."

The three humans stood in place, looking completely gobsmacked. They had also taken several steps away from me and their hands were gripping their staffs, their knuckles white. It seemed they didn't quite trust that this time I might turn feral. But I knew how to keep control.

"*Bengie, I thought we said you weren't going to do that?*" Salanraja said to me, although her voice now sounded muffled, as it often did when I was in chimera form.

"*I thought you were sleeping?*"

"*I was until I felt our bond tensing. You know, if you do that enough, you* won't just become feral, but you'll also break the bond between us. Just think what would happen to me then."

"It was necessary!"

"What? How?"

"They just wouldn't shut up, and Seramina needs to sleep."

"Oh, I knew I would have problems choosing a feline rider. If only our crystal had told me what I'd be getting myself in for. Ah well, what can you do?" And then, just like that, her thoughts drifted off to oblivion, and I heard her softly mumbling in my mind as if from her dreams.

Meanwhile, back at the campsite and outside the realm of my mind, it was Ange who broke the silence. "Well, I have to admit," she said with a shrug. "I've never seen a goat sleep."

"Yeah, me neither, come to think of it," Rine said. "Say, do goats actually sleep at all?"

Ange had now taken hold of Seramina's hand and was dragging her into the tent. "Come on," she said. "Before it gets bright. You need to get at least a couple of hours of shuteye."

Both girls vanished into the tent. Rine also lowered himself back into his tent. "I guess I'm just going to freeze by myself in here, then," he said, and he let out a yawn that looked almost feline in its vastness.

Funnily enough, the goat part of me didn't feel tired. But I could swear that the snake part and cat part of me caught a few more winks. There was nothing to watch out for though – the whole 'bandits' dilemma had been a complete farce. There weren't any bandits around to fear, and those strange noises from the mist stayed within the mist. Besides, given I had a lion's strength, a snake's venom, and a goat's speed to fight back with, I didn't feel scared of anything.

As I stared off into the darkness, my snake's tongue tasted something in the air. The whiff of rotten vegetable floating in faint streams upon the currents that smelled of rotten algae. I'd discovered a trace of more than one dark magical creature in there, and tomorrow I vowed to hunt them down.

14

BRO TIME

The next morning, Ange finally allowed us the privilege of lighting a fire.

So, I went with Rine into the surrounding woods that weren't part of the Aurorest Forest and didn't fall under its shroud of glowing mist. Admittedly, it was no longer so cold that we needed a fire, but there was a promise of mutton sausages on the horizon. Rine had already expressed his annoyance to Ange that we had skipped our age-old dragon rider tradition of roasting them on the campfire, all because of her fear of bandits that weren't there. But Ange had said she'd only delayed it and that they would still have the sausages - for breakfast, once the well-rested Initiate proved his worth and gathered the firewood.

We did, of course, need to work out the location of the forest golem. I'd had time to assess the smell, and I could also taste various streams of dark magic on my snake's tongue. Some of them, no doubt, belonged to the bone dragons and Manipulators that we'd seen here in the crystal. But anything could wait for nutritious food, particularly food that had been freshly barbecued on an open fire.

I went with Rine, not so much because I wanted to chop firewood, but because I had work to do in sealing up the rift that had widened between Ange and Rine the previous night.

I was still in chimera form as Rine and I hiked through the woods, and I scanned every single tree we passed – beeches and poplars and silver birches – wondering which of them I'd end up knocking down with my goat horns. Rine would have to weaken the trunk first with his hatchet, of course, but I'd do the hard work of actually felling it.

Rine stopped by a large horizontal trunk of dry silver birch that had already fallen, probably in a storm. He smiled and then unlatched his hatchet from his waist. I went over to sniff the bark and noticed there wasn't anything peculiar about it. It didn't smell of disgusting algae or rotten vegetable juice or anything like that.

"I thought we were going to chop down some trees," I complained. I'd been looking forward to the whole ramming down a tree part. I hadn't used my goat ability since I'd defeated the demon Maine coone.

"Why would we do that, when there's perfectly good firewood on the ground?" Rine asked.

"Well, come to think of it, why would we do any of this searching for firewood when Ange could just generate some using her leaf magic."

Rine laughed. "Have you ever tried to burn wet grass?"

"Can't say I have. Have you ever seen a cat try to burn anything?"

"I guess not." Rine shrugged. "Well, let's just say that Ange can only work with stuff that's alive, which tends to be full of water, meaning it won't burn well." He ran his hand along the branch. "This beauty, on the other hand, has dried out and will make perfect kindling. Which might make a particularly smoky fire, cooking perhaps the best mutton sausages you've ever tasted."

I chirped, liking the sound of that. "So basically, you didn't need me here at all?" I said. "Because it looks like there's nothing I can do to help you chop the firewood."

"I appreciate the company," Rine said, raising his hatchet slowly as he lined up a perfect place to chop the wood. "Besides, aren't you meant to be guarding me in case any bandits attack? I might not be able to get to my staff in time, and I'm not particularly good at throwing an axe."

"There are no bandits. I would have smelled them…"

"I know. It's ridiculous, right? Ah well, girls will be girls."

Rine brought his axe down, slicing right through a large chunk of bark and wood. He nodded, clearly satisfied that his instrument was sharp enough. I watched him for a while, as he worked away at the tree, occasionally stopping to wipe sweat away from his brow with the back of his hand. Eventually it became rather boring, and a passing dragonfly caught my attention. I started after it until I realised that a beast three size the times of a lion was meant to hunt larger things.

So, I turned back to Rine, who had just paused to take a breather, and I focused on the issue at hand. "When are you going to say it to her?" I asked him.

"Say what, and to who?"

"Ange… When are you going to tell her what you truly feel about her?"

Rine looked at me as if he was considering kicking me, but he probably realised I was much bigger and much scarier than him in this form. "Not this again. How many times do I have to tell you, Ben? Ange and I aren't a thing. I'm with Bellari. And that's how I intend it to be for a very long time."

"But not forever," I said.

"I…" Rine looked away. "I didn't say that."

"But you meant it, and do you know why? Because you have feelings for Ange… And if I keep nagging you about them enough, you'll one day act on them. Then, you know what? I think you're going to make a great family."

Rine laughed. "I can't imagine myself having little Ange babies. They'll be so bossy, and they'll think they're the smartest kids in the world. No thanks, Ben. Really."

I barked out a laugh. "Is that what you're scared of? You don't want your kids to be smarter than you? Then tell me, what has Bellari got to offer from the gene pool?"

"It's not that, it's just… Look I can't believe we're having this conversation, Ben. Just shut up. I'm not going to talk about it anymore." He brought down his axe again with such vigour that it looked like he might chop off his hand.

Now, I don't know if being a chimera made me smarter. Perhaps the goat had a bigger brain, or I just had the idiosyncratic cunning of a snake. But I realised through this that I was trying the wrong strategy with Rine. I needed to come in from the side. There was no point telling Rine what his feelings were. I had to make him realise them for himself.

"You know, I've never told you this, but I have regrets."

"What that you never had another mouthful of that fish, what did you call it, salmon, before you came into this world?" Rine said this with a smile that contained half a mocking sneer.

"No, not that. But I do miss salmon. Now, though, I'm talking about Ta'ra."

Rine stopped a while and looked up at me. "What about her?"

"I never told her about how I really felt before she left us to look after the other Cat Sidhe."

"So why didn't you say anything?" Rine asked.

"Because I wasn't honest with myself about my feelings. Whiskers, I'm not even sure cats are meant to have these kinds of feelings. We're meant to be solitary creatures that look after ourselves, unless we need to eat food, and then someone feeds us, and we go back to looking after ourselves again."

"What are you trying to say, Ben?" Rine cocked his head.

"I'm trying to say that I wish I'd have told her at least how much I wanted her to stay. Because now, I don't know, I might never get to see her again. That's how it is… If we don't seize the opportunities we have when we're presented with them, they don't tend to come up again."

Rine placed his axe down on the trunk and stood up with his hands on his hips, looking me square in the eyes. "And you think it's the same with me and Ange?"

"Oh, I know so," I said, adding a deep rumbling leonine purr of victory to my voice. "You regret getting into that relationship with Bellari and part of you wants to get out and start a relationship with Ange. But you feel too much peer pressure, because your 'friends' are so proud of you for landing such a catch. So you convince yourself that you were 'meant' to be with Bellari all along."

Rine puckered his mouth and sucked air through his tight lips, making a slight whistling sound. "Well, look at you, mister insightful."

"Are you telling me I'm wrong?"

Rine paused and stared into space. "Fine," he said after a moment. "I'm going to tell you what you want to hear, and that will be the end of it. Yes, I feel something for Ange. But of course I do, because she's been my friend all of my life."

"I think it's more than just a 'she's my friend' kind of feeling. You feel more for her than you do for Bellari. Admit it!"

Rine's face had almost gone bright puce, and he looked like he would kick me right now, with no regard for if I was a chimera or not. But when he looked into my eyes, and I yawned, showing him my huge sharp fangs, I guess he came to his senses. "Okay, I feel more for her than I do for Bellari," he said.

"Finally... A confession. So, the next question is, what are you going to do about it?"

"I'm going to do absolutely nothing," Rine said, with a smirk. "And I'll live with those regrets the rest of my life probably, just like you do. I'll be a fallen hero type. I'll complain about it for the rest of my life until I find another girl. I won't marry Bellari in the end, and I know that. I'll eventually, in the wider world, find another girl who isn't Bellari, and isn't Ange, and she'll be beautiful, and then I'll live a very happy life."

I watched Rine as he spoke, my eyes wide, trying to work out if he was serious or just having a jest with me. He waxed lyrical about the type of girl he'd eventually marry. About her upbringing – filthy rich, her hair colour – red like Asinda's, her eyes – a beautiful turquoise green, her measurements. Funnily enough, not once did he mention anything about her personality. Even worse, he hadn't even stopped to consider her quality as a chef. Not that I'm saying a woman needed to be, just I doubted Rine knew his fried eggs from his poached ones.

It seemed as if he would go on and on forever unless I did something about it. "Okay, that's enough," I said. "Go back to chopping firewood, and I might even take another nap."

"A nap? You just slept all night."

"And now it's daytime, a good time for sleeping." I laid my head against the ground and I closed my eyes. But I didn't end up sleeping. Rather, I continued to listen to Rine's chop-chop-chopping of wood, the occasional strand of bark brushing against my whiskers.

Inside, though, I was content. Because despite Rine shining me on, I had made progress. I'd finally made him admit he liked Ange romantically. Now, I had to work out how to break it to her.

15

SAUSAGES

Just as Ange was the oldest human in our party, Quarl was the oldest dragon, and so the emerald had the honour of lighting the campfire. Everyone stood behind him as he drew back his long neck. A rumbling sound grew in his belly while his nostrils smoked and whistled like a kettle ready to boil. He opened his mouth and out came a jet of amber flame. It hit the neat arrangement of firewood in the centre of the pit, casting out a bright light and long shadows from the ring of stones on the outside that Ange and Seramina had gathered while I was chopping firewood with Rine.

The fire came to life, and its flames shot upwards, reaching into the sky. I watched it for a moment, appreciating the warmth. Then Rine walked over to Ishtkar and took a huge string of sausages out of his panniers. This was so large, he had to place it over his neck before he deposited it in front of the dragons who had gathered in a loose circle. He took another smaller string, separated the links with a pocketknife, then skewered several individual sausages, and started to roast them on the open flame. He sat on a log as he did so, and I watched, mesmerised by both the fat spitting on the sausage and the wonderful aroma it sent up into the air.

Ange joined him on the log. This time she sat next to Rine, a little closer to him. Being a chimera, I was a little too big to sit on a log, and so I curled up by Rine's and Ange's feet as I stared into the flames. Only Seramina didn't sit. Instead, she stood staring into the mist, facing away from us, seemingly uninterested in our feast. Meanwhile, the dragons started to toast their own sausages. All this fire roaring around us cast such an impressive display of light that I forgot momentarily about the glow coming from the Aurorest Forest, and the shadowy shapes that moved within the mist.

"Me first," I said. "Please, Rine, let me have the first sausage."

He looked at me and scoffed. "Turn back into a normal cat, first," he said. "Otherwise, you'll eat more than we can spare."

"No," I said. "I'm staying as a chimera. That way, we have the best bet of defeating the forest golem." From behind me, Salanraja gave a disgruntled snort. But I guess she was so much into roasting her food that she didn't this time bother chiding me.

Ange, however, did. "Ben, this isn't wise," she said. "Remember what happened when you turned into a chimera in the dragon egg-and-spoon? Seramina ended up winning, because you were too heavy for Salanraja to carry."

"She would have won anyway," I pointed out. "Me turning into a chimera gave us the best chance."

I looked up at Seramina, expecting a reaction. She said nothing. She had her staff braced horizontally across her thighs, as the firelight cast pretty patterns over her platinum blonde-hair.

"This isn't the point, and you know it," Ange said. "You'll be far too heavy for Salanraja in your current form. Then, by the time she gets to the forest golem, she'll be too exhausted to fight. Without Olan here, we need all the dragons in tip-top shape. So, as the leader here, I'm ordering you to turn back into a cat."

"I wasn't planning to fly," I said. "I can go by myself through the Aurorest Forest on foot if you want?"

"You've got to be kidding," Rine said. "Great, the cat's being a moron again."

"What?"

Ange was a little more tactful in her approach. "Just because you're a chimera, Ben, doesn't make you invincible. Even in your form the mushrooms will send you to sleep if you try passing through. Then, other creatures in there will emerge and devour you whole. And all that will be before you even get to the forest golem."

"But from the air, I'll lose the trail. If we don't take advantage, we might never find the forest golem. Then, if I don't get the staff, how are we meant to defeat Astravar?"

"A forest golem won't be hard to miss," Rine said.

"Really, and you think we'll be able to see it through that thick mist? Plus, it's got Manipulators and bone dragons guarding it. If we track it on the ground, we reserve the element of surprise."

Ange was shaking her head. "Why don't you ask what your dragon thinks?" she said, her voice slightly raised. "In fact, why don't you ask what all the dragons think?"

I turned back to Salanraja, who had just finished devouring her huge mutton sausage. Still, the scent of it lingered on the air, making me feel even hungrier. I'd much rather be eating than arguing. But I knew we needed the staff as fast as possible. Maybe being part lion gave me extra bravado, but I really needed to make my point.

"*I guess you're going to give me a lecture now,*" I said to Salanraja inside my mind as she turned her head to me.

"*It's not just me,*" Salanraja said. "*Every single one of us dragons thinks you're being idiotic.*"

"*Why? Because I want to take a bit of action around here?*"

"*No, because you're letting your pride impede good old-fashioned common sense. Why don't you listen to people who are wiser than you for once, Ben? Ange, at least, has a good head on her shoulders.*"

"*Because this time I know I'm right. We need to act while we've got the advantage.*"

"*No,*" Salanraja said. "*That's how people like Prince Arran and his dragon Corralsa think. The warlocks will take advantage of such impatience when they notice it. We need to act in a measured way.*"

"*I've thought this through,*" I said. "*I had an entire night to think about it.*"

"Hah, I never thought I'd meet the day when you think about something first."

"I still let it process in the back of my mind. What do you call that place? The subconscious!"

"Did you? Because I don't think you have a clue. Tell me this if you've got such a grand plan. How will you sneak in exactly? What will, in fact, give you the element of surprise?"

"I'll be stealthy."

"What, as a massive chimera beast? You'll stick out like a mouldering talon."

Salanraja's words struck true. A chimera wouldn't be particularly stealthy. For this mission, we needed me in my true form. I could pass through the Aurorest Forest as a Bengal, undetected, much as I'd done many times through the wilderness of my South Wales neighbourhood back home. Besides, Rine and Ange had already started munching on a couple of sausages, and Rine had told me I needed to be a normal cat to eat one.

So, I let the magic seep back into my bones, the way that my crystal had taught me. My muscles gained that stretching sensation – this time due to them shrinking. I roared out in pain, and I continued this way until the roar shrank to a growl, and then a soft chirp. Rine glanced at me, smiled, then he tossed a sausage down on the floor. It smelled delicious as I approached it, and I ripped off a mouthful of tantalising juiciness.

It wasn't until I was delightfully chomping down on it that I realised I couldn't smell rotten vegetable juice anymore. Whiskers, I'd lost my trail. "Great," I said, after I'd swallowed my food. "I can't smell the golem now."

"Salanraja, this is your fault," I added in my mind.

She responded with a loud growl that caused Ange to jump slightly. Ange then gave me a stern look as if to tell me not to aggravate my dragon. Really, it seemed that as soon as she became boss around here I was destined to get on bad terms with her. But then, from the moment I'd encountered authority in this new world, I'd had problems with it.

"So we'll just have to do things the old fashioned way," Rine said with his mouth full. "The way we always did when Aleam was with us. Seramina, do you want a sausage? You've not eaten anything for hours."

But Seramina didn't turn back to us. It was then that I noticed something was off. Her hair was blowing as if moved by a wind that wasn't there, and her staff had a slight glow to it. I still couldn't see her eyes, but I could imagine they were burning like they always did. I wasn't the only one to notice something wasn't quite right, either.

"Seramina?" Ange said.

Ignoring Ange, Seramina took a decisive step forward. In my whiskers I could now feel the breeze picking up and eddying around her.

"I've got this," she said, as if speaking from a dream. "Do not worry. I must take this chance now, or we'll miss it."

She raised her staff, its gem glowing brightly. Then she ran forward, gently, as if almost on tiptoes, but at speed. Her dragon Hallinar tipped back her charcoal head and called out with a shriek, and looked ready to go bounding after her. But Quarl blocked his path, clearly afraid Seramina might do something to her dragon if he interfered.

Seramina continued to run towards the green glowing mist.

"Seramina," Ange called out again. She shook her head and then lifted her staff off her back. The gem at the top of it glowed green for a moment, and then a good dozen twisty stalks shot of it towards Seramina's ankle. Cascades of purple light streamed out of Seramina's staff, falling at the point where Ange's vines were headed. The spells collided head on, and both the vines and the light stream fizzled into nothingness.

"Dark magic," Ange said. "Gracious demons, Seramina!"

But her words couldn't stop the girl, just as her magic couldn't.

"Come on," Ange ran ahead a little, then looked over her shoulder at Rine. "We need to go after her."

Rine shrugged, then unslung his staff from his shoulder and

sprinted to catch up with Ange. "Come on, Ben," he screamed without turning around. "And don't turn into a chimera."

I had no choice, really. But before I left, I picked up another mouthful of sausage to keep me going. As I ran, a great thunderous crash boomed out from behind, followed by the flapping of wings as our four dragons lifted into the sky.

16

THROUGH THE FOREST

It took us a matter of minutes to catch up with Seramina, but then she was hardly sprinting. Rather, she sneaked as if stalking a mouse. She had her staff raised up above her head. Purple tentacles of magic whipped out of the crystal on it. Plants veered away from her path, creating a clear route through.

We were well within the forest, and the smell of rotten algae and dirt hung in the air. Around us, yellow clouds floated above nearby clusters of mushrooms. I presumed this to contain the spores that would reputedly send us to sleep. But even the clouds seeped away from Seramina.

"Seramina," Ange called out. "I'm not going to warn you again." She raised her staff to cast another spell, presumably with the aim of tripping Seramina up, or perhaps wresting the staff out of her grasp using magical vines.

I growled, but I didn't have time to warn her not to be so idiotic. Fortunately, Rine also saw sense. He leapt in front of Ange and knocked her staff down to her waist. "Don't!"

"What?" Ange asked, her eyes wide.

"Don't you see? Without her magic, we have no protection. I don't know what kind of magic she's using. But we now have to see how this plays out."

"Fine," Ange said, frowning. "But I really don't like this."

"Neither do I," Rine said. "But we don't have much of a choice, do we?"

Seramina didn't seem to realise we were talking about her. She was in such a trance, with a white glow now floating around her, giving her a spectral appearance. Then I saw why Rine had claimed he had no clue what kind of magic she was using, because there was a white light also coming from her crystal, radiating outwards, presumably casting the protection we needed to make our way through.

"It doesn't matter," I said, stalking as close as I could to Seramina in case I ended up breathing in some of those sleep spores, "because she's leading us to the forest golem."

"How do you know she is?" Rine asked.

"I just have a hunch. Maybe she has the magic to vanquish it without us even having to fight. After all, she is the daughter of Astravar."

"Seramina," Ange said. "Say something, please. At least tell us your plan."

The young teenager stopped and turned around. Ange's jaw dropped, and she gasped. I looked up, and where I'd expected to see fire in her eyes, instead, they had gone pearl white, with a slightly purple glow to them. "You needn't worry." Her voice was flat. "I have it all under control. I'm merely following the trail Ben detected. Keep close and you'll be safe."

Ange frowned. She didn't look convinced. Rine shook his head, then shrugged. I growled at Seramina, not liking that horrible look in her eyes. Seramina turned back and continued onwards, almost floating instead of walking. I looked up to get a view of the dragons. But the green glow made it hard to see far above. I could still hear them, though, or at least their wings beating.

I marched slightly to the side of Seramina so I could see her in profile, and I noticed white lines like lightning bolts streaking across her skin. They were very faint. I remembered how Astravar looked, with his eggshell cracked skin. I'd learned to fear him every time I saw him in my dreams, even if I hadn't seen him much lately. Whiskers, I really hoped that Seramina didn't end up going down the same path as him.

What is Hallinar feeling right now? I wondered.

"Are you talking to me?" Salanraja asked.

"No, just thinking out loud. But maybe... What about Seramina's dragon? Does he like her casting this kind of magic? Something tells me that if I did it, you'd be furious."

"I would," Salanraja said. "And we need to give Hallinar all the support we can right now. We don't know what Seramina is up to, but something has forced her to cut off her bond to her dragon. Hallinar can't reach her, and he's feeling terribly alone."

That was all Salanraja said, and so we trudged on silently. As we went, I could hear the heavy beating of Ange's and Rine's hearts, and they kept glancing at Seramina worriedly, unable to do anything. Meanwhile, Seramina's heart sounded deadly still.

It wasn't long until we saw a white glow on the horizon that seemed to push away the ambient green light that surrounded us.

"There they are," Rine said.

"Who?" I asked.

"Manipulators... But usually it's them that sees us first."

"Slow down, Seramina," Ange said. "We must exercise caution now."

"No," Seramina said through clenched teeth, and her hair whipped out in many directions. "I've got this."

"But you have no idea what Astravar put there..."

"Oh, I do," Seramina said. "I do..."

Rine and Ange now had their staffs gripped tightly in their hands, the white of their knuckles showing. Part of me still wanted to turn into a chimera so I could join the fight.

"Don't," Salanraja told me.

"Whiskers, I wish you weren't reading my mind all the time."

"I'm just saying this to protect you. You're better stealthy against a forest golem as a cat than huge and visible as a chimera."

This was one of the rare occasions I knew she was right. Or at least I thought she was...

We continued to follow Seramina, me staying close behind her ankles while Rine and Ange stayed on either side of her. Not long after, the forest golem came into view. It wasn't facing us but looked out towards the direction of the camp as if it thought we were there. The glowing spectral forms of seven Manipulators hovered close to its massive feet, each one having a bone dragon splayed across the ground in front of them.

They didn't seem to see us. In fact, the entire scene was unnaturally still. A bitter wind seeped through the forest, singing out as it whisked past the surrounding strange bulbous plants that leaned away from Seramina as if afraid of what she had become.

"The time is nigh," Seramina said. Then her voice changed, and she spun around to face me. Her eyes went a haunting, glowing purple colour, and those white cracks that I'd seen ever so faintly on her face before shone even brighter.

"Now, young Dragoncat," she said. Her voice was deeper, and I knew it wasn't really Seramina who spoke – I'd seen this kind of magic before. "It is time for you to face your destiny. As for the rest of you, you are fools to bring one of my own blood into my domain. My daughter shall join me soon and share my power. It won't be long until she learns who she truly is."

"Astravar," I hissed, as the hackles shot up on the back of my neck.

The wind picked up around Seramina, sending up a sudden putrid smell of rotten vegetable juice, as if this place didn't smell horrid enough.

She stared back with terrifying, glowing eyes, and I knew well that a battle was nigh.

17

GOLEM BATTLE

So much happened at once.
There came a great roar from the forest golem, and a creaking sound like wood about to snap. Seramina shrieked out shrilly and spun to face Ange. She thrust her staff forward and cast a purple beam of energy right at Ange. This met a wall of ice that Rine had magicked out of the blue shimmering crystal on his staff.

Ange joined the battle by casting a flurry of vines right out of her green glowing staff. These twisted over Rine's wall like fast-growing wallflowers. They travelled back downwards and crept along the ground at super speed, kicking grey leaves up off the forest floor. Then they gripped Seramina's staff, and the features on the teenager's face contorted into a wicked grin of concentration as purple flames crept along the vines towards Rine's wall of ice.

Meanwhile, the forest golem was glowing green as a powerful wind buffeted around it. The bone dragons screeched as they lifted their necks and they pulled up into the air, and the Manipulators warped into life, their forms shifting until staffs extended from their glowing bodies. From these, they sent up powerful beams that fed the bone dragons with magical energy.

Our dragons crashed through the glowing shroud of mist and

dived at their quarries. Seramina's charcoal dragon, Hallinar came down first, heading straight for the bone dragon closest to us. But the bone dragon had chosen its target like an arrow and hurtled back towards Hallinar. Out of its terrifying jaws came a column of green, gaseous flame. This hit Hallinar on the left wing, and he screeched, and then corkscrewed downwards. He tucked his wings into his body, sending him diving towards the ground so fast that I thought he might hit it. But at the last moment, he opened his wings again, the injured one seeming a little limp, and soared back into the air.

On the ground, the purple flames from Seramina's staff shattered Rine's ice wall, creating a sound like breaking glass. Another more concentrated white beam went straight from the crystal on Seramina's staff towards Ange's forehead. Ange ducked underneath it and she changed tactics. She pointed her staff at the ground just in front of Seramina, whipping up a column of leaves into a vortex. This spun slowly towards Seramina, gaining strength.

"Isn't there anything I can do?" I asked Salanraja, watching as she fled from the bone dragon's acidic flames.

"*The Manipulators – take them down, while Rine and Ange work on Seramina.*"

"It's not Seramina... It's Astravar."

"*Bengie, we really don't have time to discuss our enemy's identity!*"

I wasn't looking at the Manipulators though, because there was something odd about that forest golem. Last time we'd fought one, it had attempted to smash the dragons out of the air with its fists while, at the same time, it had stomped chaotically with its massive feet in an attempt to trample its enemies to the ground. But this time, it hadn't moved to assault anything.

Instead, it had its fists clutched to its barrelled chest, and was hunched over itself, its head drooping low, its legs stiff and its feet still. The cracks between its joints let out an amber glow that grew in intensity, and the pieces of wood and forest that it had collected resonated with a rapidly increasing frequency. It also let off a loud hum; the pitch sliding up to an ear-piercing intensity.

It was about to blow.

"Watch out!" I screamed, and I was glad I wasn't a chimera, because I had to dive out of the way of a tree stump that would have flattened me whole if I was any bigger. Other pieces went flying towards Ange and Rine, who cut off their magic so they could flatten themselves against the ground. In the chaos, the debris hit the Manipulators, knocking the crystals out of their centres. The spectral creatures dissipated on the spot while the forest golem remained in place. The golem had transformed into a massive whirlwind, spinning around a red illuminated blurry object that hovered at its centre.

Seramina laughed a wicked and hysterical laugh that clearly didn't belong to her. Her image then split into what must have been twenty versions of her, which danced around her in a second, smaller vortex. "You could also be a powerful warlock," she shouted. "I can see the potential in you. It's such a pity that you'll die so young."

In horror, I realised she was sending both whirlwinds – the forest golem one and the one composed of images of Seramina – towards Ange. I screeched, remembering how recently I'd also been torn apart by a whirlwind-transformed forest golem which tried to lift me off a tree and feed me to wargs. Then, I'd thought it was going to kill me, until Salanraja turned up and scorched it down with her dragon fire. Now, if we did nothing, it would indeed kill Ange.

Quarl and Ishtkar were already on it. Both dragons plunged down through the mist, and they shot towards the forest golem. Out from their mouths came intense gouts of flames, which washed over the vortex of gathered leaves, dancing around that red object – the crystal that powered the golem. The flames converged at a single point, and the crystal within the vortex glowed bright white for a moment. It looked for a moment that the flames would cut the thing off.

Smoke gathered as the dragons flew away, but it was quickly drawn into the larger vortex. The wispy golem form continued onwards unscathed, the smaller whirlwind now getting dangerously close to Ange.

It took me only a moment to see what was going on. A thick white beam came out of the smaller whirlwind towards the larger one. It was hard to see, because of the dozens of images of Seramina spinning around the central point. It seemed that Seramina – or Astravar should I say – powered that golem, much like a Manipulator powers a bone dragon.

"*Gracious demons, that magic is powerful,*" Salanraja said, and I spotted her hovering a safe distance away from the golem, as if getting ready to attack. The glowing mist silhouetted her form, and the spikes on her back curled upwards, the sharp points looking more prominent than usual. But despite her menacing appearance, I knew if Quarl and Ishtkar couldn't bring down the forest golem, there was little she could do. Added to which, there was no time.

It didn't matter, because I was already working up the courage to do what I had to do. This time, I couldn't be afraid, and I couldn't cheat and become a chimera. I needed to be spry old Ben.

"*I'm going in,*" I told Salanraja.

"*Bengie, no!*"

Her words came far too late to stop me, because I was already springing towards the larger whirlwind, my gaze focused on the crystal. It felt like I was entering the embrace of a massive invisible creature as the whirlwind whipped me up into its arms.

I spun around and around, trying to make sense of the rotating world. I saw Ange and Rine lying on the ground, pinned in place. I saw dragons hurtling through the sky. I saw the forest floor and the winding thorny plants that seemed to now be leaning in towards us. I saw the world as if in frames, everything spinning so fast I thought I might throw up. At the same time my legs flailed around, and I felt like a puppet where some huge demon was orchestrating my every movement using huge dangling strings.

But I couldn't give in – I needed to focus. I turned towards the single red crystal. It was like a beacon, calling out to me – my target. I only needed to swipe it out of place. It was also a little easier to focus on, because while the exterior of the whirlwind spun by like the drum of a washing machine, this crystal had a much slower, steadier rotation, remaining fixed in place relative to the vortex as a whole.

I swam like I might swim underwater. The seconds it must have taken to cross that gap felt like minutes. But eventually I managed enough control of my front legs to get nearby and knock at the crystal with my paw. It didn't move, and a paralysing jolt came off the crystal and sent me spinning towards the edge of the whirlwind.

I exited the whirlwind, and my stomach churned as the ground sped towards me. That was it. I was about to get pancaked to the ground. But as if it didn't want me to leave, the whirlwind picked me up again. It carried me up into the air, and I caught a glimpse of Seramina's smaller whirlwind getting ever closer to Ange, who lay supine on the floor. In moments, it would tear her in two.

I turned to the centre, and I focused on the crystal again, squinting my eyes. I clearly needed to be light to stay aloft in this vortex, but I would need to be much stronger to knock the crystal away from its magical perch. I summoned courage once more, and swam towards the crystal, using thin measured strokes to find my way across the eddies. There was a flow to it, I realised, and if I concentrated, I could find the currents that would take me closer to my goal.

I was soon in front of the crystal, spinning around it so fast, but feeling calm inside. I heard a voice then, reaching out to me from a distant land. It had a Welsh accent, and a female soothing voice. "*Remember your destiny, Ben*", my crystal told me. "*Embrace the chimera within.*"

I drew upon the memory of her testing me in that imaginary desert. I had seen my crystal floating above an oasis then – a beautiful transparent lake with fish, all of which had been purely a construct of my mind. I summoned the energy once again to my muscles, and partly transformed into the chimera. But I used only what I needed to build power in my forelegs and swipe at the crystal with all the strength I had within, and then I let go.

It must have been a mighty swipe – the power coming not just from my superior chimera lion strength, but also from the magical energy emitted by the transformation. I hit the crystal, and it shot out of the whirlwind like an arrow and then tumbled across the ground.

I hadn't transformed into a chimera, and I still had my beautifully lithe Bengal body. I stretched myself out so wide that I floated gently down to the ground, like a feather might if suddenly ejected from a hamster wheel. I tracked the smaller whirlwind as I did, terrified that I'd been too late and I was about to lose Ange. But she'd rolled out of the way of the smaller whirlwind while I'd been focusing on the crystal. That whirlwind was also losing momentum. I caught occasional glances of Seramina spinning slowly inside it. The doubled-up images of her had now vanished, and her own eyes had returned to normal. The features on her face looked worn.

I landed on the ground, and I took one more look at Seramina. Her legs buckled, and she fainted. Her staff was no longer aglow, and I could see that mustard yellow mist creeping in – the one with the sleepy spores Salanraja had told me about. Another wind picked up, this time coming off a shock wave that brushed right over me. A blue light flared from behind, and I turned to see a portal had opened up.

Everything seemed to move so much slower. The wind coming out of the portal felt like it was made of treacle. Sound stopped – the silence so dominant it seemed to roar.

Meanwhile, my staff was nowhere to be seen. I could only guess that it was beyond that portal.

Ange had picked herself up now, and words came out of her mouth so slowly they were incomprehensible. But she also pointed at the portal. Clearly, she felt we should enter. The land on the other side of the portal looked kind of dark, with glowing blue outlines around the edges of the rocky, barren terrain. In the distance, a village lay on a hill, also only visible because of its illuminated edges.

In my experience, we only had moments before that portal winked out of existence. But Rine and Ange also seemed to realise what was at stake.

Rine picked himself up, strapped his staff to his back, and took Seramina in his arms. Ange picked up Seramina's staff and strapped it onto her back next to her own. Then, both of them sprinted forward – and I say sprinted, because they did so in such slow motion it wasn't actually sprinting at all. I matched their pace so slowly it felt almost choreographed.

We reached the other side, and time accelerated. Hallinar flew towards us, the other three dragons trailing behind. But I could see they wouldn't make it in time. It wasn't just for the fact that the portal was much too small for them, but also the fact that it was shrinking ever so fast. As predicted, it winked out of existence, leaving us in a world without an aroma.

I felt then the tearing of my soul, much stronger than I'd felt it before. We had just entered another dimension, and I couldn't hear Salanraja in my mind, nor could I feel what she felt, or taste her last meal still lingering upon her tongue. In the pained looked in Rine's and Ange's faces, I could tell they were going through the same.

Rine shook his head. Then he deposited Seramina on the ground. We waited in silence for her to wake.

18

A VACUOUS WORLD

I have no idea how long Seramina took to wake up. The passage of time seemed to go on for hours upon hours, with despair sinking from my heart right down into the pit of my stomach.

I felt despair for being cut off from my dragon, which seemed much worse here than the last time it had happened. I guess because my bond for Salanraja was growing stronger daily. Despair for not finding my staff waiting for me once we defeated the forest golem. Despair for not even knowing what dimension we were in, and not particularly having the will to find out.

Besides, Rine and Ange seemed pretty depressed as well. We just sat on the floor there, Rine and Ange with their legs crossed, me sitting like a cat does. For a long time, we said nothing.

There was something about this place, the bleakness of it, with no natural daylight or moonlight. Just complete darkness with only a faint blue luminescence around the edges of objects to identify shapes by. Even we had glowing outlines that cast only a faint blue light, strong enough to see our faces but not to see our expressions and details. There was no smell. No sound. No taste of anything upon the air. We had, it seemed, entered a vacuous world.

It made me long for the tastes, sounds, and smells back home in South Wales. The taste of roast chicken straight out of the oven. The scent of catnip drifting upon a warm breeze. The call of the mistress telling me that supper was ready. Such memories made me long for a familiar life. But the worst feeling was not having Salanraja nearby, perhaps never being able to see her again. My connection to her had been severed.

Eventually, Seramina opened her eyes. She didn't look around her yet, but at the three of us sitting nearby. While before I remembered the fire, and then the purple light burning in her eyes, now it seemed to be guilt that burned there. This strengthened when she turned to Ange – the one she'd tried to kill.

"What happened?" Seramina asked. "I—He took control, didn't he?"

Ange reached out and took Seramina's hand in hers. She squeezed it, and I wasn't sure if it was so that she'd be ready to restrain Seramina if she tried anything else, or true empathy.

"Seramina, before you say anything else, I want to know that it's truly you that's with us." I'm surprised she didn't restrain Seramina using her leaf-magic. But then, Ange looked as if she knew what she was doing.

"My fa—" Seramina stopped herself. "Astravar. He tried to kill you, Ange. He—I lost control."

"Seramina, this is important," Ange said, squeezing Seramina's hand even tighter. "Do you know what Astravar was planning? What do you remember?"

"He... I don't know. He wanted Ben to enter this place. And he wanted him to come alone after I'd disposed of the rest of you, including the dragons."

"So he couldn't be here to orchestrate the battle himself," Ange said, shaking her head, "and he took control of his daughter to do his dirty deeds. But why would he want Ben in here?"

"Probably so he could have him locked out of the way, so he can't interfere with Astravar's destiny," Rine said.

"But why not kill him?" Ange said. "After all, Astravar seemed to want us dead. It just doesn't make any sense."

Seramina sat up, then she lowered her head, unable it seemed, to look at any of us. "I don't know. I don't remember that part... But when Astravar took control of me last time he knew he couldn't hold it forever. He knew little about me back then – had hardly known I'd existed. I think he must have implanted a little magic in me, lying dormant until it was time for him to take control.

"Since then, he must have been studying me to gain a stronger grasp on how I tick. That's why I need to keep control of my mind, because I hear him in there sometimes. That's what Aleam's been training me for. So that I can protect myself from him. If only Aleam were here this would have never happened."

"Well, he's not here," Ange said. "You'll need to accept that, Seramina. If you convince yourself that only Aleam can save you, then you'll make yourself more vulnerable to Astravar. You need to learn to rely on your own wits."

Seramina lowered her head and placed her hand on her forehead. She spoke without looking up. "You don't think Driar Aleam will come, do you? Even if he escapes Prince Arran, how will he know where to find us? I really do wish he was here. He'd know exactly what to do now."

"I guess you have to put all this out of your mind for now," Ange said. "Just focus on the present moment and on what we have to do now. That was why he was teaching you to meditate, right? He wanted you to become stronger within."

"It doesn't matter anyway," Rine said. "Astravar won't find us here, unless he's crossed into this dimension. I doubt he's a threat to us anymore."

"And where exactly are we?" I asked.

Ange let go of Seramina's hand, crouched down and stroked me at the back of the neck. I wasn't sure if it was to comfort me, but it sure felt comforting in this strange alien land. "This is the Ghost Realm. The Third Dimension – rumoured to be filled with the souls of the dead. I recognise the pictures from books. It can't be anything else, can it?" She looked at Seramina, as if for confirmation.

"Astravar wanted to trap Ben here forever," Seramina said, "so he could never interfere with the warlock's destiny."

A wind picked up from the hill with the distant village on it. It was strong, and strangely didn't cool or warm as you'd expect wind to do. But it chilled me emotionally, causing a deep wave of depression to sink within me. It howled through the barren landscape, whipping up glowing trails of dust in its wake. Everything around us seemed to shimmer, making me wonder if we were actually standing on solid ground or if it was about to give way and send us plummeting into an abyss full of the tormented souls of hippopotami or something. I shuddered at the thought.

"Do you mean we're dead?" I asked, examining my paw – it looked solid enough, and the claws seemed sharp, as they should be. "I knew it. I shouldn't have gone into the whirlwind. I killed myself, didn't I? And Seramina killed the rest of you."

"I—" Seramina said, and she turned away, looking up towards the glowing village in the distance.

"She did not," Ange said, scowling at me. "We came through the portal, remember? Stop worrying the poor girl."

"What? And you don't think I might be slightly anxious too? We're going to die because it doesn't look like there's any food here. Don't you remember how Seramina attacked you?"

"She wasn't herself," Ange said. "Gracious demons, Ben, you can be so selfish sometimes."

I growled, not expecting to hear this out of Ange of all people. I had thought she would have always sided with the cat, but that shows how wrong I was. Girls would always stick together. I needed Ta'ra here if I was going to have any chance of winning an argument against them. But then, knowing Ta'ra, she'd probably side with the girls too.

Rine stepped in front of me. He had his staff clutched in his hand, which he leaned on as he looked out towards the village. "Look, folks, we've not got any time to be wasting by assigning blame." He stared daggers at me. "Nor have we any time for feeling sorry for ourselves," he then looked at Seramina. This look was softer than it had been with me, but still pretty harsh. "We're in the Ghost Realm, and we need to get out of here fast."

"Is that right, smart Alec?" Ange said with her hands on her hips. "So how do you propose we do that?"

"My guess is that Ben's staff is here. So, if we can find it, then hopefully it has some magic to lift us out of here, or at least Ben's crystal will intervene."

"There's no telling what Ben's crystal can do," Seramina said. "Or any of our crystals. If I'd thought about it earlier, I might have tried to read them, to at least have some idea of our futures. But I was keeping away from the magic. It's all my fault…"

"We can't change what's been done already," Ange said. "But what we can do is start towards that village." She pointed at it, as if none of us had already seen it.

I gazed not at the village but at the darkness beyond it. It seemed to stretch on into infinity, and it gave the impression that there was nothing behind the village, except perhaps a chasm that plummeted into oblivion. Though I knew Ange was right, a huge part of me didn't want to move anywhere in this alien barren land. In many ways, it seemed like a good place to curl up and go to sleep forever.

"What exactly do you expect to find in the village?" I asked.

Rine looked down at me and smiled. "Ghosts I guess. What else would you find in the Ghost Realm?"

I groaned. "I don't want to meet any ghosts…"

"I don't think any of us do," Ange said. "But it's our only chance to get out of here." She looked again at Seramina, as if to check she was okay. I also checked that Seramina's eyes weren't glowing any funny colours, but everything looked normal, fortunately.

Rine grunted, then marched onwards, without looking back. Ange huffed and then trailed after him, with both hers and Seramina's staff swaying with the rhythm of her strides. Seramina followed, but she seemed to want to fall back a little, as if wanting to be alone.

Nobody seemed to care right now if the cat came too, which was odd given it was my staff of destiny we were looking for. In other words, I was the key to getting out of here. But they knew me too well, because it didn't feel right to be left alone here, surrounded by nothing but sheer barrenness. I growled a complaint that no one heard, and then I raced to catch up with Rine and Ange, respecting Seramina's wish to walk alone.

19

INTO THE UNKNOWN

As we climbed, we expended energy. My legs were sore, my tummy rumbled loudly at me, and my throat felt completely dry. I regretted secretly that I hadn't taken a little extra time to eat more sausages at this morning's campfire before taking off after Seramina. If there was food in the village, then it would no doubt be ghost food, which meant that it might have been dead a long time and potentially decaying – in other words completely inedible.

But the more pressing issue was thirst. If we didn't find anything to drink soon, we'd surely die here. Then we'd become ghosts, and we'd be destined to live here forever, roaming this boring place with nothing at all to do.

Seramina still trailed at a distance behind us, but close enough, I noticed, that she could probably hear what we said. I could also hear her footsteps, which was why Ange probably wasn't checking every ten seconds or so to see if she was still there.

"The thing I don't get," Rine said, "is where are all the ghosts? I mean if everyone and everything in all seven dimensions end up here when they die, then there should be millions here, surely."

We were halfway up the hill by that point, and Rine was right. Really, we should have been trudging through wispy stalks of grass, spectral dragonflies, bees, wasps, and butterflies flitting and buzzing around us, cats of all types and ages stalking their prey across rolling meadows. Whiskers, for a moment I wondered if I'd even meet my ancestors here – the great Asian leopard cats of old. But everywhere I looked I saw nothing but darkness with faint glowing lines around its edges. Even the ground I stepped on was pitch black. Fortunately, we could see each other, but only because of those weird glowing outlines around our bodies.

Ange put her hand to her chin as she walked, as if in thought. "Maybe the ghost realm is not quite what we expected it to be. Perhaps we're making a discovery of our own."

"But people must have explored this place, surely?" Rine asked. "I mean what did the books you read say about it? It's not like the Fifth Dimension and Sixth Dimension, is it? We at least understand something about this place, right?"

"Well, if there are ghosts in here," I suggested, "maybe we can't see them. Aren't ghosts meant to be invisible after all?"

"That's not what the books say," Ange said. "There are reports of men and women coming into the Third Dimension, but they don't stay long. The explorers see a village, then they see the ghosts, and then they decide to leave."

"Why would they do that?" Rine asked. "They could learn so much about the place."

"Some reports say it's because of their respect for the dead. They don't want to disturb them. Others claim it's because of their sheer fear of what they see, and so they decide they'd much rather stay in the safety of their own home than face what lives in this place. No one, after all, wants to see a ghost. So they just summon a portal and vanish home."

"You didn't tell me we could summon a portal," I said. "Then let's get out of here. I don't want the staff anymore."

"We can't use portal magic, you idiot," Rine said. "That's done by the White Mages and the warlocks, but never dragon riders. For some reason the crystals never gifted us with that kind of magic."

"Come to think of it, I've never met a White Mage."

"That's because you haven't become a full-fledged dragon rider yet. When you do, you might go on expeditions with them, or you might even fight alongside them in larger battles against the warlocks."

"Then why hasn't the king sent any White Mages to protect us in Dragonsbond Academy?"

"Didn't you listen, Ben," Ange said. "Prince Arran did say that reinforcements were on the way. I guess they're a little late arriving. Perhaps Prince Arran wanted to establish his authority before the rest of the men came in."

"Or they're marching on foot... Travelling by horse carriage, perhaps," Rine said.

"That's a possibility too," Ange said. "I really don't know. Why do you ask?"

"Because I don't know anything about your world. Or at least I didn't until I was forced into it. But at least it's familiar. I really don't like this place, and I don't know what's worse - here or the Seventh Dimension."

"From what you've told me about the Seventh Dimension, I think I'd choose here," Rine said. "At least you don't have, what was that thing, a demon hippopotamus threatening to eat you?"

"I think I'd rather be eaten than die hungry," I said. "Wouldn't you?"

Rine snorted. "No comment," he said. "It's funny how since I've known you've made everything out to be about food. I would have thought you'd have changed by now, at least a little."

I said nothing back to him, and we were all silent for a moment, the only noise being our footsteps and the soughing of the wind, with Seramina pattering along behind. We were close enough to the village now that I could see the structures within it. The houses looked like the old-fashioned hovels we'd seen in villages back in Salanraja's world. But these buildings completely lacked colour, except for their weird glowing blue outlines that cast a cold light over everything. The village also wasn't showing any signs of movement. No sign of ghosts, whatever they were meant to look like, prowled the streets.

We entered just as that strange wind picked up and rushed through the streets as if it wanted to blow us away. I wondered if these invisible ghosts were calling that wind to push us back from where we came. Perhaps they actually didn't want us treading on their ground, peering into their houses, catching glimpses of their eternal lives.

"I don't like this," Rine said, and he shuddered visibly. I could hear his heart pounding in his chest.

"I don't either," Ange said, her heart pounding too. "It feels as if we really shouldn't be here. No wonder all those scholars turned back." She edged noticeably closer to Rine. But I didn't care at that point. If we were trapped in here, it didn't matter if they got together or not.

"Why do you humans always go around stating the obvious?" I asked. "Sometimes don't you think it's better not to say anything at all?"

Seramina had caught up with us by this point, and her heart wasn't beating as heavily as the other two. I wondered if for a moment Astravar had taken possession of her soul again, because she now seemed a lot more spritely. "I think it's this way," she said, and beckoned us forward.

"Seramina," Ange said, and she reached over her shoulder for her staff.

Seramina frowned at her. "Don't worry, I won't cast any magic. I don't need my staff to detect destiny. I've been reading the possible threads of the future, and how they surround people, all my life."

The young teenager pushed on ahead, and we had no choice but to follow.

Seramina led us over what must have been the main road. Beneath us, the glowing lines running around and over the cobblestones made them look shiny, as if covered with water. But there was no rain.

The outlines weren't the only thing that cast light in here. There were also these strange-looking oil lanterns hanging off rafters that jutted out beneath the eaves of the hovels. They didn't have flames in them, but instead they emitted blue glows as if lit from the inside by crystals.

Seramina turned off into a narrower alleyway, with a lantern shining out so brightly at the end of it, I couldn't see what was behind it. The wind howled loudly, startling me. It came from behind and pushed us down the alleyway, this time seeming to want to edge us towards our target. I screeched and tried to pull away from the light, but the wind came even stronger so that it almost lifted me off the ground.

Seramina opened her arms, and she let the wind carry her towards the light, floating upon it like a stray bin bag caught in a storm. Ange tried to resist the wind like me, but it spun her around and propelled her onwards. Rine ran forwards instead, gaining momentum from the wind. He screamed out in ecstasy, his arms windmilling around him as he went.

Once we'd all accepted there was no turning back, the wind died off. Seramina executed a well-balanced landing, thrusting out her arms and then drawing them back into herself, as if she'd predicted exactly when the wind would stop. But it had carried me high on its currents, and I ended up twisting one of my ankles as I hit the floor. I shrieked out, and rolled over, and then limped forwards towards the light in pain.

I had the sudden sensation of being watched. I turned every which way, expecting at least to see eyes glowering at me from the darkness. They weren't there. But I heard breathing, and whispers in all kinds of languages. Having the gift of languages from my crystal, I understood every word. But as soon as I tried to attach meaning to any sentence, I'd hear more ramblings from another random direction.

These random ideas continued to assault me as if I was on the edge of madness and hearing them in my mind. But I knew these voices weren't in my head. They were out there somewhere.

I shuddered, and I thought it would be saner to focus on the light ahead. Seramina led the way, Rine and Ange slightly behind her. Their figures were framed in silhouettes and cast long shadows well behind me. Not wanting to get left behind, I matched their pace, trying not to get distracted by the voices which got louder with every step I took.

I could hear heavy breathing from the shadows now, and I had this strange itching sensation against my fur. Yet I didn't dare stop to scratch myself – as much as I wanted to.

The light ahead faded slightly, and then a shape seemed to emerge inside it with a slightly darker outline. This continued to gain definition until it took on human form. It wore a cloak that billowed around it, and it had a staff. At first, I thought I was looking at a Manipulator, and I next expected to see bone dragons rise out of nowhere, screeching violently.

But this definitely wasn't a Manipulator. The shape warped even more until I could see the creases on its clothes, the folds underneath its eyes, the cavernous wrinkles in its skin.

Recognition dawned on me. Before me stood Aleam in spectral form.

20

GHOSTS OF OURSELVES

Ghost Aleam looked at each of us. First, he studied Rine. Then he turned to look at Ange. Next, he looked down at me. Only last did he turn to Seramina, and then he gave a nod as if in approval.

"Everyone's here, I see," he said. "Just as I've always expected."

His sudden appearance had caused us to freeze in shock. I could see the sides of Rine's and Ange's faces from where I stood, and their mouths were agape. I couldn't see Seramina's face from here, but her straight-backed posture had been replaced with a full slouch.

"Aleam," Seramina said. "This wasn't what I foresaw. You can't be…"

Aleam laughed loudly. "Dead, you mean? We all must pass sometime, you know, and I was getting old. This is one thing that everyone needs to learn to accept."

"No!" Ange said, her face even more blanched of colour than before. "Prince Arran? Did he do this?"

Rine took and squeezed her hand. The outlines of their hands seemed to glow in the light that Aleam emitted.

I walked forward, unable to believe my eyes. Part of me was wondering if ghosts emitted a smell, but there was nothing here. Strangely, I couldn't even catch whiffs of Seramina's or Ange's perfume, and I longed for the aromas so much. I longed for any aroma, really, for a sense of realism to this world.

The wind picked up again, but this time it pushed me away from Aleam. "Not too close, Ben," he said. "There will be time for that later. For now, our friends are waiting. Will you please follow me?"

He turned slowly, and as he did the light from his body flared up once again. It grew, and seemed to surround him, although ever so faintly did I make out the outline of his form drifting away as if disappearing into the light. "One at a time, now," he said from behind the light. "Don't go too slowly or you'll get left behind."

Rine had let go of Ange's hand. He looked at us in turn as if trying to assess what we all felt. But in all honesty, I've never known a human who can read a feline expression. They all seem to think we're sad when we're happy and happy when we're sad.

"Do you think we can trust him?" he asked, looking again at Ange.

She shook her head and put her hand to her chin but said nothing.

Seramina did though. "We can. I didn't lead you here for nothing. I think I'm beginning to understand." She took a deep breath and walked right into the light.

"Seramina!" Ange called out. "Gah, that girl."

Rine laughed, and then reached out for Seramina's staff on Ange's back, touching it lightly. "Well, her crystal didn't break. So, I guess that means she's okay."

Ange swallowed, then stepped gingerly forward. "I guess we have no choice." She stepped forward and disappeared behind the light.

"My turn," Rine said, and turned back with a cocky smile. He drew his staff from his back, then he charged forward with his shoulder. As he did, he screamed out, "Goblins beware!"

I didn't know what a goblin was, and I wasn't sure I wanted to meet one. If I did, I hoped they were edible, because I was starving. I also knew one thing – I didn't want to be abandoned here, sad and alone. With that thought in mind, a rush of adrenaline coursed through me, and I sprinted forward. As I did, that strange wind without temperature picked up behind me, throwing me forwards.

I hit something cold and wet, and a powerful force pulled me downwards. I couldn't breathe, and whatever was rushing against my fur from above was so cold, I felt paralysed. The next thing I knew I was drowning, my eyeballs bulging so hard I thought they were going to pop out of my sockets.

Sudden dread came over me, as I thought this must have all been a horrible trick. We'd not just seen Aleam, but a Manipulator controlled by Astravar. Annoyed that he'd not killed us with the forest golem, he'd come after us in the Ghost Realm, and used this apparition of our old friend to lead us into a trap.

I was going to die.

Or at least I thought I was, until I tumbled out of the other side, soaking wet but very alive. I sputtered out water, and then a few anchovies flopped out of my throat too and spasmed on the floor a moment before coming to rest. Instinct took over, and I pounced on the anchovies, and I took them into my mouth. I bit down on their crunchy, salty goodness, and then I swallowed them in one bite.

"Those weren't real," Aleam said. "Which means they're absolutely lacking in nutritional value. You realise that don't you, Ben?"

"Yes, but they still tasted so good," I said, and I took some time to look around. We had left the Ghost Realm. Or at least, it seemed that way, because some colour had returned to everything around us. Green verdant hills rolled towards a sun hanging high above. But something about it was off – the sun just didn't seem as bright as it should be given its position in the sky.

Dandelion seeds floated around everywhere, but they lacked definition, as if their fronds weren't separate but instead seemed to be welded together in places. I scanned around looking for butterflies, or birds, or at least something interesting to chase. But I found nothing of interest. I chased after a dandelion seed instead, but I lost it very quickly and that was enough to get bored.

Rine, Ange, and Seramina had already gathered around a campfire – looking kind of blurry from here as if I was looking at a photograph with the background out of focus. Still, I could see my three companions clear as day. I stalked over to them as the light from the campfire got brighter, and the warmth washed over me. Finally, this place had invented heat. The breeze coming off the hills also felt a little cooler. But somehow, the fire didn't feel as warm and the wind as cool as they were meant to be.

You couldn't get too close to a fire, comfortably, without it burning you. But this one felt as if I could step right into it, dance around for a few minutes, and then step out uncharred. I didn't try it though. Every cat knows not to play with fire, and this was no exception.

It was then that I noticed what Rine, Ange and Seramina were looking at.

We also sat on the other side of the campfire, duplicated in blurrier, paler forms. There was a version of Seramina, a version of Ange, a version of Rine, and a version of spry old Ben. Except they all looked slightly paler as if the colours had been bleached out of their hair, skin, and fur. They weren't completely colourless, but somehow everything in this place looked desaturated. They also emitted a faint glow around the outlines, weaker than before but still noticeable.

I wondered if this was like the Faery Realm where everything I saw was made of some kind of glamour spell. If so, this magic was a pale imitation to what those tiny fairies could do.

"How's this possible?" Seramina asked.

"They must be ghosts," Rine said. "Which means we must be dead after all."

"Don't be stupid," Ange said. "If they were ghosts, then we wouldn't be looking at them like this. *We'd* be the ghosts then."

"Really, and do you know how things work here?" Rine said, his hands on his hips.

I growled, loudly, to let the nascent couple know that I couldn't take another one of their arguments. Aleam made his way over to us using his staff, balanced almost unnaturally on it as if he didn't need it for support at all. He also now had a little colour and emitted a faint glow.

"But they are ghosts, you see," he said. "Just your concept of a ghost isn't what you expect it to be."

Rine looked at him with wide eyes. "Okay, please explain?"

"You need to change your perception of this world," Aleam said. "Ghosts are nothing to fear if you lead a good life. But they are everything to fear if you lead a bad one."

Seramina had leaned in and was watching Aleam with interest. "I can feel something in this place. As if I was meant to be here. The more I study it, the more I recognise things as if I'd known them all along."

"And that is because you are a very gifted child," Aleam said. "You see, the Ghost Realm is the world of the future dead and contains everything that happened in the past and that will happen in the future. It's a timeless place, one which no living creature is wise enough to understand yet. But the crystals understand it, which is how they connect to it to draw off its magic as a source."

"Does that mean you're not dead?" Seramina said, a flash of hope in her eyes.

Aleam gave her a warm smile. "In one version of the future I might be, in another I might not. You know well how this works, girl. After all, destiny magic is your school."

Ange scratched at her forehead and shook her head slowly. She also seemed in better spirits, as if the puzzle of this place had given her energy. "This is the source of magic? Does that mean that this place belongs to the crystals?"

"Not at all," Aleam said. "The crystals learned to project this place onto the world. They are windows, their facets planes that display the essence of existence. What you see in this place are threads of the future, how they might be. You can learn a lot from this place if you have the courage to look through the lens."

"So what you're saying," Ange said, rubbing her chin, "is that anything we see here is a possible thread of the future. Now we're seeing us around the campfire like this, because we might end up there sometime in our lives."

"Or it's already happened," Aleam said. "Don't forget this is a timeless place, so you can gaze across the threads of time."

"Hang on a minute," I said, and stepped towards Aleam and examined him. He emitted a faint Aleam kind of smell now – a combination of sweat and flaky skin. But it wasn't strong enough for me to trust him. "This doesn't make any sense. The visions we saw in the crystals were so vivid. They had lots of colours, and everything here is faded and yucky."

Aleam smiled. "Because you don't put much importance to this," he said. "This vision isn't so strong in your minds, and so you only see it faintly here. But if you use your memories and your imagination to your advantage, the vision will become stronger."

"But how can a vision of the future be in our minds at all, if we've never experienced it?" Ange asked.

"Oh, you have such little faith in this realm. Your mind can transcend time here, if only you let it. Trust the magic of time, and you can see the past and future. Once you learn to do so, then your path here will become clear."

It was then that I realised what ghost Aleam was talking about. Because I recognised the scene, it had only happened this morning after all. We were sitting around the campfire, Rine now cooking sausages. I hadn't noticed the tents yet, because they were so faint. But now they stood there billowing in the wind. I saw the green glow from the Aurorest Forest in the distance, and I smelled that horrible scent of putrid algae coming from it.

The other version of me wasn't a Bengal, I realised, but a chimera. As soon as I recognised this, that version morphed into its expected form. The snake tail had bright yellow and green stripes along its body that I'd never noticed before. Nor had I noticed the deep black around the eyes of the goat's head, creating a stark contrast against its otherwise alabaster coat, fading into a golden colour at the base of its neck. The lion's head had mustard yellow teeth, and its breath absolutely stank.

"I wanted to take you somewhere I knew would be familiar to you," Aleam said. "Now, it's time to explore each of your futures. But I see only one of you is ready." He turned to Seramina. "Shall we begin?"

Seramina shook her head. "I'm not sure I want to see the future. Every time I've used my magic lately, it has ended in disaster."

"And that is the problem we need to work on, young lady." He reached down into a pocket in his cloak, which now was its normal deep brown colour and wasn't glowing at all. From it, he produced a closed pouch, lumpy over its folds, and tied tight at the top. He pulled this back and threw it onto the fire.

For a moment, everything went bright white. Then, the surrounding light faded to reveal Seramina's future.

21

THE HERMIT

"Just assume, for now, that you've defeated Astravar," the ghost of Aleam said, as the light died down even more. "Because it is not time yet to show you what happens if you don't."

I stood in bright green grass, which looked incredibly vivid compared to how it had looked before. Birds chirped out from the surrounding trees. Some of these trees had lime green leaves with catkins dangling from the winding branches. Others had darker leaves and supported white flowers. The air was heady with pollen, and I saw butterflies and dragonflies dancing around, the way it was meant to be. One butterfly landed nearby and perched itself on the biggest dandelion I'd ever seen in my life. But I was interested in the butterfly and not the flower. I readied myself to pounce on my prey.

I landed on the flower, but the butterfly had already flown away. I chased after it and tried to paw it out of the sky. My blow knocked it aside, but it flapped its wings and fluttered high enough to survive another day.

I growled, then looked up to see a hovel across the field. There was nothing around it, no path leading to it, and it was surrounded by a mystical purple mist that stank of rotten vegetable juice.

"The question is," Aleam continued, "though this place might look beautiful, will you be truly happy here? Or will you become a tormented soul? Seramina, this is your potential future. And, if you ask me, this version of you doesn't seem happy at all."

Aleam pointed with his glowing staff at the porch of the hovel. Behind a rickety wooden balustrade, Seramina's ghost sat on a rocking chair. Her eyes had rolled back in her head so only the whites of them showed. They also had a slight purple tint to them. As she rocked back and forth on her chair, she clutched a staff in her right hand. It had a purple crystal on the top of it, glowing brightly.

"What is this?" the real version of Seramina asked. "Why am I here all alone?"

I didn't like it either, and so I backed away from her, scouring the terrain for butterflies. But everything had run away, and the bird sounds had died down. All that remained was a grating buzzing coming from ghost Seramina's staff.

"You chose this life," Aleam said. "Or rather you lost control, and the dark magic chose it for you. Because you became an even greater enemy to the most powerful in the realm."

"Will become," Seramina corrected. "But, no, I won't. I will never let it happen to me."

"But if you keep hiding from who you really are, you will. You have power, Seramina – it's in your blood. And, if you don't acknowledge that power, then it will consume you whole."

I wasn't the only one who had backed away from the evil version of Seramina. Ange and Rine stood back-to-back, clutching their staffs in front of them. The real Seramina stood close to them. She tapped her fingers against her legs, and she kept glancing at the staff of power in her doppelganger's hands.

"Don't worry," Aleam said. "This is just a vision."

Evil Seramina gazed out at the horizon where a thick carpet of purple clouds loomed. There came a screeching sound from the distance, and then six birds of prey suddenly shot out of the clouds. There was a seagull, a vulture, a buzzard, a condor, a bald eagle, and a hawk. But there was no crow…

Carrion eaters, I thought. All cats knew to stay away from such birds, and if we ever saw one wheeling above or even smelled one nearby, to run and hide. The six birds landed, and greyish purple plumes of smoke billowed around them. These soon dissipated to show six pale skinned figures, in fancy cloaks just like Astravar's.

"That's the other warlocks," Ange said. "What do they want with Seramina?"

One warlock – the one who had been a condor – stepped forward. She was a woman who looked even older than Aleam. She moved with one hand behind her back, the other resting on her staff for support. This staff glowed as she stopped and lifted it into the air. From it came this terrible screeching sound, and two wispy looking purple dragons lurched out of the crystal at the top. They were formed of clouds and circled around the old warlock in a figure-of-eight motion, casting a light across the sky that gave the warlock's silver hair a kind of spectral glow.

Evil Seramina stood up from her chair, whilst the Seramina we knew so well glowered at her but didn't move as if frozen in place.

"What do you want, Lasinta?" evil Seramina said. "All of you… Why do you disturb me? All I've ever wanted is to be left alone."

"Because you hold too much power," the warlock said. "Not only are you a threat to our kind, but you can help us break the treaty with Illumine Kingdom and finish what Astravar started, fool as that man was. This is your last chance. You either join us, or it all ends here."

Evil Seramina narrowed her eyes. She raised her staff high above her head, and it also glowed purple. The ground quaked so hard it sent my cheeks wobbling. I hissed out, crouched, then I dug my claws into the soil to help keep purchase.

Seramina's voice rose in both volume and pitch as she continued to speak. Her words were laced with anger, and an undertone of spite. "I owe you nothing, Lasinta. My father is dead, and you will be soon too if you don't leave this place."

She pointed her staff at Lasinta and out came an intense white beam. Lasinta screamed, and she swung her staff downwards. A vortex shot out of Lasinta's crystal, that sucked in the beam, and the two cloud-shaped dragons spiralled around the vortex as if powered by its circular motion. The other warlocks sprinted into position, clutching their staffs, and casting spells all around them. An incredible light show filled the scene with flashes of purple and white. It reminded me of the scariest night in Wales every year – bonfire night when fireworks screech and crash and bang high above tall roaring fires. That used to be the worst night of the year.

For a while, I thought this would be the end of Seramina. Her life would end here, lonelier than she'd ever been. Spells of light and terror whooshed towards the ghost form of the teenager. I saw skulls made of thick glowing fog, thorny purple vines, intense beams of light, and burning purple fireballs.

Some dark magic, or perhaps the magic of the Ghost Realm, also slowed time, meaning I had to wait longer to see who the victor was. Really, given Seramina had turned evil, I didn't know who I wanted to win.

The evil version of Seramina also had tricks up her sleeves. She glowed bright white, just like we'd seen her glowing in the Aurorest Forest, her hair whipping against her face as if stirred by an intense wind. She opened out her arms and her feet lifted off the floor. There she floated as she watched the warlocks' spells approach ever so slowly, her eyes narrow slits and her jaw clenched. Then, she clutched her staff in both her hands and extended it to the sky. Time accelerated back to normal, as Seramina placed all her weight down on the staff, plunging it into the ground.

The whole earth shook, much more violently than last time. I slid across the ground, growling, screeching, and hissing, as it tore at my claws. Around me, the earth had already been torn asunder. Great rents led down into it, leading into enormous pits of boiling magma. Heat raged from beneath, and the smell of rising sulphur reminded me of the time I was in the Seventh Dimension. The earth rocked again, and I slid down towards one of the cracks.

"Ben," Ange shouted. She scrambled over to me, then plunged her staff in the ground. It glowed green, and thorns tore out from her crystal into the earth, rooting her in place.

Just as I was about to slide into a chasm, she scooped me up in her arms and clutched me tightly. She squeezed a little too tight, but I knew it would be stupid to try to claw myself out from her grasp. Rine had also cast a spell, freezing his feet in place, and he'd done the same to the true version of Seramina.

Meanwhile, evil Seramina still floated in the air, her staff glowing brightly as it fed energy into the ground. From the rents in the earth came great roars, and I saw all manner of creatures rise out of it – all of them incarnations of the Seventh Dimension.

First swarmed out what must have been tens of thousands of demon rats, scurrying as if a lion had just disturbed their nests. Then came swans and cormorants and ravens and other birds as large as giraffes, with gaping cracks in their skin, molten rock glowing underneath. The demon dragons followed them, filling the sky with such a racket it seemed to be crashing down on us. After that flooded out every creature I could imagine, including the terrifying demon hippopotamus. Also, there came a wave of demon salmon, flopping out of the abyss. For a moment I thought I'd never like salmon again.

I knew what would come next, and I hated it. Once the Seventh Dimension had emptied, the First Dimension would become the demons' dominion. They'd flood across into other dimensions, and I doubted very much my old master and mistress in South Wales were equipped to handle them – particularly the demon salmon.

That was enough, I didn't want to see any more. I sealed my eyes shut whilst Ange clutched me in her arms, careening from side to side with the motion of the earth.

A warm light filtered through my eyelids. I opened them to see the entire scene flooded with white light and the vision faded to darkness. We were back in that place without warmth or cold, the glowing outlines rolling over the hills. The village was nowhere to be seen now, and I felt terribly alone. Rine's and Ange's hearts were beating faster than I'd ever heard them beat before, and even Seramina's heart was pounding.

Yet, I couldn't detect a heartbeat in the ghost of Aleam's chest. He didn't smell of anything anymore either. No one smelled of anything.

"I can't do this," Seramina said, this time the good version of her. "Please Aleam, this cannot be my fate."

"But you've seen it yourself," Aleam said. "It comes to you in your dreams. You must learn to take responsibility for your own power. Eventually, you will become even more powerful than your father. That fact is written in the annals of time. But either you'll learn to take risks upon yourself, or fate will destroy you. Only the first of those will allow you to then use this power for good."

"I can't live up to that," Seramina said. "I'll never be as powerful as him…"

"This place doesn't lie," the ghost of Aleam said. "This is only one possible thread of your destiny. The worst imaginable. I showed it to you because you need to get over your pride."

Seramina cheeks puckered, making a whistling sound as she sucked in air through her teeth. Her eyes were now filled with tears. "Don't you get it? I have no pride. I was born a monster, and I will die a monster. What does this prove?"

Aleam shook his head. "Your pride isn't in what you believe yourself to be, but what you believe others to be compared to you. It's that desire for pride you have to let go of. A desire to belong to a family, a desire to be accepted amongst your peers. You are already great, Seramina. Accept that and then store it in a tiny compartment inside yourself. Only then, will you become strong enough to be who you are destined to be. Once you accept who you are, Astravar can no longer control you like he just did, because you will be complete."

Seramina said nothing, but her gaze had gone distant and tears welled at the bottom of her eyes. She clearly had a lot to think about. Aleam turned to Ange and Rine who had huddled a little closer together. He smiled, and then Ange stepped back from Rine. She looked down at her feet, her cheeks red. She then shook her head hard and glared at Rine as if to warn him away from her.

Rine shook his head and turned his shoulder away from her, just as Aleam turned to look at him.

"Now it's time to see both of your futures," Aleam said with a smile. "What, I ask, might destiny find?"

"Please, no more apocalypses," I said. "I've decided I hate apocalypses."

"Not this time," Aleam said. "To most of you, this one will seem quite mellow in comparison. Although something tells me, young Ben, that you will hate it more."

He raised his staff above his head, and spectral glowing outlines passed over its tip, like water running over its surface during a heavy rainstorm. The ethereal crystal on the staff glowed, intensifying into a blinding white light.

I squinted as the light faded, and I was seeing dots at first, as we entered the vision of Rine's and Ange's future.

22

A FAILED ROMANCE

We stood on a ledge in the centre of a massive chasm leading down into swirling darkness. It looked like a pool of that gross smelling stuff that the master used to eat in South Wales – I think it was called yeast extract.

The stuff swirled and stank as it flowed towards the horizon. It tainted the bases of the cliff walls that led up on both sides to two houses. Both of these were opulent mansions, with massive gardens. The one to the left had low overhanging gables, crab apple trees surrounding it, and yellow brick walls. The other led to a mansion made of heavy stones, with a slate roof adorned with gemstones and a coniferous hedge with red berries shining out from between the soft needles.

Both gardens looked like two wonderful places that I would love to explore. Only, I couldn't decide which one I'd prefer. I certainly didn't fancy a life where I was trapped on a rock with a steep drop into a pool of yeast extract. This ledge was wide enough for us to walk around a little, but also sheer enough that we could fall to our hideous deaths should we misstep.

"What's with the abyss?" Rine said.

"Visions of the future often use symbolism," Aleam said. "It fills them with rich meaning, and multiple interpretations. This is how soothsayers have always been able to make a living."

"But it's full of that stuff that smells amazing. It's almost as if I could crawl down with a butter knife and spread it upon my toast."

Ange's eyes went wide. "You've got to be kidding me. You'd eat that stuff?"

"What, wouldn't you?"

Aleam laughed an almost bitter laugh. "This food item, once discovered, will spawn divisions across millennia and multiple dimensions. But for now, there's more to see, and what's in the chasm isn't as important as it might seem."

There came a call from the mansion on the right. A female voice that was instantly familiar. Ange stepped out onto the porch, except it was a much older version of Ange, with greying hair and wrinkles under her eyes. She still had that slight squirrelly look to her though, which is how I recognised her.

"Oh Ben," she called out. "Ben, are you out here?"

This caused everyone to smile, including Seramina. The young teenager wiped the tears away from her eyes, but another emerged and dripped from her cheek. She seemed to notice I was looking at her, and so she turned away from me.

"Ben?" The apparition of Ange called again. "Oh, Ben, don't tell me you've gone over to visit Rine again. I—"

Another figure ghosted into view. At first, it looked like a Manipulator, glowing white with every single one of its limbs seeming to warp around its body. But as it moved towards Ange's apparition's doorstep, it gained definition. After a few moments, it took the form of Prince Arran, standing as tall and mighty as that man does, his nose almost higher than his forehead. He wore lush velvet purple attire and a long trailing red cloak. There were other ghostly forms standing nearby, in two sizes – man-size and dragon-size. Presumably they were the guards who had flown in with Arran. But they probably weren't important for this vision, and so they all looked blurred out.

Prince Arran knocked on the door. Ange's apparition turned around and noticed him there, and so she walked over and curtsied slightly. It's strange, while they were so far away, I could see them as if I was standing right next to them, despite the precipitous chasm that lay between us.

"Driar Ange," Prince Arran said. "Have you completed your target for the day?"

"Yes sir, I've delivered what you expected," Ange said. She reached down to the porch and picked up a small bag. From it, she produced some berries. They had the same colour as the berries on the hedge. "These will produce three times the output of normal crops. I infused them with a little leaf-magic. I believe my research will be quite satisfactory for the king's purposes. Just plant these, and they'll grow into fruitful trees in a good six months. I cannot count on two hands the number of diseases they will prevent."

"Very well," Arran said, accepting the bag. "I'll pass them on. Meanwhile, I don't suppose you've considered my offer of accompanying me to the Royal Gala this year? The king is supposed to be throwing quite a celebration."

From beside me, the true Ange gasped. "Please don't tell me I accept, Aleam," she said. "I would never even consider an offer from that pompous oaf."

"Just watch and see what happens," Aleam said. "Now fate is set in this thread, it will unfold as it was meant to."

I looked up at the real Ange, and then I turned to Rine, as he puffed out some air that he'd been holding between his cheeks. Meanwhile, over the chasm, the apparition of Ange cocked her head as if she was considering a moment.

The prince looked behind him at his guards and dragons. "Please," he said. "I've not got all day for you to consider this. I need an answer now."

That caused the apparition of Ange to immediately straighten her neck. She gave a slight curtsey. It looked lazy, as if she was mocking the prince. "I'm sorry, sir. I'm meant for the fields, doing my work here, and you're meant for higher circles. Somehow, I don't think I would belong at that ball."

Arran shook his head and then turned back to his dragons. He looked over his shoulder for a moment, though I couldn't see from this angle the expression on his face. "Very well, I gave you a chance for a higher life. I guess you're right though. You'll always be meant for a life like this." He placed the pouch to his waist and tied it to his belt. Then, he walked off in his characteristic haughty manner.

Time sped up. The prince walked at a sprinting pace towards his dragons and flew off. Ange scurried about her garden pruning the trees and sprinkling some kind of dust on them that glowed gold.

The sun soon set on her side of the chasm. But strangely, the sun remained up there in the sky over the second house – the one made from yellow bricks on our left. From it came a boisterous laughter, pealing out from inside as the front door swung open.

An older version of Rine emerged on the doorstep. Surprisingly, his features looked edgier on his face, and he'd also bulked up. While when I'd first seen him, he'd been a spotty teenager, now he seemed kind of handsome.

A blonde-haired woman in a free-flowing sequin dress waltzed out the door after Rine's apparition, giggling out in a high-pitched voice. She leaned over to him, gave him a kiss on the lips. Rine took her into his arms and then dipped her down to the ground. She gave a whooping sound as he planted an even longer, firm kiss on her lips. She giggled again.

"Hah," I knew it, the real version of Rine said from our position on the ledge. "I'm a stud."

"I guess blonde is your type," Ange said with a sigh.

"Who cares? She's beautiful, don't you think? I knew it. I guess my time spent with Bellari really paid off. They say you can learn a lot from young love."

The vision of Rine released the woman, and she skipped down the path towards a horse-drawn carriage that was waiting for her. She had a real spring to her step. But Rine's apparition didn't look too happy. As he stared after the girl, he had this long, forlorn expression on his face. Perhaps it was an expression of boredom, or perhaps even loneliness…

Rine's apparition turned towards the chasm, and it looked as if he was almost looking at Ange's house. But he didn't seem to notice anything. Instead, he put his hands to his mouth and hollered out through them.

"Ben," he called. "Ben, where are you now? Don't tell me you've run away again. Ange can't look after you. She doesn't have time. You know you're better here, Ben. You know this is where you belong."

Now my heart was thumping in my chest. I looked up at Aleam, who was glowing and his face had lost form so I could no longer see his wrinkles. "Hang on a minute," I said. "If I'm not at Rine's and I'm not at Ange's, what happened to me? Please Aleam, don't tell me I've died. That would be a sorry end to this story."

Aleam didn't answer me. Instead, he raised his spectral staff to the sky with both hands. Out of it, he cast a light that filled the entire space. It created a beam that split into two and hit both houses on the sides of the walls. The houses folded outwards, so we could see each individual room inside.

Now, both Rine and Ange were in their bedrooms, lying on their beds. Rine had an incredibly opulent four-poster bed, with satin sheets and covers, coloured rose-red. Ange lay on a single bed, with a plain brown blanket. Ange was sobbing, staring at a painted portrait. Rine didn't sob, but he also had a portrait in his hand.

"Let's just stop time there shall we," Aleam said.

He clicked his fingers, and everything went silent and eerie around us. Then those two beams latched on to the pictures in Rine's and Ange's hands. They pulled the two portraits towards us, so close that we could see them clearly. They were both the same portrait, an oil painted replica, with only slight variations in the features. On the left side stood Rine in a red cloak and a black flat hat, with his emerald dragon, Ishtkar, peering over his shoulder. On the right stood Ange in the same attire, with her Sapphire, Quarl peering over hers. They both had a scroll in their hands, each wrapped with a red ribbon.

Each picture was set in a wooden frame with a glass pane at the front. And both frames had the glass cracked, forming what looked like a chasm between the couple.

"Our graduation," Ange said. "But why would I break that picture?"

"Yeah," Rine said. "I have no reason to smash that. I mean it's only a paint—"

Aleam cut him off. "Maybe it's time for some introspection. What could the symbolism in this vision actually mean?"

His words fell to silence. Then, Ange turned slowly to Rine and Rine turned slowly to Ange.

"There's no time for that now," Aleam said, and a white light plunged through the surroundings again coming from the staff that he held high above his head. "We are now about to enter the final vision, and this is the most important of them all. Unfortunately, you three must stay behind."

The ground wobbled underfoot, and the scene changed again.

23

BATTLE FOR THE CLOUDS

The first time I'd flown up on Salanraja's back, I'd felt vertigo like I'd never felt it before. It had made me nauseous, and I'd thought that I'd never fly again. But then, at least we'd taken off from solid ground.

Now, I had suddenly materialised thousands of feet above the ground and flying with nothing underneath us. At first, I thought we were going to plummet. But we continued onwards, as if I stood on an invisible floor. The ghost of Aleam looked at me, and his expression seemed to wonder why I was looking so terrified.

Then he looked down. "Oh, sorry," he said, with a slight chuckle. "Looks like I forgot something."

A light came out of his staff, and a beam leading downwards. It hit something at a point right beneath our feet and spread out into an undefined blob. This took definition – warping into a tangled mass of spikes around us, and a scaly floor beneath our feet. As the vision crystallised further, I noticed myself to be nestled within Salanraja's corridor of spikes. Now, I could hear her inside my mind again.

Yet, it didn't feel good to be connected with her all of a sudden. Because her thoughts were gibberish. *"The hamster. The owl in the bottom of sky dawn. The beauty is oblivion coming to us all.*" She said in the dragon tongue, and more nonsense not worth repeating.

I was alone with her, just as Aleam had promised. No Rine. No Ange. No Seramina. Just Ben, in the sky with an insane dragon not having a clue where he was going. Not even Aleam was there, although I sensed him watching me from nearby, just as I sensed Rine's, Ange's, and Seramina's watchful eyes as they waited for good old Ben to do his stuff. But I couldn't sense where they were watching me from, and I couldn't see their eyes or hear their voices. The thought of it sent my hackles shooting up.

"Where is everyone? Why can't I share this vision with my friends?"

Aleam's voice trickled out of the sky, as if from nowhere. "You will fight this battle in the sky alone, Ben, and none of your friends will mean anything as you battle on the threshold between life and death."

"What does that even mean?" I asked. "Where are you, Aleam? Reveal yourself."

"As I said, you are in this vision alone."

"But what about my ghost? Why can't I see a ghost of myself like Seramina and Rine and Ange did?"

"In this possible thread of time, you don't have a ghost," he said.

"What do you mean I don't have a ghost?" I considered this a moment. "Does that mean I'm going to end up immortal?" Really, I wasn't sure I liked the thought of living forever. After all, one day the world would surely run out of food.

"Because," the haunting voice of Aleam said. "The darkest magic in the universe can obliterate a soul from eternity. If this happens, you wouldn't have a future nor a past."

I tried to fathom that idea. But thinking about it gave me a headache – I just couldn't process all the possibilities.

Salanraja's gibberish continued in her head, and because I was bonded to her, it continued in mine too. "*Night and day and chocolate and treacle. They haven't been invented yet. But my cat, he knows of such things. Dragoncat. The fate of the world belongs to Dragoncat. No one else. Time incarnate, and time existing not at all. There is no time. Time is an illusion. Tick-tock tick-tock boom!"* Really, she sounded like that faint voice you hear just before you go to sleep. If you can focus on it, then sleep comes. But if not, it can drone on for what seems like eternity.

The sky was streaked with wispy clouds and a crimson sunset. Out of the reddening light, another blurry form appeared. A discordant broken sound came out from this, which soon formed into an ear-piercing shriek. Then the shape became two – a glowing dragon, and a glowing humanoid shaped figure perched on top. More time passed until I saw the humanoid carried a staff, glowing purple. Then the sharp bones on the dragon became visible, as well as the white beam that fed it from the staff. As the figure's features gained definition, I recognised the man who carried that staff.

There came a raucous cackling sound of laughter derived purely from evil intent, and I saw Astravar's wicked grin. His eyes glistened purple as he rushed past me, then he wheeled his mount around again, his staff poised ready to knock me off Salanraja with his magic.

"My staff," I screamed out. "Aleam, I need my staff. This isn't fair. I can't fight this battle without it."

"It's not your staff you need right now. You have other lessons to learn."

"No, I need my staff. Give it to me, and all this can be over. I can save the kingdom of Illumine, and I can save all the dimensions. Then, I can retire and live a perfect, happy life."

I stared, hissing and yowling, as Astravar swung round for another pass of taunting me. He was surrounded by these hideous bat-like creatures that I'd seen in other visions. Well, I say bat like, but they actually had sharp beaks that looked like they could pierce through anything.

Astravar swooped around still cackling with laughter, and I remembered from all my dreams how I'd seen his eggshell-skinned face laughing at me in the sky.

"Aleam, help me!" I shouted. "Please, I need my staff!"

Aleam didn't respond. Instead, I heard another voice. A familiar female voice with a lilting near-Welsh accent. The voice of my crystal.

"*Initiate Ben, are you not a great warrior, descendant of the great Asian leopard cat? Haven't you always been destined for remarkable things?*"

That's what I'd always told people. And I'd said it over and over again. "What are you saying?" I asked.

"*You are Dragoncat. Destined for perfection. The most remarkable creature that ever lived. Have I got you right? You don't need your staff. You can do this alone.*"

Now her words stung so harshly they made me growl. She was right; I was destined for greatness, just as my ancestors were. I imagined them prowling through the jungle, mighty creatures like lions that stalked their prey with ease. Then, it occurred to me – I didn't know what my ancestors looked like at all.

"*Answer the questions, Dragoncat. What is it you see in yourself? Who are you? Who must you become? What is your destiny?*" Her voice had once again taken on that scary Boudicca quality.

"I don't know!" I screamed, and I'm sure I screamed it out loud at the top of my voice. "I don't know who I am. I don't know who my ancestors were. And I don't know what I'm meant to become."

As if acknowledging the request, my crystal continued the conversation out loud. "Then you have taken the first step towards becoming a hero of legends," she said. Her voice hung for a moment in the air, then it seemed to bounce off the clouds, and the bat-buzzard creatures, and filled the scene with a momentary warmth. "Remember, Ben you must sacrifice yourself to become complete."

Time had stopped for a moment, but it was only going to be for a moment, because soon enough everything accelerated around me. The creatures swooped in to attack Salanraja, and a searing purple beam came shooting out of Astravar's staff.

A jolting searing pain came in my right-paw side, and I wasn't sure if it belonged to Salanraja or myself. Then I smelled something burning – fur, scale, or flesh – and I tumbled down into a bright light that faded into darkness.

The last thing I heard as I fell into the abyss was Salanraja's voice in my mind, still plagued by madness. "Alas," she said. "*This is the end of us all.*"

24

GHOST TA'RA

I hit hard solid ground. The impact was so strong that I thought I'd broken every single bone in my body. I yowled out in pain, then for a while, I lay there, unable to budge an inch. Again, there was no heat or cold in this place. There was no wind, no sensation of anything other than my muscles throbbing in protest. There were no glowing outlines of objects to see my way by.

Nothing surrounded me but darkness, and a horrible thought came to me. I was dead. Dead, and perhaps even about to be erased from eternity.

I considered turning into a chimera. It could probably take the pain better than I. It was far, far tougher than this fallen Bengal who didn't even know who he was. Whiskers, I couldn't even claim to be like my ancestors, the great Asian leopard cats. I was an imposter – a fraud. There was no way I could live up to their legacy – the great agile beasts that stalked through jungles and caught anything they wanted to eat. I was nothing; I was worthless; and I belonged in this vacuous, dark place.

With such thoughts rolling around my mind, I lay there for a while, pity consuming me. Perhaps this was how you got lost in this place. You first got lost inside your own mind, and then you forgot who you were.

"Get up, Ben." The voice floated over the air to my ears like pollen on a warm breeze. It didn't belong to my crystal, nor did it belong to Aleam. It didn't belong to the mistress who had looked after me in South Wales, either. Yet, it had a sweet familiarity to it. "Ben, you can't lie there forever. But you know that already..."

"I can't move," I said, trying to work out why I knew that voice so well. But my head was throbbing, and I couldn't think straight.

"Of course you can. All injuries in here are only in your mind, and you didn't just really fall from the back of your dragon. It was just a vision, and now that you've experienced it in your mind, I really hope you've learned not to fall like that again. If you ever do, remember, cats always land on their feet. You taught me that, remember? *'Make sure your feet are always facing the ground before you touch down against it... A cat who cannot be graceful doesn't deserve to be called a cat at all.'*"

I blinked in astonishment – slowly because my eyelids still felt incredibly painful to move. "Ta'ra... Is it really you? But that means..."

"Oh, don't worry. I'm still alive in the real world. At least in most of the possible threads of time. You probably won't lose me yet."

I groaned and then rolled over. I grimaced when I felt a sharp sting at my side. Though I couldn't yet see Ta'ra, her familiar smell drifted over to me. She'd never quite smelled completely of cat. She'd always been cleaner, preferring to bathe herself in fresh water and lavender salts whenever she could.

Pain coursed through my legs as I lifted myself up on them. But it wasn't as intense as I'd expected. I stretched, my legs shaking as I did so. The pain felt like the kind of pain you get a couple of weeks after an injury. Still evident slightly on movement, but not strong enough to impede it.

It was almost as if this darkness had an ability to consume you if you let it latch onto you for too long. An ability to weaken the muscles, soften the mind, and numb emotions to the point of despair. But now, Ta'ra's presence was setting me free.

"Ta'ra, where are you?" I asked.

Though I didn't have to because I soon picked up on her scent. I followed it, and the next thing I knew I was brushing against her soft fur. Then I felt her wet nose against mine, and I slid my face across hers, and we rubbed against each other.

A faint light emanated from behind me. I turned to see her blue outline shimmering around the detail of her fur. She'd told me before that Cat Sidhe's were often thought of as ghosts that haunted the night, and now she truly looked like a ghost, with her green eyes and the white crest on her chest shining out from the blackness of her fur. She looked truly spectral – the kind of shade that inspires fairy tales. But I wasn't afraid of her.

"I've so missed you, Ta'ra," I said.

"Don't tell that to me," she said. "For I am now a version of Ta'ra long into the future. Tell it to the Ta'ra in your world, when you see her next. Because, trust me, she longs to hear those words more than anything. And I should know…"

"Oh, I will," I said. "If I ever see her again."

"That is up to you."

I was only half listening to her advice, because really, I didn't care so much about it. This might not have been the version of Ta'ra I wanted to meet, but still it was a version of Ta'ra. I was purring, and I knew I had so much to tell her. "I really thought that I would never see you again. I thought I'd lost you forever."

"And why did you think that?" Ta'ra's ghost asked as she gave me a sidelong look.

"I don't know. Because… I guess I didn't quite believe that we'd win. I didn't think that I'd ever be able to get the staff, and then we'd be stuck in Dragonsbond Academy, unable to leave, and I'd never thought that I'd be able to visit. Meanwhile, you'd be too busy looking after your Cat Sidhe brethren, you wouldn't have time to visit me."

"I thought you wanted me to come and live with you and Rine and Ange in your version of the future. I've talked to versions of you, Ange, and Rine in the Ghost Realm and they've told me everything."

I lowered myself to the ground, stretching my paws against it. But there was nothing there to dig my claws into, as if the ground below was made of incredibly fine sand. "I wanted to believe all of that," I said. "But, whiskers. I never truly believed it. Not deep inside."

The ghost of Ta'ra was now purring. Around her, the atmosphere seemed to sing. At first, the sounds were unrecognisable – a faint unidentified chiming amidst a chorus of what sounded like violins. Lights of all kinds of different colours and shades peeked out of the darkness. They took on angular shapes, displaying smooth polished facets.

I peered at it, trying to work out what I was looking at, as if I was awakening from a pleasant dream and trying to make sense of the real world. Soon enough, it took on enough definition for me to recognise it.

Right after my first flight on Salanraja, she had taken me to the Versta Caverns. In these caverns, I had encountered the crystal that had given me the gift of languages. Without it, I wouldn't have been able to talk to Ta'ra in the first place, as she spoke fairy and not cat. Salanraja had explained that these crystals that glowed from the walls of the caverns were the source of all magic in the first dimension. Now, I could see them as clear as bowl water, displaying visions I'd never imagined possible before I saw the magical creatures of this world for the first time.

In them, I saw humanoid creatures with enormous arms and long legs, so stretchy that they looked like they'd topple over themselves. I saw golems of many shapes and sizes – not just the clay and forest golems I'd encountered, but a golem made of molten metal, a golem made of clouds, a golem made – it seemed – of pure water. I saw dragons aplenty, flying around the stalks of mushrooms which were as tall as trees.

"Ta'ra," I said, looking at her. She'd gained definition now and no longer looked like a creature of the night. "Why did you come to me? And why did you bring me to this place?"

"Don't you think I wanted to see you?" she replied.

"No… I think there's more to it than that. What's in here, Ta'ra?"

She let out a soft, drawn-out chuckle. "You know, there's a cave of crystals like this in every dimension. In your world, so it is said, it was buried deep underground a long time ago, to prevent misuse by rogue monarchs, false theocrats, and eventually corrupt politicians. In the ghost realm, it is only accessible to those the crystals deem worthy of an audience. That's why Astravar could never reach here."

I growled in slight frustration. Not only had she failed to answer my question, but she'd also introduced more questions. "I thought Astravar was controlled by dark magic," I said. "Surely the dark crystals would have let him have access."

"It's not as simple as that," Ta'ra said with a very human shake of the head. "Crystals are always pure at their source. They are forces of nature after all and there's no dichotomy to them – no black and white. Only an intelligent creature can breed essence into the crystals, and then the crystal draws magic from either the darkness in the Ghost Realm or the souls who exist here independent of it.

"Those who use the power for decay will taint the crystals towards darkness, whilst those who use them for growth will steer the crystals towards the light. This is the distinction so few humans understand. The warlocks aren't the only threat to your kingdom, but anyone who binds themselves to dark magic. It's truly a dangerous power, one of which the most powerful should always beware."

"Even dragon riders?" I asked.

"Even dragon riders," Ta'ra said. "As you soon shall learn."

I considered a moment. I was hardly the kind to listen during lectures back at Dragonsbond Academy, and now there was so much to take in. But I felt I had to learn about it, just like I once needed to learn how to hunt. "So, explain something to me," I said. "If crystals don't have will, how can they know what's right and wrong?"

"They don't," Ta'ra said. "But they know what's natural, and they make judgments that work towards preservation of this world."

"Isn't that what I just said."

"It depends on how you look at it," Ta'ra said. "There's always so many perspectives when you study such things." Really, I had never thought she would become this wise. But then I guess looking after a colony of thousands of Cat Sidhe would change her somewhat. Though she was much older than me, I liked this version of Ta'ra. She behaved now a lot more like a cat should, as if she'd never needed my tuition.

"I'm guessing you brought me here to collect my staff," I said. "Is it here?"

"It most certainly is. But I warn you, getting it will not be easy."

"But I thought you said that I'd proven my worth to the crystals. Surely I'm now ready..."

"No," Ta'ra said, and her eyes flared bright green. That strange wind without temperature once again gusted out from behind her. It was almost strong enough to knock me off my feet. "The test is yet to come, Ben. The crystals need to know you're strong enough to pass."

Of course, I thought. There was always going to be a catch. "I'm ready," I said.

Ta'ra's gaze seemed to bore into my mind, as if she knew exactly what I felt within. "Are you?"

"Yes!"

"Well then. I guess we're about to find out. Come..."

Ta'ra stalked away down a narrow passageway leading between rows of neatly stacked glowing crystals. They jutted out from the bottom of the cave walls like the teeth of an invisible beast – a beast that would either swallow me whole, or I'd emerge from its belly victorious.

The outcome, I guessed, was down to fate. With that thought in mind, I followed Ta'ra within.

25

AN IMPOSSIBLY MIGHTY STAFF

I only had to get a little way down the passageway when pitch darkness again enveloped me, and I couldn't see a thing. I navigated using Ta'ra's scent, and soon that faded too, along with any sound she emitted. I couldn't even hear her soft footsteps pattering in front of me.

I stopped, wondering if she'd left me alone. But I knew that was stupid. It was just the darkness trying to consume me, and if I lingered too long, I had no doubt it would suck me down into it again.

I carried on, and I soon felt a sharp tearing sensation in the side. It must have been one of the crystals cutting me. I licked my fur there, the sting intensifying. I tasted sticky blood.

But still I pressed on, confident it would do no good to curl up at all and go to sleep in this place. I'd seen enough of it. It wasn't a suitable place to lie down and retire. It was dark, boring, and lacking in both food and water.

My throat was so dry it was sore. I thought I must have been so thirsty, in fact, that I was hallucinating. Maybe Ta'ra and the crystal cave and all the other weird things I'd seen here were just illusions – constructs of my own mind.

Despite my doubts, I still pressed on. It was better to be wrong about this than right. Besides, Ta'ra's ghost had said that the crystals might test me, and this felt a lot like a test.

A faint light coming from in front of me gave me hope. Ta'ra wasn't there, but some crystals were glowing in faint hues from both sides of the dark cavern wall. The passageway had widened out significantly. I turned back to check the cut from earlier, to see if it had gone deep. But I didn't yet have an outline. Then I remembered what Aleam said about having to believe in something to see it. So, I projected an image of my silky fur into my mind, the stripes and leopard-spotted jungle patterns painted over it. Miraculously, my body took form behind me, and I saw that there wasn't a cut there at all. There wasn't any blood either.

My surroundings lit up too. Now, I could see the glowing outlines of a meadow. It had long grass, dandelions, tulips, poppies, lupins, buttercups, and all kinds of other pretty flowers. Bumblebees buzzed around the place, and I thought about chasing one. But then I remembered what had happened the last time, and I didn't want to get stung again. The passageway I'd come from had completely vanished. I wondered for a moment if I was still within the Versta Caverns.

But it was all illusions. I was in the Ghost Realm trying to find light amidst the swirling darkness. I was starting to realise how this place worked.

The surrounding objects continued to warp and coalesce into recognisable shapes. The meadow stretched out in all directions, fields of grass and flowers leading to nothing beyond it except clouds as far as my eyes could see. There was no visible sun either – rather the light came from the blue sky as if from all directions at once. Yet I felt comfortably warm.

An enormous oak tree stood in the centre of it all, massive acorns hanging off its massive boughs and twisty branches. Its bark looked gnarled and whorled by time. There were many owl holes inset into the trunk, and the tree's upper boughs looked gravid with leaves. It cast no shadow, for the light seemed to have no direction here. Yet, the wrinkles in the bark housed deep ambient shadows that seemed to push the light away – making it look as if the tree itself was fighting against the darkness.

Soon, I could sense everything around me in vivid detail. I could smell the grass, and the soil, and the pollen from the flowers. I sensed something watching me from the tree's branches. Growls seemed to come from it, and there was another smell – of cats that had recently sprayed. But this didn't smell of house cats back home in South Wales, or in Dragonsbond Academy for that matter. This smell was muskier – more feral.

I also caught a whiff of the more familiar scent of Ta'ra from behind. I turned to see her approach. She still looked older than the Ta'ra I knew but had now lost her spectral appearance.

"You said my staff was here," I said. "But all I see are flowers and grass and a gigantic tree."

"Then you've found your staff…"

I blinked in confusion. "What, the tree?"

"Precisely," Ta'ra looked up at the tree, with an awfully proud-looking posture. "Your staff is the tree."

"What the whiskers do you mean? I can't go into battle with an oak tree in my mouth. I mean the thing's ginormous."

"You can change its form," Ta'ra said. "Remember, a lot of what exists in this place is to do with belief. A tree donates its spirit to become a magical staff, and then you only need to find the crystal that was meant for it."

I didn't understand. I thought this version of Ta'ra must have been having a joke with me. "So what? I just go up to it and say, excuse me tree, will you turn into a staff for me? This is absurd."

Ta'ra laughed that sweet laugh again. "Not precisely. You will have to defeat its guardians first."

I paused a moment as I took in that foreign scent of cat spray above me. "It's guardians…" I said, my jaw clenched tight with anger.

"Exactly," Ta'ra said. "Behold your ancestors, the great Asian leopard cats…"

I looked at her in astonishment. This really had to be a joke, albeit a very bad one. The older version of Ta'ra was getting her revenge for all the mackerel she thought I'd stolen from her. She'd taken it too far.

Just as I turned away from the tree, ready to find my way to somewhere else, my ears perked up and honed onto some rustling sounds coming from the thick clusters of leaves. Little pink noses emerged first, followed by three pairs of amber eyes.

Three blue shimmering forms stalked along the branches and down the trunk, their bodies seeming to cling to the tree. They found their way to the ground, and then they sprinted towards me.

26

ANCESTRY

The next thing I knew, I had three cats circling me. They still looked like ghosts, but it didn't take long for their fur and features to gain definition and the glow that outlined them to fade. Soon enough, before me stood three Asian leopard cats, and other than their distinctive oriental look, they looked no different from common house cats.

Disappointment sank into my chest as I took in their size and stature. These were my ancestors, the great Asian leopard cats, and they were hardly great at all. In fact, one of them was even smaller than me. I'd expected the great Asian leopard cat to be a great hunter, like a jaguar or a lion. How was this creature meant to claim any prey it wanted? Your everyday deer would just trample it into the ground.

As a cocktail of confusion and dismay whirled in my mind, I spun around, trying to get glimpses of my ancestors' features. But they moved so fast and seemed so wild it was hard to focus on them for long. Still, I noticed the beautiful markings on their fur. Just like mine, except with more spots and fewer stripes. One of them – a tom cat – had an incredibly long neck, and much of its mass seemed distributed towards the back of its body. Another – a she-cat – had a heavy fur coat, making it look a bit like a Maine coon except much smaller. The third – another tom, and the one that was smaller than me – had a tiny head and massive ears that made it look a bit like a caricatured fox.

"These are my ancestors?" I asked. "The great Asian leopard cat? Then why must I fight them? They're practically family."

Ta'ra wasn't there to answer me. She had disappeared now into the magic of this place. The three cats had one thing in common – their eyes all sloped downwards towards the centre, as if they wore permanent frowns.

"I'll talk to you then," I said to my ancestors, hoping that one would answer. I could, after all, speak their language. "Why must I fight you?"

"You have to prove yourself worthy," the long-necked leopard cat said.

"If you are truly an Asian leopard cat, then you must fight like an Asian leopard cat," the thick furred she-cat said.

"Show us what you're made of, Bengal," the small leopard cat with the large ears said.

Just as the smallest tom cat held my attention, the other male with the long neck pounced on me from behind. Its claws tore into my back, and then it bit through my fur with its teeth, sending a painful shudder up my spine. I shrieked out, and I shook the creature off me. I turned to see it coming at me again with flailing paws. I dived out the way and watched it pass. My heart pounded in my chest, and my breath was so heavy it hurt. I'd never seen a cat move so fast.

While I watched the long-necked cat, something massive leaped out at me from the concealed grass to my side. A fluffy mass of fur sailed towards me, and I turned towards the bared yellow fangs of the female leopard cat. It extended its sharp claws and scraped them across my face. The force of it sent me rolling across the ground, and I tumbled right into the third leopard cat.

I thought this one would be a complete wimp, and I couldn't have been more wrong. Because what it lacked in size, it gained in ferocity. It executed a flurry of movements with its paws and gnashed at me with teeth so sharp I thought they might shred me to fur balls.

I scrambled out of the way, and I hissed and yowled as I ran towards the oak tree. I leapt at the trunk, and I caught myself on the bark with my claws. Hisses and growls came from behind me, and I looked up towards the top of the tree and pulled upwards. The tears in my knotted muscles screamed at me as I went, but I persevered and eventually clambered on to a branch. There, I lay down and watched the leopard cats hissing and growling at me from the bottom of the tree.

It was stupid really because I knew they could also reach me here. They had come down from here to fight me. But they didn't even seem to want to bother coming up. It didn't take me long to realise why.

I looked up to see more leopard cats on the tree, staring at me from higher branches. They wore a variety of coats – some of them in brilliant fiery colours, others in desaturated greys, and others in russet browns. They stalked down the high branches, their fangs bared.

"Come down to the ground, you coward," one of them said.

"Face up to your past," another said.

"Embrace your destiny," said a third.

Still the three Asian leopard cats stalked the bottom of the tree, looking even more ferocious than their brothers and sisters up here. Then I remembered. I had the power to turn into a chimera. I willed the magic into my muscles. But the magic didn't work.

My part of the branch was wide enough to fit three leopard cats side by side. They stalked forward, and I could smell the wildness in their breaths. It wasn't as foul as the breath of the chimera I'd caught a whiff of before, but still it stank of rotten meat.

I never had actually killed an animal and eaten it raw. But these creatures must have done it daily. In other words, they were seasoned killers, and now they were coming to get me. They backed me down the length of the branch until I was right at the edge, the leaves tickling at my shins.

The branch snapped underneath me, and I fell. I yelped out, twisting my body as I fell. Fortunately, I landed on my feet. My heart was pounding, and at first, I thought I was about to taste bitter defeat.

But then, I realised I had no choice. I had to fight. I couldn't run from this. I was a Bengal, a descendant of the great Asian leopard cat. Which meant I must have evolved and adapted to be better than them.

The leopard cats I was meant to face were lying in the grass in wait. As soon as I hit the ground, they charged. The long-necked one pounced first, and I dashed underneath it, swiping up with my claws to scratch underneath its belly. I didn't turn to see it clumsily roll through the grass behind me, but I'd already known from its trajectory that it would.

The small Bengal with the big ears came next. It moved so fast, dashing around me so swiftly that it made me dizzy trying to track it. But still I focused on its small head and the long ears that bobbed over it. When it came in to strike, I was ready. Its flurrying swipes were fast – full of feints and jabs and all kinds of complex manoeuvres. But they were designed to keep larger enemies at bay, and to make the leopard cat seem larger than it actually was.

I pretended I was a goat and lowered my head. I think I even pushed some of the chimera's magic into me, and I charged. I rammed the smaller creature across the ground, and it skidded away.

Finally came the leopard she-cat in the fur coat with the super strong swipes. Without my power as a chimera, I had no chance of defeating her in a paw wrestle. So I ducked the first swipe that it sent at me, darted around the second, then I knocked the leopard cat down from behind. I growled in triumph as I pinned it by the shoulder, and I was just about to bite down on its neck, when I realised something.

Astravar had wanted me all this time to turn feral, which is kind of what dark magic had done to him. It had destroyed his mind, so he didn't care about those who should be close to him. If my lust for this battle won within me, then I'd have lost, because I'd be no different from Astravar.

This was surely the test.

I calmed myself and stepped back off the furry leopard cat. She glared over her shoulder at me, confusion evident on her face.

"This is enough," I said. "I will not fight you."

"What do you mean you won't fight us?" the long-necked leopard cat sputtered back.

"Are you telling us you're weak?" said the small one. "Incapable? Are you a coward?"

"Explain yourself," the thick coated one said.

I took a deep breath and tried my hardest to ignore the adrenaline surging in my legs, shaking in such a way that they compelled me to re-join the fight. "I do not want to win. I only want to save the kingdom, save myself, and to save those I—" The words caught on my tongue, as if I didn't want to admit them to myself. But really, who was I kidding?

"I want to save those that I care about," I said, "including my friends and my dragon. And I'm sure you do too. If you stop me from getting that staff, then all the leopard cats in our world will perish. Is that what you really want?"

The three leopard cats I'd fought remained silent. They stared at me with wide eyes, as if waiting for me to say something. Instead, a loud voice boomed out from the distance. "No," it called out. "That is not what they want."

A cat jumped down off the top of the tree. It wasn't a leopard cat like the others. Instead, it was your typical mongrel tomcat tabby – with a round face and a strong-looking body. One of its eyes was dead, and it looked as if it had been in a lot of fights.

He strode up to me, and then looked me straight in the eyes, recognition painted on his face.

"Who the whiskers are you?" I asked.

He looked a bit taken aback by that reply, but he didn't express this for long. "I'm your father," he said. "And I'm incredibly proud of you, son."

27

THE MIGHTY GEORGE

The old Ragamuffin back home in South Wales had told me it's rare that a cat will ever meet their father. "If you do," he said. "Then you are either incredibly lucky, or you've committed such terrible crimes against cathood that he's spent the rest of his life hunting you down to make you atone for them."

I hadn't committed any crimes – or at least I didn't think I had. But given how battered this cat looked, I didn't quite feel like one of the lucky ones.

I observed him cautiously because I really believed this had to be a trick. At the same time, disappointment bloomed inside me like a toxic flower.

"No," I said, with a bitter laugh. "You can't be my father. I'm a Bengal descendant of the great Asian leopard cat. One of these ghosts is my father, but not you."

As if wanting to wound me, he said it again. "No, Ben. I am your father. Your mother was a Bengal, and her mother before that, and then her father, and her mother, and her mother. You do come from a great line of Bengals, but that doesn't mean your line is pure."

Really, I'd never heard anything so ridiculous in my life. Now, adrenaline was really pumping through me. I felt I should fight this imposter, and then I'd show him not to make up terrible lies.

"If you're really my father, then why are you telling me this? Isn't it better for me to be proud of my heritage, so I don't need to worry about it when fighting Astravar? If I know I'm descended from mongrels, how can I expect to defeat him?"

"That is your problem," my alleged father said. "For a long time, Ben, your pride has been wounding you. It doesn't matter who your ancestors are. All that matters is that you've made it this far, and you have the will to do good."

"How do you know all this? How could you possibly know who my ancestors are?"

"When you live in the ghost realm long enough, you get to trace back your entire family lines. You meet members of your family going generations back, and you learn revealing things about your past you couldn't have possibly learned in the land of the living."

He sounded genuine enough. But I still didn't – or rather I couldn't – believe him.

I stalked over to him, and I sniffed his fur, searching for familiarity. I smelled behind his neck first, and then down his back, all the way to his tail. He had the scent of a normal moggie tomcat – there was nothing special about him.

"There's no way you can be my father," I said. "It's impossible. You don't even smell like me."

"You really think a father and son should smell the same?" the foreign tom cat said, and he cocked his head.

"I mean, you're not even a warrior. You couldn't defeat these great Asian leopard cats."

"Really? Do you want to fight me and test that?" He puffed himself up and arched his back.

"No, it's okay," I replied. I'd really had enough of fighting for one day.

The sun suddenly emerged at the highest point in the sky. Its rays filtered through the blue, limning everything with soft, warm hues and filling me with warmth. It revealed, in this cat's fur coat, familiar markings. The patterns in my fur were made of stripes and spots, and here I saw the stripes.

"You can trust him," a voice said in my head. It was my crystal speaking. "He has no reason to lie to you."

"But he's not a Bengal," I replied in my mind. "Nor is he a leopard cat."

"Does he need to be?"

I stopped to consider that for a moment. Though I had no reason to trust this strange cat, I also had no reason not to believe my crystal. It had, after all, guided me through this world and other dimensions, during the times when I was most lost. I turned to the cat. Now, the other leopard cats were nowhere in sight. It was just me and him, standing alone by a massive shimmering oak tree set amongst tall, green grass.

"Father," I said. "Let's say for a moment you are my father... Most cats don't get to meet their fathers, do they?"

"Until they reach the ghost realm," he said. "And yet here you are."

"Then why are you even here in this vision? Surely the entire purpose of this dream – or whatever it is – is for me to get my staff."

My father was purring now – a deep rumbling sound that filled me with comfort.

"I discovered your crystal," he said. "It spoke in this soft Welsh accent, much like the humans back in our home. At first, when it said that I was destined to meet you, I thought that I'd gone crackers. But then, when it showed me visions of you in your litter, with your five brothers and sisters, I was filled with joy. It told me your story – about that evil warlock, and what he tried to do to you. It showed me what he intends to do to the world, including the destruction of my old family home, and all the other little kittens I've fathered, too." He fell silent for a moment.

I meowed at him because I realised he needed a little comfort. I'd never found it easy to watch those visions of Astravar, just as my dreams of him had always spooked me out. I felt grateful that I'd not had to deal with those dreams for a while. Even so, the memories of them remained.

"How many sons and daughters do you have?"

My father laughed. "Oh, I don't know. Hundreds, perhaps. You know, your mother and I knew each other since we were kittens. She really was a beautiful cat."

"And my crystal… What did it tell you to do?"

He turned back to the tree, but it wasn't a tree anymore. I was staring right at my crystal, spinning slowly on its vertical axis. It was showing a vision from my kittenhood. In it I was a kitten when I loved to swipe at pieces of string the mistress' and master's son dangled from a fork. Then when I got the string, he'd hold the fork over my nose, and I'd swipe it out of his tiny fingers. I remember my feeling of pride whenever I did that. But then both me and the child were still young.

The thing that struck me most of all about the vision was my appearance. I still had the long neck and huge ears of an Asian leopard cat. But the markings on my coat were definitely similar to my father's, and my face also had his shape.

The vision of the crystal changed, and it stopped spinning. One of its facets faced us, showing both of us staring forwards, as if at nothing. It took me a moment to realise that this wasn't a vision at all, but my father and I were looking at ourselves in a mirror. Indeed, there were so many similarities, that there was no doubt in my mind who this cat was.

I no longer felt the dismay I'd felt when my father had told me the news. Rather, I felt good to finally have an identity. Now I knew who I really was.

I turned to my father, and I bowed my head. "Father, you never told me your name," I said. "Because I'm going to tell everyone I'm descended from you from now on and be proud."

"George," he said. "I am the great mighty George. Or at least that's what the humans called me."

I laughed. "Much, much better than Bengie. Well, I am Ben, descendant of the great Asian leopard cat and the great mighty George."

"Very well," George said, and he blinked his one good eye, then rubbed his nose against mine. I turned back to the crystal, because it had started to glow white and was spinning once again.

"Can you accept this, Initiate Ben?" the crystal said. "*The fabled Dragoncat and descendant not only of the great Asian leopard cat, but many other breeds of cat as well.*"

"*I think so,*" I said.

"No," the crystal said. "*There is no 'think' about it. You either do or you don't.*"

"Okay," I said. "*I accept it, and I accept my destiny. My father is right, it doesn't matter where I come from.*"

"Then let it be so," my crystal said, glowing as it spoke. "*Initiate Ben, the fabled Dragoncat, who will one day be spoken of in legends. Descendant of the great Asian leopard cat and the much-revered George. I must warn you of the powers of this staff, because there is only one other of its kind in existence. It contains dark magic, and we hope and have forecast in most of the possible threads of the future that this dark magic will not corrupt your soul. Can you accept this responsibility?*"

"*Of course I can,*" I said.

"*Then, it is done. Here is my final gift to you. After this gift, I will only help you if you call on me and you truly need my aid.*"

The crystal resumed spinning, and it went faster and faster until its facets were completely blurred, and it soon resembled a whirlwind – except this time not a dangerous one. The surrounding light intensified. It got so bright that I saw spots before my eyes.

I couldn't see my father anymore. I couldn't see the great Asian leopard cats around me. Nor could I see Ta'ra, but she had vanished quite a while ago now. The crystal sang like sharp metal blades slicing through the sky. The pitch continued to intensify until it hurt my ears, and it got so loud that I thought my delicate ear drums would rupture.

I lay down and buried my head in the ground as I clutched at my ears with my paws. This shielded me from both the light and the noise. The ground shuddered, and then everything went still.

When I looked up, the crystal, the oak tree, the grass and everything around me had gone. All I saw was a human-sized hand holding a staff with a purple crystal on it. Both hand and staff had that spectral glowing outline to them I'd become used to in this domain. The hand floated around me, as if attached to an invisible body. I tried stepping away from it, but it stayed firm by my side – my new companion.

"The crystals also decided to gift you with a staff-bearer," my crystal said in my mind. *"It will go with you wherever you travel. You will need this, for obvious reasons. Once you call upon the staff, it will place it in your mouth. Only then, can you use it, and you will know instinctively how to do so. But to master its use will require some training."*

I chirped, happily. Finally, I'd got the staff I was destined to retrieve. *"Is that it?"* I asked. *"So now I can return to Dragonsbond Academy, rescue Aleam, defeat Astravar, and end this once and for all."*

"No," said the ghost of Ta'ra, as she was suddenly standing right beside me. I hadn't realised she could hear the voice of my crystal, but I guess everything was possible in the ghost realm. "I think you'll probably want to return to the Caldmines Forest first."

"You mean the place where all the Cat Sidhe are?"

"Yes," ghost Ta'ra said. "Because your friends are in danger, and they urgently need your help."

"What? What's happening to them. Ta'ra?"

She said something in reply, but I didn't quite catch it because her voice and smell were trailing away as the scene filled with white light again.

28

SERAMINA'S SECRET

Once again, darkness enshrouded me. A haunting silence enveloped everything, so still that for a while I thought myself surrounded by voices. But my mind had created these voices to fill the spaces where sound should have been. I also sensed other things in the darkness – the mistress from South Wales laughing as she called me in for a roast chicken dinner, flames spouting out of Salanraja's mouth onto a raw slice of beef, butterflies and catnip and the warming sun. But none of these really existed. I just longed for them in a darkness that would have consumed me if I didn't hold onto my hope.

Later, the ghost of Ta'ra's words came back to me, now only a memory. *"Your friends are in danger, and they urgently need your help."* Those words echoed around my mind as if they were ball bearings bouncing off the walls of my skull. I wished I knew more. Why hadn't Ta'ra's ghost told me exactly what was wrong?

It could be that they were facing complete annihilation. If that was the danger – Ta'ra had told me nothing. It might be they were bracing against a terrifying flood, or they were stuck in the centre of a raging forest fire, or they'd all been sent to the Seventh Dimension and were stuck on a rock surrounded by glowing, sulphurous magma.

Or Astravar could have sent his lackeys, and the only way to defeat them would be through my staff. Whiskers, for all I knew, Astravar could have left Dragonsbond Academy to fight them. Or maybe he was going to possess them all again so he could use their magic to destroy Dragonsbond Academy.

I imagined a purple mist looming on the horizon, bone dragons flying in from afar, keeping pace over armies of Manipulators, glowing forest golems, and shifting clay golems. Then, in my mind's eye, I saw an image of the Cat Sidhe, their teeth bared and ready for battle. That's all they had for weapons – teeth and claws. And I guess they could also turn into fairies and use their special magic.

Now I had my staff I could now go and help Ta'ra. Yet, I was trapped in this place, surrounded by the darkness that wanted to consume my soul.

As I considered my terrible situation, the darkness and the silence weighed down on me. I growled, I hissed, and I writhed on the floor, clawing at myself to try to get a grasp on reality.

Fortunately, a female voice jerked me out of my downward spiral. It was slightly monotonous, but at least familiar. "Ben," she said. "Is that you?"

I latched on to the smell of snowdrops coming from some place nearby. It was only faint, but strong enough to remember that I still had friends in this lonely place. "Seramina?" The smell intensified. "Seramina, where are you?"

"Here, Ben. I'm right in front of you."

Her voice drifted off into emptiness, and at first, I thought that the silence had returned, and I'd lost her. But then I recognised the roaring of a well-lit fire, crackling and spitting. From my right, a hearth emanated a warm red light. Within a nest of roughly hewn stones, flames lapped up from behind iron bars, stretching up towards a stone chimney. A cloud of soot danced above these, disappearing again into the darkness.

I shivered as the firelight bloomed out and filled the room. I could now see everyone around me. Seramina, Ange, and Rine sat in incredibly comfortably looking armchairs placed around the fire. A fourth armchair lay between Rine and Ange. Both seemed deep in thought as they stared at the fire.

I stepped towards the fireplace. The fire within felt like a real fire. If I was behind those bars, I wouldn't be happy, but here on the comfort of the rug that covered the loose floorboards, I could lie down and have a well-earned nap. I rolled over onto my side so I could feel the warmth of it on my belly. There I lay, purring to the rhythm of the crackles.

"Ben," Rine said, and his eyes lit up when he saw me. I was glad to see some amusement in his eyes. "Here, you might appreciate this."

He pointed his staff, and at first, I thought he was going to freeze me in place. Instead, the blue, frozen beam hit a point on the floorboard next to me. A block of ice sprung out of the ground there. It was as big as my head, and close enough to the fireplace that it immediately started to thaw.

I let out a chirp of appreciation. Then I scrambled over to the ice block and licked off my first drop of water. It tasted amazingly fresh, and I continued to lick away until my tongue was numb. Something shimmered from next to me, and the hand – my staff-bearer – appeared. It had my fabled staff clenched tight between its thumb and fingers, and it glowed blue as a spectral hand should.

Ange also seemed to perk up a little bit when she saw me. I guessed that all three of them had been so worried about me that they had almost become lost in this place. Ange smiled as she looked down at me, then clucked softly. I was about to go over and jump onto her lap when her eyebrows furrowed and her expression twisted to disgust. She wasn't actually looking at me, but at the spectral hand and specifically the purple crystal on the staff that it wielded.

"Ben…" she said through clenched teeth. "Your staff… You have dark magic."

"I do," I said. "The crystals entrusted me with it."

"But how? I was worried when you became the chimera and saw that you could use more than one school of magic. I guess it makes sense, but… You cannot use this staff, Ben. You're not strong enough… The dark magic will taint your soul, and you'll end up just like Astravar."

I blinked at her in surprise. I hadn't expected this from Ange. But then I'd seen how quickly she'd almost turned on Seramina. I guessed she was testing me and wanted to know I still walked in the light. "It's tainted the souls of all humans that have connected with it," I pointed out. "Cats, however, haven't had a chance to try it yet. Maybe we'll be okay."

She shook her head, and then gazed at Seramina, who approached my spectral staff-bearer. Seramina carried her staff in one hand, whilst the other she had cupped over her staff's crystal, which was glowing white.

"Might I suggest something?" she asked. Her hand glowed red as the light suffused from her staff through the skin. She lifted her hand away from the crystal, keeping the palm facing downwards. She carried away a ball of light, hovering just underneath her hand. As it floated across, clinging to her hand like a magnet, it pulsed in a mesmerising way.

Seramina placed the ball over the purple crystal on my staff. It lowered from her palm into the crystal on its own accord, and it touched the crystal, then flared out brilliantly. When the light had faded, all that was left was a white crystal on my staff, just like the one on Seramina's.

"What?" Ange said. "A glamour spell won't change the issue. It's still dark magic."

"Yes," Seramina said. "But no one will have to know now. Ben can just say he's a master of alteration and mind-magic, just as we've always thought." She bit her lip, as if considering something. "Trust me, it worked for me…"

It was as if someone had just smashed a plate in a quiet room. For a moment, Ange seemed stunned into silence. Then her jaw dropped, and she stood up.

"Y-Y-You're a dark magic user as well?"

"I am," Seramina said. "Is that a problem?"

Ange had placed a hand to her temples, and I could sense anger burgeoning inside her. "Well, that makes sense. You had everyone fooled, thinking that you're a mind-witch and destiny-mage when you're actually just as dangerous as the warlocks. That's how Astravar managed to take control of you, and that's why we saw you destroying the world in that vision."

Ange drew her staff off her back as she studied Seramina. She had clearly given Seramina's staff back to her whilst I'd been off fighting the ghosts of my ancestors. Now, her expression said that she thought it had been a mistake to do so.

"I didn't choose my discipline," Seramina said. "I didn't choose what was in my blood, and I didn't choose who my father was." The fire next to Ange flared, and a flame lashed out against the iron bars as if it wanted to escape. At first it seemed Seramina had done this. But then I remembered that this place seemed to feed off our emotions, and the fire was probably all a part of the show.

"And what does the Council of Three think about all this?" Ange asked as she stepped forward and slightly to Seramina's side. "Why would they let you loose in the world if they knew you had the power of a warlock?"

"The Council of Three already knows. I came clean after what happened during the battle with the Cat Sidhe. I'd been hiding it before then. I never knew why I had this power until I learned who my father was. But Aleam and the Council of Three always suspected my powers, and when Aleam saw what I was capable of, he took me under his wing and taught me how to control myself. He knows how to handle dark magic, and he knows how to stop it consuming me."

"But how can you do so without breaking your connection to the dragon? None of this makes any sense."

"I don't know," Seramina said.

Ange took a deep breath, and she turned towards the fireplace and gazed into the flames. "It's not just the warlocks we have to worry about, but the threat of such vile magic consuming us from within our society."

"It's not just me. There are other dark magic users in Dragonsbond

Academy. Aleam can still use dark magic. There's also another child of a warlock, I believe."

"What? Who?"

"The way that you're talking about this dark magic, I'm not sure I want to tell you. Anyway, I don't know for sure. I only have my suspicions – and in truth, if I'm right, I don't think she knows either. But you have to understand, we have to keep this a secret. If Prince Arran found out, then there's no telling what he might do. You've seen what he's like."

"So why did you tell me in the first place?" Ange said.

"Because it's about time that people saw who we were," Seramina said.

"But what if it consumes you? What if you become just like the warlocks? You should be stripped of your magic."

Seramina squinted her eyes. "Even if we need it to defeat the warlocks?" she asked. "You've seen Ben's visions, and I've had many of my own as well, that I've kept secret for a long time. Until now, I was even more scared of this power than you are. But Aleam, or at least the future Aleam, made me see sense."

Ange had definitely calmed down, at least a little. She backed away from Seramina and lowered her staff to her legs. As she continued to speak, she no longer sounded angry, but confused, as if she were trying to work out a way to accept this in herself, as if she wanted a way to reason with herself.

"Someone should tell King Garmin," she said. "Why keep it a secret? He would see sense and he could tell Prince Arran that he can't hurt any of you."

Seramina lowered her head. "Not everyone trusts King Garmin. Aleam feels we should keep this a secret from him, and Driar Yila agrees. On the other hand, Driar Brigel and Driar Lonamm think the king could help change things. But everyone agrees – the more people who learn about this, the more at risk our dark magic users become. We think there are many more inside Cimlean City, and if the warlocks learn of this, they will take the opportunity to corrupt those who don't have the power to control their abilities yet. This secret must be guarded closely, Ange and Rine. I'm only telling you this because I just couldn't stand seeing you turning on Ben like that. But I've kept quiet about it because I worry what people might think of me." Her eyes had gone puffy underneath, and her nose was scrunched as if she was about to cry.

Ange lowered her staff, then bent down and placed it down on the ground. She opened out her arms to Seramina. "Come here," she said.

Seramina nodded, then placed her staff down on the ground. She entered Ange's embrace and held her there.

"It must have been hard, keeping this a secret for so long," Ange said.

"It was. But I don't think vanquishing the warlocks will ever be the end of it. Dark magic will always exist in the kingdom in some form."

"We have to do what's right," Ange said. "We've got to fight for a better world. For a better life."

All this time, both Rine and I were happy to take a backseat and watch Ange and Seramina get over their differences. There came a slightly high-pitched buzzing sound from next to Rine, and suddenly the ghost of Aleam stood there. He looked slightly alarmed.

"You've all fulfilled your purposes, I see," he said. "You've reconciled your differences and Ben has got his staff."

Rine stood up from his seat and looked at him, his head askew. "What's wrong?" he said to Aleam.

Aleam looked over his shoulder to where the light from the fire couldn't reach. "You've each encountered the darkness here in various forms, and you've all fought it off in your own ways. That darkness is your enemy – not just the source of dark magic, but the source of dark emotions and dark thoughts. It powers the night, and those who draw magic from it, and it powers the emptiness between spaces. You must use it wisely, Seramina and Ben, but you must fear it and respect it too."

I stood up, and I looked at Aleam with wide eyes. "Aleam?"

He didn't seem to hear me, and he continued to stare onwards. Meanwhile, his ghostly outline was shimmering and seemed to be fading. Even his voice was getting fainter and fainter, though I could still hear what he said.

"Here, in the ghost realm," he continued, "we call it *Cana Dei*, and us ghosts can only travel through it because we exist independent of time. I've held it away from you long enough, and I can't hold it anymore. You must run, or it will consume you." He pointed off towards the darkness – the place I least wanted to go. "In that direction you can find a way out to the Caldmines Forest. Open a portal, Seramina, and get everyone out of here, before it's too late."

29

THE DARKNESS

"Too late... Too late... Too late..." Aleam's words seemed to echo as if bouncing off the walls of a massive chasm. Meanwhile, the darkness seemed to gain strength. It was as if everything around it seemed to dissolve into it, melting away.

The fireplace went first, the heat from it dissipating instantly. Then went the stonework, then the railing – everything dripping into nothingness as if composed of drops of black liquid. The chairs and the rug went next, followed by the floorboards. The floor felt as if it was made of that horrible yeast extract stuff, and it smelled of it too.

Then I noticed myself sinking ever so slowly into the ground. I lifted my feet, and the act of moving seemed to pull me up again. Even so, I knew if I stayed still long enough, the smelly floor would suck me into the darkness, and I'd become lost forever in its depths.

If I ever got home, I would tell the Savannah Cats that the worst deaths didn't happen underneath the belly of the hippopotamus, as they had claimed. Instead, they happen at the bottom of a pool of yeast extract. A bottomless pit of the stuff that shows no remorse, even to vegetarians.

"Hold on," Rine shouted out. "I've got this." He lifted his staff and its crystal glowed blue. He pointed this at the ground in front of us. A sheet of ice cascaded out to where Aleam had directed us. I turned around to see that the old man had disappeared, and nothing remained of what had been in that warm, cosy room.

Rine stepped onto the sheet, then he yelped out as he went skidding forward. He would have slid off if he wasn't quick enough to cast another spell just next to his foot. This created a block of ice that clung to the sheet and stopped his foot in place.

"Idiot," Ange said. "What will all this be worth if you end up getting killed, Rine?" She cast a spell of her own from her staff. A row of vines sprang out of it, and they quickly crawled along the edges of ice, creating a makeshift balustrade. Rine looked back at Ange and gave her a nod of appreciation. He used the vines to pull himself along his magical sheet of ice, sliding with his feet as he did so.

Seramina stepped forward next, her staff clutched in her hand as she focused on a point at the end of the sheet of ice. She pulled herself along gently with the other hand. Then Ange stepped on, and she kept casting vines that wrapped around the ice, as if to secure it in place.

Meanwhile, I'd forgotten myself while watching Seramina, Ange, and Rine, such that I was up to my knees in the black goo, and I couldn't see my feet. Once I got deep enough in it, I forgot my muscles were even there. In a way, I wanted to sink down all the way into it. Fortunately, I still had that rational part in my brain that told me it wasn't a good idea. The goo hadn't consumed that part yet.

"Come on, Ben," Ange said, turning back to me from her perch on the ice. "You can't stay here." Something also nudged me from behind – my spectral staff-bearer pushing me forwards with its fist.

I summoned my strength and pulled myself out, then I rushed forwards and stepped onto the ice. It was cold against the bottom of my paws – which meant that at least it was real. I slid across it, and I hit a wall of springy vines. I was lucky, really, that Ange had thought to cast vines low enough to support me. I skated after the three teenagers, my feet so cold I thought they might develop frostbite and fall off. I'd said many times that I hated walking on snow, but walking on ice was much, much worse.

Eventually, after what felt like hours of pain travelling along this sheet of ice, with Rine casting the sheet of frozen ground, extending ahead of us, and Ange casting the supporting balustrade and scaffolding, we reached the end of the journey.

Rine stopped first. "What in the Seventh Dimension?" he asked. At first, I noticed the light had gone out on his staff. But then I saw that the darkness had closed around it.

"It's got me too," Ange said. "We can't go any further."

"It doesn't matter," Seramina said. "This is the place, I think."

"You don't sound so sure," Ange said. Her legs were bowed, and her gaze was focused on Seramina's staff, as if she were considering wrenching it from her grasp.

"No, no," Seramina said. "This is it." She raised her staff, and the crystal on it glowed purple. Then, she reached into a pocket, and produced a smaller crystal, again purple and not attached to anything. "Courtesy of Aleam. This should lead us back home."

"You had that all along?" Rine said. "Why didn't you use it?"

"Because Ben needed to find his staff first. Anyway, it doesn't matter now. Just let me concentrate." She closed her eyes and both the crystal on her staff and the crystal in her hand lit up purple. A beam then shot out from her staff into the purple crystal and refracted through it, shining out again into the darkness ahead of us. The faint outline of an oval shimmered there – wide enough for us to pass through it. But there was nothing on the other side to step into yet. There was only an abyss.

I turned back to look at the path from when we'd came. The blackness was edging closer and closer, like water coming in from the sea. It ate away at anything it touched, and it was far too close for comfort. I gave it a matter of seconds before we all fell into it – and this time I doubted we'd be able to crawl our way out of it. If the darkness shrouded our magic, then we'd have nothing left to fight back with.

Strangely, though, it didn't seem to want to cut off the purple crystals. It made sense, I guess. If dark magic fed off this thing, then perhaps it could push it away.

"We've not got much time," I said.

"State the obvious, why don't you, Ben," Rine said. "Seramina, whatever you're doing, you need to hurry."

"Hold it," Seramina said, as a thin film of energy developed over the inside of the oval. "I need just a little longer."

Ange said nothing. Instead, she was wrestling with her staff as if trying to pull it out of the darkness. Still, whatever she did seemed to pull the darkness closer towards her. It had almost reached the bottom of her staff now and would consume her arm.

The light from the portal was growing, but strands of darkness had already crept under our feet, and what used to be ice and vines below us resembled a spiderweb more and more. I clenched my jaw and plucked up some courage. This one was on me.

I glanced at my staff-bearer, that had my staff held tight within it. Just as my crystal had instructed, I reached out mentally and summoned it towards me. It lurched forward, and then it was as instinctive as putting a paw in a hole. It placed the staff in my mouth, and I clenched down on it. Then the crystal on my staff glowed and brimmed with power.

It felt like I had a long pole clenched between my jaws, with the other end wedged underneath a washing machine at the peak of its cycle. It vibrated so hard that part of me wanted to drop it. But still, with such intense power surging through me, I didn't want to let go.

"Ben, no! You're not trained." It was Ange who said it, but her voice seemed so distant now. Instead, I focused on the magic. It was so addictive that part of me wanted to become part of that magic – to lose my mind to it. It felt as if something invisible was reaching out inside me and trying to control my soul.

I had to keep focused. I had to get us all out of there. So, I imagined the most powerful spell I could possibly cast. An explosion that would push the darkness away for miles, revealing the light of the ghost realm that resided underneath it. It would strengthen the ice and vines beneath it and even feed a little magic into the portal. Meanwhile, it would leave Ange, Seramina, Rine, and me unscathed. Plus, it would bring some delicious food with it for good luck.

That was what I hoped for. What happened instead was salmon.

Out of my staff, I shot this tiny pulse of blue light that floated in the darkness for a moment, pushing it away. Just when I expected the explosion that would save us all, the first salmon flopped out, shredding the darkness with its sharp teeth as it sailed through it. Then came another, and another. Before I knew it, what must have been thousands of salmon were all leaping out of this magical spell. They flopped at the darkness, pushing it away in swathes. It looked as if they'd tried to leap up a waterfall, but instead of getting to the other side, they'd been dragged through time and space into this world, just as Astravar had done with me. Alas, in this realm, these salmon wouldn't last for long.

"It's done," Seramina called out. "Quickly now."

She beckoned us forward. Ange and Rine stepped through first. I could feel the ground sliding underfoot as well. It seemed that my magical salmon trick hadn't worked for long. I scrambled across the floor, almost losing my footing several times. Just before I went through the portal, I noticed a salmon flopping on the floor. I wanted to drop my staff and pick it up, so I could take it with me.

"Come on, Ben!" Seramina shouted. "There's no time."

The wind without temperature was howling around me now, and I couldn't see anything except what was really close to me – the salmon, Seramina, the portal, and the sparse yet remarkably strong gossamer threads that supported us.

I had no choice but to leave my favourite fish alone here. I sprinted out the portal, and I passed through a cold cascade of what felt like water. I emerged in what seemed a warm and safe world.

I was in forest dense with alders and poplars, birds chirping, the sun shining bright and high in the sky. Then, I caught a whiff of rotten vegetable juice, and dread came over me once again.

ALL THAT GLAMOURS

The smell of rotten vegetable juice was somewhat different than it was at Dragonsbond Academy. It wasn't as potent, and I couldn't smell the distinct variation of Astravar or any of the other warlocks in it. The mist on the northern horizon was also fainter, meaning there probably wasn't a fully equipped army of dark magical creatures waiting behind it. Even so, an army of any size of magical creatures was something to fear.

Despite the looming threat, life thrived in this forest. Blackbirds called out their melodic songs from the high tree branches, and there was a natural mossy aroma to the whole place, quite distinguishable from the smell from the mist. This was what forests should smell like, and I took a breath of fresh air, happy at last to breathe something.

I sniffed around. Cats had definitely been here. They'd sprayed the trees and done their business in the leaf mulch. Unfortunately, I couldn't detect a sign of Ta'ra anywhere. She'd always believed that she shouldn't spray just to leave a scent and mark her territory, much as I'd tried to reason with her.

I continued to follow the scent as I tried to determine where the cats had come from. The trail led me to a hollow with a deer skeleton within it, stripped bare of meat. Around this, some leaves lifted on the breeze and danced around the carcass.

Whatever the Cat Sidhe had been up to, they had been eating well. Rine, Ange, and Seramina didn't follow me, but my staff-bearer did. It floated nearby, wobbling along in a way that looked like the staff might topple out of its hand. I wondered if I could ever lose it or make it invisible. It was so obvious there, glowing all the time, that it would surely ruin my chances of successful hunts.

Seramina had already concealed the colour of the crystal on the staff, using her glamour spell to make it white. Which was fortunate, because in the distance, from behind a thick fog, two golden glowing wisps came into view. They danced around like fireflies, as if searching for something. Then, they must have seen me because they shot right towards me.

They took me by surprise until I remembered this was exactly what fairies looked like. Which meant either they had come from the Fairy Realm, aka the Second Dimension, to visit, or some of the Cat Sidhe had used up one of their transformations. If they had, they would have needed good reasons to do so. Cat Sidhe could only transform eight times in their lives before they would become cats forever. As far as I knew, none of the Cat Sidhe wanted that to happen. They wanted to return to their fairy homes and live amongst their folk again, and they couldn't return to their homeland when they could become cats at any moment. Most fairies don't trust cats, apparently – although I can't imagine for the life of me why.

A plume of golden smoke seeped out of one fairy, as if it had suddenly become a burning ember. This led downwards and soon morphed into a humanoid shape, looking almost like a golden Manipulator. The features formed on this to reveal a familiar figure clad in a short rainbow coloured dress and golden hair. Although, apparently, fairies can display any form they like, they tend to use just one. Most of the time, they liked to be recognisable.

The fairy floated forward in a way that wasn't quite human – her legs crossed like a ballerina's. Once she reached me, she slid to a halt and spoke in a high-pitched voice that, just like last time, reminded me of a cartoon mouse.

"Ben," she said.

I'd seen her last in the fairy realm when I'd first met Ta'ra's grandfather. She'd claimed to be the sister of Ta'ra's ex-betrothed, Prince Ta'lon. But I couldn't for the life of me remember her name.

"I'm sorry, remind me…" I said.

"Remind you what?"

"Your name?"

"Oh…" She put her hand to her mouth and giggled. "I'm Go'na, Prince Ta'lon's sister."

"Yes," I said. "I remember your relationship with the fairy prince. But why are you here and, more importantly, why did you use your transformation? Don't you want to return to your family and once again attend court?" It wasn't that I had any problem with these fairies turning into cats. I just didn't think this fairy woman would make a particularly good one. I guess I was more worried about her ability to survive than anything else.

"We take it in turns to go out and scout," Go'na said. "When we saw the portal emerge from a distance, we decided it was my turn to investigate. None of us want to change forms, really, unless we have to. But anything could have come out of this portal, and we need to stay safe."

"So why not go over as cats?" I asked. "You'd be stealthy and fast in that form."

"Not as stealthy and fast as a fairy in flight. Plus, we can't use magic if we need to, when we're cats. We might need to defend ourselves, you know?"

Her implication that cats couldn't defend themselves sounded ridiculous to me. I turned to see Rine walking over to join us.

"Hello," he said, as he eyed Go'na down then up, as if trying to work her out. Then, when he looked into her eyes, his cheeks went slightly red in a very un-Rine-like way. It was almost as if she'd cast an enchantment spell on him. Whiskers, for all I knew she might have done.

The fairy bowed to Rine, a warm smile on her face. "I'm Go'na, and I was sent here to assist you." She cocked her head rather demurely, her gaze locked on Rine's. "So long as you turned out not to be a threat."

Meanwhile, Seramina studied the fairy from a distance. As a mind-witch, she probably saw right through the glamour. Also, if this fairy knew Seramina's relationship with Astravar, then she would surely consider her one of those threats. So Seramina's caution was wise.

"Knock it off, Rine," Ange said as she approached, and she punched Rine hard on the shoulder, jolting him out of his trance. "Fairies aren't your type, I'm sure…"

He looked away, as if embarrassed to be caught in her enchantment.

"I'm pleased to meet you, Go'na," Ange said, and she stepped forward to shake the fairy's hand. "We all are, in fact. I heard you mention Ta'ra. Is she nearby?"

"She is," Go'na said, looking over her shoulder. "Well, I guess we should take you to her. Come…"

Golden smoke billowed out around her until it concealed her. When it had vanished, she was once again a golden wisp – a ball of light floating in the air. She drifted ahead, circling slightly around the other fairy who hadn't revealed his glamour form.

They shot off through the forest. I was the first to rush after them, excitement brimming in me. After all, I knew that I was once again about to see Ta'ra.

31

THE COMMUNE

It wasn't cats I first encountered when we reached the Cat Sidhe's new home. Rather, I smelled human sweat, and then I saw a burly man stalking through the forest. I could smell cats, of course – lots of them – their scent getting stronger with each step we took. They just weren't visible yet.

The man sat on a small stool on the porch of a wooden hut. Welcoming firelight glowed out from the open doorway behind him. He had a staff in one hand with a yellow crystal at the top of it, just like Aleam's. On his back, he carried a thick bow and a quiver full of arrows, fletched with peacock feathers. His face sported a full growth grey beard, salt and pepper hair, and intense blue eyes. Behind the man, lay a royal blue dragon, bathing in the patterns of speckled sunlight coming through the canopy.

"You've got to be kidding," Rine said.

"What?" I asked

"That's Driar Reslin."

"You mean, Bellari's father?" Ange asked and she didn't sound happy about it.

"Who else?"

The man watched us approach, his hand on his hips. When he saw Rine, he let out a loud and hearty laugh, his chest shaking and the sound of his laughter seeming to bounce back from every tree bole.

"Well, look who the cat dragged in?" he said. Then he looked down at me and gave me a nod. "You know, I've been waiting to use that line for so long now, and you finally gave me the chance. Rine, how are you, son? I've not seen you in donkey's years." He barrelled forwards and embraced Rine in a massive bear hug that looked like it would break Rine's body in two. He didn't seem to notice anyone else here.

I shrunk away. If that was how he treated Rine, then I didn't think I'd survive getting picked up by him.

Driar Reslin released Rine from his embrace and stepped back. Then he looked at Ange and Seramina. Go'na had also appeared from a puff of golden smoke, and his eyes finally fell on her. He looked at her as if he'd never seen her before, and probably he never had in this form.

"Well, aren't you going to introduce me to your companions, Rine?"

"I, er…" Rine glanced nervously at Ange.

"Always been one for the ladies, haven't you, son," Driar Reslin said. "You know what I say, don't you? It's okay to have eyes for others of the fairer sex, as long as your heart's always with your true love. Know what I mean? You still have a heart for my Bellari, don't you?" He elbowed Rine in the ribs and laughed raucously once again.

Rine looked as if he didn't know what to say, glancing between Ange and Driar Reslin as if he really wanted to give the game away. Ange had her hands folded beneath her waist and stared at the ground as her foot tapped rapidly against it. The silence was awkward, and I was just about to break it when the other Cat Sidhe did it for me. Rustling sounds came from the trees, and the black cats stalked down from the high boughs where they'd concealed themselves amongst the leaves. One by one, they dropped from their perches, emitting the purrs of a happy and well-fed commune.

I latched onto the familiar scent of Ta'ra nearby, and then I saw her, standing on a catkin carpet next to a beech tree with a thin yet sturdy bole. She was looking at me with her bright green eyes, seeming even brighter as they shone out from her dark fur. The white diamond crest on her chest seemed even larger than the other Cat Sidhe's, and also contrasted sharply against the surrounding fur.

When I returned her gaze, she blinked contentedly. I could hear her purring from here, and I could also smell fish on her breath.

I bounded over to her and then rubbed my body against hers. "Ta'ra... It's been too long. You're okay, and I'm okay. I couldn't have asked for better."

She laughed, then she turned away from me. "Come on," she said, and she glanced back over her shoulder. "Let's go for a walk. The other Cat Sidhe will no doubt have lots of questions for you all. But for now, let's keep this moment just between us two."

She stalked off a little into the forest. I went with her, and as we walked, the surrounding trees got a little thicker, offering better privacy.

"You know," Ta'ra said, "I've been practising since we last parted. See, I can walk even better in a straight line now." She stepped along the ground, her feet landing with absolute precision. Her back paws hit exactly where her front ones had been. She looked graceful, and elegant, very unlike she was when I'd first met her.

Yet, although she'd mastered the first step, she still had a long way to go. "So how well can you climb the trees?" I asked. "And have you mastered jumping yet? If you crouch low enough, you should be able to jump up to six times your height."

Ta'ra cocked her head and blinked heavily as if she couldn't believe she was hearing this. But she had been fishing for compliments. It's well known that proper protocol when a cat does this is to demonstrate how far they have to go. It's the only way you learn.

"Well, I've still got to work all that out, haven't I? But I have learned how to fish, and I've taught the other cats too. Say, we caught some mackerel today, and Driar Reslin here cooked some for us. Would you like some? I remember you liked mackerel."

Now it was me who was purring – loudly. "Mackerel... I'm so hungry. You know I almost brought some salmon for you. I found some in another dimension, but then I tried to take it with me, but I couldn't because I had my staff in my mouth."

"Your staff?" Ta'ra glanced up at my staff-bearer which did a little dance of appreciation in the air. "Ben, you did it! You can now go and defeat Astravar."

"Yes, but I met your ghost, and it told me you were in trouble and then I knew I had to come here first."

"Really, my ghost?"

"Yes, of course. Who else do you think I might meet in the ghost realm. I also met my father, and my ancestors – the great Asian leopard cats. And I fought them, and I won..."

"But what was I like? I mean will I turn out okay?"

"You'll turn out much older than you are now," I said. Then I added, "as a cat." I think that was what she really wanted to know.

Ta'ra turned towards the purple mist that stretched out in the distance. The sun was waning in the sky behind it and was suffusing it with a red glow, making it look like it was burning.

"It's not Astravar," Ta'ra said. "There's no sign of any warlocks. But there are all kinds of different golems and wargs. Every so often we think we detect danger, and so we send two of our own out in fairy form to help. That's how you met Go'na. Whoever sent these creatures, I fear they're trying to get us to use up all our transformations. I heard you're under siege, right? Perhaps they've posted them there to use up all our fairy magic so if you need us, we won't have any magic left to help out with."

"We can fight them," I said. "We can get rid of all the horrible magical monsters over there. I have my staff now, and we've got Seramina and her—" I stopped myself just in time, perhaps because Seramina was staring at me, that burning look behind her eyes. "Mind-magic... And Ange, and Rine, can use their magic too. Our dragons aren't here yet, but they're coming. I can feel them."

Ta'ra looked up at the floating hand hovering near me. At first, she hadn't shown much interest. But now she seemed rather impressed. "You got that from the Ghost Realm?" she said. "I recognise the glowing effect…"

"We did."

"And you got out of there okay?"

"Somehow," I said.

Her eyes went wide as she gazed at me. Her pupils had gone from narrow vertical slits to almost full circles. I knew I was meant to do something at this point. There was something I'd meant to say to her at this point. But I couldn't quite remember what it was.

Meanwhile, I could feel Salanraja trying to tap into my thoughts. Part of me wanted to respond to her, but another part of me was enjoying my private time with Ta'ra and I didn't want anyone – even my dragon – butting in on the moment.

Before I could put any more words to thought, a thundering sound came from the distant south. I spun around and saw four silhouetted forms approaching through the bright sky, looking like geese with jagged wings. They were still quite far away. Another roar came out, but there was nothing threatening about it.

"Your dragons are here," Ta'ra said. "I guess the help you promised is here after all."

But that wasn't all, because I heard Rine call out, and he pointed at something with his staff. Then, as if to drown out the sound of his voice, Reslin called out even louder. "Ahoy!"

All four humans were looking not at our dragons, but at another small flock of them approaching from the west.

They were even nearer than our dragons, and I could see that they were going to land first. I recognised the leading dragon, which was twice the size of the others. Its white scales shimmered in the waning light, and an old man was perched on top of it with his staff's crystal glowing yellow.

"Aleam!" I said. "He made it out. It's a good day for everyone."

He had three other dragons with him. One of them was a charcoal colour, just like Seramina's dragon, Hallinar. The other two were citrines, and I racked my brain to remember who amongst those I knew rode a massive, flying, scaly lemon. High Prefect Lars rode one – his dragon Camillan. Which meant that Asinda must have been with him on her charcoal, Shadorow.

But I couldn't work out who would be on the other dragon. She had her staff lit up, fire drifting out from it, letting off smoke as if to create a signal. Her blonde hair whipped back in the wind, and her face looked almost as red as the crystal on her staff. It seemed like this girl had caught the sun a little.

My heart leapt in my chest. It was Bellari, sitting on her dragon – called Pinacole – with a tremendously haughty posture. Whiskers, I had worried that I might meet Astravar soon, and instead the powers that be had sent me my second worst enemy. And she was here just when Rine and Ange were about to seal the deal.

They were soon almost upon us. The Cat Sidhe cleared out of the way to give them room to land. Meanwhile, our dragons were still pinpricks in the ever-darkening sky. It would take them a while to reach us yet. Salanraja tried to say something in my mind again. But I wasn't interested. Not while everything was going all wrong.

Olan landed first, sending up billows of soil from the ground. Then Camillan came down with Lars, followed by Shadorow with Asinda. Finally, Pinacole hit the ground, and he lowered his neck to let Bellari slide off. Bellari immediately strolled over to where Rine and her father stood. She ignored Rine completely, and she let her father embrace her in a gentle hug.

I perked up my ears to listen in as she spoke.

"Oh daddy, how I've missed you," she said. "How many years has it been?"

The loud-mouthed man didn't seem so loud-mouthed with his daughter. He mumbled something in her ear. Rine slinked away from them as they talked.

After a few moments, Bellari broke the hug. Then she spun around and stormed over to Rine, who had been getting closer and closer to Ange as if seeking comfort. I walked up to get a closer look, the hackles rising on the back of my neck.

Bellari glanced at Ange, huffed, and I could only imagine the scornful look she gave her. Her voice was so sharp it hurt my ears.

"Rine," she said. "We need to talk. Now!"

She took hold of Rine's hand and pulled him off into the forest just as our dragons arrived.

TALK WITH THE DRAGON

As soon as Salanraja touched down, tossing up a mass of leaves from the forest floor, she let out a roar. It was so loud that it seemed to shake the trees in the forest. The leaves to the side of her and behind her quivered, and those in front of her shot forwards as if propelled by a blast. Many Cat Sidhe arched their backs as they turned towards Salanraja in surprise.

The incident reminded me of the first time I'd met her in her tower. Back then, I'd apparently tried to steal her dinner – because she hadn't understood that food left untended is up for grabs by anyone who discovers it. It's not my rule, it's one of those universal laws that virtually every living creature seems to understand other than humans and dragons. Salanraja had threatened to flame me alive, and I'd believed her, not realising that she would never do that to a poor innocent cat.

Now, she seemed even more angry than before, and I hadn't a clue why. *"You did it again, Bengie,"* she said. *"After me specifically telling you not to."*

"I did what, sorry?" I asked. *"Oh, and nice to see you, too. It's been so long... I almost died, by the way, not that you seem to care."*

Salanraja didn't seem to be concerned about any of that later stuff, though. "You blocked me out of your mind. I wanted to talk to you, and you just shut me away as if you had more important things to do."

"Well, I had a very important cat to talk to." I looked at Ta'ra, as she gave me that endearing blinking look again.

"And what's that meant to mean? Are you telling me that there's a living creature out there that's more important than your dragon? Do you truly understand what our relationship means?" Smoke rose from her nostrils, and I was glad that I was still a safe distance from her, surrounded by a clowder of Cat Sidhe. In the ghost realm, I really had thought I'd missed my dragon. Now, I wasn't so sure.

"Look, it's like Ange and Rine," I said. "Though they don't admit it, Ange is the most important to Rine, and Rine is the most important person to Ange. It's like that with me and Ta'ra, or at least it's going that way. Come on, Salanraja. I hadn't seen her in ages. She deserves a bit of my private time."

"That's what you've never seemed to comprehend, Bengie. There is no private time to dragon riders, or at least as far as your dragon is concerned. We're meant to share everything, so I can protect you, and you when you finally learn how to, can protect me. The most important thing to Rine is Ishtkar, and the most important thing to Ange is Quarl."

"I can't believe that."

"Really? Then who do you suppose is with them every moment of their waking lives? From what I've gathered, I'm not sure Rine and Ange have spent much time together at all. It doesn't seem a good basis for a relationship if you ask me."

"You are so wrong," I said.

"Am I?"

"Yes..."

"And how would you know?"

"Because I've seen it. I've been to the ghost realm, and I've seen their future, and mine, and Seramina's too." I wondered how far I should take this. How would Salanraja react if she knew Seramina was really a warlock? Had she talked to Hallinar about it? Or Olan, perhaps? Whiskers, could she even hear my thoughts right now? Fortunately, it seemed I'd learned to mask them better from her and I wasn't planning on telling her how I was now a budding warlock anytime soon.

"So that's where the portal led," Salanraja said, and she lowered her head. Her nostrils had stopped smoking, and she seemed to have calmed down a little. *"I'm sorry, Bengie, perhaps I overreacted. You'll learn one day, as you grow stronger. I guess it takes time to become less feline and more..."* She paused briefly, as if to think. *"Human."*

"What? Don't be so ridiculous."

"Of course you are," Salanraja said. *"Who knows, you might even develop opposable thumbs soon. How would you like that? You'd be able to use human tools and cook your own sausages."*

"There's no way I'm getting rid of my claws," I said, and I extended them, admiring their sharpness. One thing that was great about this realm is that the humans didn't bother clipping cat claws. They needed them for a purpose, or perhaps they understood we needed them too.

Salanraja laughed. *"I've missed you, Bengie. You make me complete, you know? I'm so glad you made it out of the ghost realm. I don't know what I would do without you."*

"I've missed you too," I said, and I went up to rub my nose against her massive talon. I turned to see Ta'ra staring after me, as if thinking, *What the whiskers do you think you're doing?*

I'd heard the students say that dragon riders never dated anyone but other dragon riders. Now, I think I understood why.

33

ALEAM'S STORY

After Rine, Ange, Seramina, and I had time to bond with our dragons again – because we needed to after being through such a terrible ordeal – Aleam called us over to Driar Reslin's porch. By 'us', I meant me, Ange, Seramina, Lars, Asinda and Reslin.

The Cat Sidhe had been instructed to stay away, as if the information that Aleam was about to divulge, or at least the implications of it, might scare them. We still couldn't see Bellari and Rine, but I could hear her haughty voice cutting through the forest.

The approaching night brought with it a fresh chill. I could still catch that whiff of rotten vegetable juice upon the breeze every now and again. After being in the ghost realm and having to deal with that wind without warmth or cold, I appreciated this breeze, even if it made me shiver a little. Still, I made sure that I stayed as close as possible to the door and the fire roaring within so I could soak up any warmth that seeped out of the hut. Seramina hung close to me, as if she also wanted to savour the heat too.

"Should we wait for Rine?" Aleam asked, looking to where the voices were coming from.

"Oh, I'm sure he'll hear plenty enough, after Bellari has given him her *'talking to'*," Ange said in a sardonic tone. "That's if he survives."

"Whatever she has to say, I'm sure she has good reason to do so," Reslin said. "One thing I can say for my daughter is that she's a smart lass."

Ange looked at the older man with narrowed eyes and a peculiar frown. "I'm sure she is," she said, her voice dry.

"I can't imagine why my Bellari would be angry with Rine," said Reslin, shaking his head. "He's always seemed such a noble, honest lad. And I can tell he's the type who's great at relationships. I guess it's just her time of the month." He gave a lopsided grin.

Ange nodded slowly, and her jaw looked clenched. She was probably biting her tongue to stop her from saying something unwise. I didn't particularly like this Reslin man either. I wanted to tell him that if Rine was so good at relationships, then he would choose to have one with Ange instead of Bellari. But Aleam had just turned up out of the blue, and he had too much to tell us. I was getting impatient.

"Aleam, what happened?" I asked. "Last I saw, you were throwing thunderbolts at Prince Arran, trying to bring down all his dragon riders like that wizard who helped the king pull the sword out of the stone I saw on the television once."

Seramina kicked me as if to tell me to shut up. But I didn't realise why at first. There was nothing wrong with kings pulling swords out of stones, surely.

"You went up against Arran?" Reslin said, and his hand twitched by his hip.

It suddenly dawned on me that it might not have been so smart to mention this detail in front of a member of one of Prince Arran's dragon corps. Mind you, I never claimed that I was good at human politics. The crystal had never gifted me with that trait.

"I did no such thing," Aleam said. "There was no violence. There was only thunder from the sky, and a bit of lightning flashing around. The worst it hit was a gargoyle."

"You still haven't explained why you needed to do this," Reslin said. He leaned against a pillar on the porch, tapping his foot. As he did, he moved his hand towards his shoulder.

"I did all this to allow Seramina, Ange, and Rine to come here and help Initiate Ben get his staff. Prince Arran would have sent the cat out alone against a verified forest golem and other magical creatures who guarded the staff. And every dragon rider across the realm should know by now that Ben's getting that staff is crucial to Astravar's defeat."

Driar Reslin narrowed his eyes. "That is mutiny," he said. "You went against a direct order from a superior officer. This…" He drew his staff from his back. "I can't allow this."

A rush of air whooshed by me, and some vines sprung out from Ange's staff. These vines shot straight out towards Reslin's staff and wrested it out of his grasp. More wrapped around his shoulders and underneath his armpits, pinning him to the pillar.

"You," Driar Reslin growled. He glared daggers at Ange, and it seemed like he wanted to scream more at her. But he took one look at the glowing green crystal on her staff, and then her cold stare, and he seemed to think better of it.

Seramina also had her staff in her hands, but she hadn't used any magic yet. If she wanted to, she could wipe Reslin's mind or something. He never had to remember Aleam's story. Come to think of it, he never even had to remember that we were here. Maybe if I asked Seramina nicely enough, she could also wipe Bellari and her father's memories of Bellari's relationship with Rine. That would get us all out of an awkward situation very quickly.

"I'm sorry for the sudden surprise, sir," Ange said. "But, with all due respect, who has been loyally serving the king for longer? Aleam or Arran?"

"It doesn't matter," Reslin spat back. "We have chain of command for good reasons."

"Yet he got the position through his royal blood and not his skill at what he does," Aleam said. "It's fair enough that our good King Garmin appointed him to the rank. But when he did so, Garmin intended for Arran to just remain a figurehead. I can't quite understand why the king now has him giving orders on the battlefield. Have you ever thought something is off about this?"

"Are you suggesting a conspiracy?" Reslin said. He seemed much more relaxed now, with his head cocked, as if the idea of a mystery fuelled him with power. He didn't seem to mind being wrapped in vines, almost as if it was a hobby of his.

"I don't know what I'm thinking right now," Aleam said. "I haven't had the time or headspace to investigate this. But believe you me, once this is all over, I will."

The old man looked down at me, then he looked at my staff-bearer. Unlike me, the small human hand seemed rather allergic to the fire coming from the hovel and edged as far away from it as it possibly could. Perhaps it thought the staff would burn if it got too close to the flames.

"Well done, Ben," Aleam said. "So, you finally did it after all. Olan tells me you got the staff from the ghost realm, and you met me, of all people, there. I hope I aged well…"

"You should see what I can do. I can conjure salmon out of my own dimension and use them as a weapon." My tummy rumbled, and I remembered I'd never quite had that mackerel Ta'ra had promised me. "You know, I should do it now. You can finally taste the best fish in the Seven Dimensions."

As I spoke, Aleam was glancing warily at Reslin as if trying to tell me not to reveal too much. But Bellari's father didn't seem to be listening to me. Rather, he had his ears turned towards his daughter's and Rine's voice coming from the forest.

"Okay," Ange said. "We've waited long enough, Driar Aleam. With all due respect, why don't you tell us what happened? Then Driar Reslin can decide if he wants to cooperate or not."

"Very well," Aleam said, and he tugged at the wattles under his neck. "After you left, Prince Arran got worse and worse. I didn't hear his conversations with the Council of Three, being locked up and all. But Lars and Asinda here relayed information to me in my cell underneath Dragonsbond Academy.

"The prince started ruling the castle with an iron fist. He further restricted food rations not because we couldn't spare food, but he reasoned that the hungrier the students were, the more aggressively they'd fight in a battle against the warlocks. He was proposing an all-out charge."

"You've got to be joking," Ange said.

Lars and Asinda shook their heads no.

"He wanted to send every single dragon and dragon rider out there," High Prefect Lars said, his red cloak blowing out behind him in the breeze. "Including Calin's injured dragon, Galludo. But if there's one thing that every Driar and student of Dragonsbond Academy agree on, it's that the warlocks must have a good reason that they've not attacked yet."

"So, what happened?" I asked. "Did you throw that stupid prince in the cell?"

Aleam laughed. "Actually, yes, we did," he said. "Or rather the Council of Three did. After realising Prince Arran wasn't acting in our favour, they locked him up. But they gave him a luxurious bedroom fit for royalty of course, and they locked the door using magic and cast escape-prevention wards on his windows."

"And what about Corralsa?" Seramina asked. "I don't think Arran's dragon would have gone down without a fight."

"It was a shame you weren't there to cast a mind-spell on her," Aleam said. "But we found ways to do it using a little coercion." He glanced at Asinda and then gave Seramina a knowing wink. I guessed either he or Asinda sent the dragon to sleep with their dark magic, now I knew they could use it.

Aleam nodded at Ange. "I think you can release him now."

Ange looked at him with a curious frown. She lowered her staff, and the light went out on the crystal. The vines that had entangled Reslin wilted and dropped to the ground. He stretched his arms and then looked at her. "Never do that again, Initiate. Unless you have a good reason to, of course," he said, but he didn't sound angry. Rather, he said it almost half-heartedly, as if about to deliver the punchline to a joke.

"Yes sir," Ange said.

Reslin turned to Aleam. "Well, old man. I guess you won't get any interference from me on your quest. You seem to know what you're doing." He continued to tell us about the magical creatures stationed nearby and how he'd been trying to work out what to do with them. The fairies had been worried, and he'd told us it had been quite a tense time here in the forest. He also knew that he couldn't defeat all those golems between him and his dragon. But now that they had more dragons and dragon riders, including Aleam – the fabled mage of legends, Reslin thought they might stand a chance.

"Presumably you have a plan," Reslin said after he'd finished his story.

Aleam looked towards the purple mist. "I'm guessing we have no choice but to throw everything we've got at them except the garderobe. I have a feeling we'll need the Cat Sidhe for the ultimate battle, and most of all, this would give Ben time to try out his staff."

I mewled contentedly as I looked at my staff-bearer, hovering slightly above and in front of me now. I was going to show everyone here how powerful Ben the Dragoncat, descendant of the great Asian leopard cat and the great, mighty George could be.

34

ACHOO!

I'd had enough of talking for one day. In all honesty, back home in South Wales, us cats didn't talk much. Occasionally, we'd meet for a couple of minutes and let either the Savannah Cats recount a brief anecdote about beasts that we might face in the Savannah, or perhaps let the old Ragamuffin tell us a wise thought that would help us through the day. One of us might come forward and give a report if a new cat or dog had entered the village that we would need to be cautious of. But we wouldn't convene for long, before sniffing each other to check that we were healthy, and then heading back off to guard our individual patches of territory.

It was a simple life – a pleasant life. I've never been able to get used to how humans seemed so compelled to make everything so complicated.

I went off for a walk, but I found myself gravitating towards Bellari and Rine. Perhaps I wanted to engage in one of my favourite hobbies of taunting her about her 'allergies'. Or perhaps, an even deeper part of me wanted to know how big a threat she was to my dreams of an easy retirement.

I found the couple standing under the boughs of a large beech tree, catkins occasionally falling around them from the high branches.

They were hard to miss, really, given how loud Bellari had been screaming. She had her hands on her hips and her red face thrust out at Rine. She poked her finger into his chest as she spoke, and Rine shrank back from her slightly.

"I can't believe I'm hearing this," Bellari screamed. "You just can't stop humiliating me, can you? It's like a little hobby of yours. Do you know what all the other girls in school have been saying about you? Do you know what they've been saying about *us*? Why do you always have to be so selfish?"

"I'm selfish?" Rine shouted. I liked it when he argued back against Bellari. She deserved nothing less. "You saw me in the forest, and what was the first thing you said? It wasn't, 'hey are you okay, Rine?' Oh, no... You said, 'Rine, we need to talk,' right in front of everyone, as if you really wanted to embarrass me. You didn't think that I might have been in danger here? I could have died out here, you know. But you don't care, do you?"

"Gah! Do you really blame me, Rine? What am I meant to say? Hey, you run off to do what you want, without even warning me. But you know what? It's okay because you almost got yourself killed. So now I forgive you... Really, Rine? How naïve do you think I am?"

Rine took a deep breath. Both of them were so focused on verbally assaulting each other that they didn't notice that I was there. Which was fortunate, because with Bellari's mood and given what she thought of cats, she'd probably kick me to the other side of the forest.

Rine's voice came across a little softer. "Look, Bellari, this relationship isn't what it used to be. When we first met, it was romantic, and you were... Well let's say, decent to me."

"Decent?" Bellari said, her arms flailing about in the air. "You don't think I'm decent anymore?"

"I think you're controlling, and you're a power freak, and you want someone who will do what you command, without question."

"Is that right?" Bellari asked, tapping her foot.

"No, that's not all... Now, it seems that everything you do is to prevent me going near anybody else. You even won't let me breathe, Bellari. Do you know how that makes me feel?"

"And why exactly do you think I'm like this?" She was hoping for something. I could see it. She wanted ammunition. But Rine now seemed well prepared.

"I think you're jealous," Rine said. "And it's changed you. To be honest, I'm not sure I like you anymore. I don't like what you've become."

Now we were talking. This is the kind of talk that I'd been prompting Rine to have for a long time. I just wished that I had my cat snacks with me so I could munch on something while watching this entertainment from a distance. Soon Rine would deliver his coup de grâce, his ultimate conclusion. I could see it boiling within him. All I had to do was wait until Bellari's insults had beaten him so hard that he could take no more.

A rustling sound came from behind me, and I smelled Ta'ra as she approached. "Ben, what are you doing here?" she said, and she brushed her nose up against the side of my chest.

"Shh," I said. "You're going to miss the good stuff, Ta'ra." I'd already lost track of what they were saying.

"Don't you think these two deserve a bit of peace?"

"Not yet... I've been waiting for this moment for ages, and now it's going to happen."

"What moment?"

"Just hang on..." I took a deep breath, inhaling the aromas of the forest. The moss, pollen on the breeze in the distance, the earthy soil, and through it all the smell of rotten vegetable juice, getting stronger I could swear. But I couldn't let my fear of dark magic spoil the occasion.

Bellari was still screaming, her voice getting louder and higher. Really, I'd stopped comprehending what she was saying, and I'm not sure if it was because I couldn't be bothered listening anymore or that she'd just started spouting nonsense. I just caught random words and phrases like 'humiliated', and 'selfish', and 'moron', and 'you just keep going around and doing what you want'.

Meanwhile, Rine looked like he was caught in a battle, bracing himself against an unending volley of arrows. This time, though, he kept his shield up. He stood strong against the barrage, and I could sense him tensing up like the coil of a winding crossbow. Then he executed the all-out assault that I'd been waiting for – a volley of rage so strong that it cut off Bellari in her tracks.

"It's over!" he screamed. His voice twanged through the forest and seemed to bounce back from every direction.

Bellari looked at him, her eyes wide. "What?"

"You heard me. This relationship is over. I'm sick of the lack of respect you give me. I'm sick of you always telling me what I should and should not do. I'm sick of *you*."

I expected even more recoil from Bellari. I expected her to scream back even. But she just narrowed her eyes and glared at him. Heavy, angry breaths rocked her shoulders back and forth. Her next words came out quieter, almost as a whisper, except with a sharp bite to them.

"This is about Ange, isn't it? You have… feelings for her… You've been lying all along, haven't you? Admit it, Rine. This has never been about us."

"No," Rine said. "This *is* about me and you. We aren't compatible, and I don't want to do this… I don't want to do us anymore."

Bellari shook her head slowly, and she turned a moment to gaze at the purple mist. "You know what… You don't get to dump me. I'm going to dump you. It's over Rine! I'll find someone better than you. Someone who 'respects' me for the lady I am. You'll see."

She turned on her heel and stormed off in mine and Ta'ra's direction – her face bright puce. As she passed us, she looked at us. Then, and I could swear this time was deliberate, she let out a horribly loud sneeze.

WHAT IS LOVE?

Bellari left the scene under the cover of low sun emerging from beneath a layer of clouds. It sent a warming magical red glow through the forest.

"Well, that was dramatic," Ta'ra said, as she watched the girl go.

"I think it was perfect," I said. "Rine couldn't have performed better."

"Poor girl," Ta'ra said.

"What do you mean, poor girl? You're not telling me you have sympathy for Bellari, do you? She's evil…"

"She's not. Only misguided. And after having worked with her father, I must say, I'm not surprised. He never takes her seriously, and he's always cracking jokes at her expense. If I had a father like that, I don't know how I'd grow up."

I growled. Bellari didn't deserve this sympathy. Not after how horrible she'd always been to me. I changed the subject, as I realised that Ta'ra and I could argue for hours about whether Bellari was 'evil or misguided'.

"Do you reckon I should tell Rine how proud I am of him?" I asked. He hadn't turned to watch Bellari go. He just gazed off at that purple mist that seemed to be getting smellier and smellier. In all honesty, I don't think he even realised that Ta'ra and I were there looking at him.

"No, no," Ta'ra said. "I'd probably leave him be. He needs time to stew – to process it all."

"What's to process? All he needs to do is to go to Ange, profess his love for her, and then they can be together forever – hopefully with you and me by their side."

The sun dropped out of the sky, and twilight befell us. The world suddenly became a cold place again, and I longed for the fire in the hut. But still, I could see that I also needed to close things up with Ta'ra. I just didn't know what I was meant to do.

Ta'ra took a step back from me, and she gave me a discerning look. "If you really think love is that simple, then I'm not sure you really understand it. But, of course, you don't. You're a cat after all. Love is a human emotion... Well, humanoid."

"I know," I said. "It's part of human society. Us cats don't need it. But we do know how to bond."

"Like you bond with your dragon?"

Oh, here we go again, I thought. I was about to have the same lecture with Ta'ra as I'd had with Salanraja. Fortunately, Salanraja was now sleeping off the effect of a long flight alongside the other dragons, and so wouldn't have heard those thoughts.

"Have you got a problem with that bond?"

"No, not at all. I just wonder, if your thoughts are with her all the time, do you ever have space to think about anyone else?"

"Of course I do."

Ta'ra cocked her head and regarded me. Her green eyes seemed to glow, cutting right through the encroaching darkness.

"What? I do!"

Ta'ra said nothing in response. We stood in silence for a while, watching Rine. I still don't think he'd noticed we were there. He made a loud huffing sound – almost a grunt – and he drew his staff. I stood alert, ready to scarper off if he decided to take his anger out on us. It wouldn't have been the first time he'd tried to freeze me using his magic. But instead, he pointed his staff at the high canopy on a tree and sent a massive bolt of ice towards it. The tree quivered, and a cloud of leaves fluttered to the ground.

Rine turned and stormed off, failing to acknowledge Ta'ra and I.

"Can you smell it?" Ta'ra asked as she watched him go.

"What? Rine?"

"No... Not Rine. The magic. It's coming closer, right?"

I took a sniff of the air. "I can smell it... But it's probably just a change in the wind."

"I hope so. But I've sent a couple of fairies out to investigate just in case." We waited for another moment, watching the light fade out of the sky until we couldn't see the mist anymore.

"I never asked you," I said, "what happened to Ta'lon?"

Ta'ra laughed a bitter laugh. "Oh, that fool. His words were just honey on toast. He never came back, you know. He probably went back to court and forgot about us. Even Go'na hasn't heard from him. And she's his sister!"

"Do you think he never loved you?"

"I don't think he does now. He could at least have sent a sign or visited once. But it doesn't matter anymore, I guess."

I growled. I'd known there was something about that fairy as soon as I'd smelt him – both in Cat Sidhe and later fairy form. He wasn't to be trusted, and now he was proving my point. "Couldn't you use your last transformation and visit him? You can turn back into a fairy once more, can't you?"

"Oh, it's not worth using my last transformation for that. I can think of thousands more circumstances much more worth saving it for."

"But that way you can tell him what you feel. Perhaps you can visit his kingdom in fairyland and say to your old fairy prince that the Cat Sidhe are all getting along fine, thank you, and you all want to stay cats forever."

Ta'ra laughed, and she brushed her face gently against my whiskers. "Most of us don't want to stay Cat Sidhe. But, you know, I think I do. Perhaps being a cat isn't so bad after all."

"What do you mean 'isn't so bad'? Come on, you've got to admit it. Being a cat is the best thing in the entire world."

"Sometimes," Ta'ra said, and she chuckled again. "But now at least, I've got to see you, Ben. A good old friend."

"Friend..." The word came out so quietly, it must have drifted off in the breeze.

"Isn't that how you see me? As a friend?"

"I..." Of course I didn't just see her as a friend. But I really didn't know how to say it to her. I mean, it wasn't just that I hadn't practiced bringing out the words, as I'm sure Rine had many times. I was also divided about what my feelings meant. I mean, cats shouldn't have such feelings, should they? Maybe, as Salanraja had said, I was becoming more human, and that thought scared me.

Fortunately, I was cut off from my dilemma by two golden wisps drifting over from the darkness that now concealed the mist. Unlike the first fairies we'd encountered, these weren't darting around without a purpose. They were heading right towards Ta'ra and I, as if following a scent.

The fairies stopped in front of us, and both of them emitted glowing golden clouds of mist. These dissipated to reveal Go'na standing on the right and another male fairy with purple eyes and a rounded face on the left.

Go'na looked alarmed. "It's good I got here in time," she said. "Because I worried I'd turn back into a cat again. It's not long before my time is up, and oh, you should have seen them."

"Go'na," Ta'ra said. "Slow down, please. What did you see?"

"Wargs," she said, and the hackles shot up on the back of my neck. "There must have been hundreds of thousands of them, coming in from nowhere, with slaver dripping from their mouths. They were thin looking, as if they'd charged without food all the way from the Willowed Woods."

"Whiskers," I said. "We're doomed."

"No, we're not," Ta'ra said. "Ben, you must never think that way. Didn't you get your staff so you can fight back after all?" She looked up at my staff-bearer, and it twisted around in the air, so the staff pointed downwards as it gave the Cat Sidhe a thumbs up.

"How long have we got, Go'na?" Ta'ra asked.

"I don't know... Fifteen minutes, maybe. If even that."

"Then we must warn the others. Quickly, get word back to Driar Aleam and the rest of the Cat Sidhe. I'll be right behind you."

Go'na nodded, and the two fairies quickly turned back into their true golden-orb forms. They shot off towards the camp. Without a word, Ta'ra darted after them. It didn't take me long to realise that I didn't fancy hanging around here to get devoured by hundreds of thousands of wargs. So, I promptly followed in her wake.

36

DEFENCES

As soon as the fairies reached Aleam and told him the news, he sprang into action. The first thing he did was to rouse the dragons. With his alleged school of magic being lightning magic, he could cast a thick cover of clouds over the sky, visible against the rising moonlight. From this he commanded a great bolt of lightning to crash down, accompanied by the loudest thunder I'd ever heard.

I got skittish, and I fled up a tree, which is apparently the worst place to go during a thunderstorm. But then, I never said every single feline instinct makes sense, just as a lot of human ones don't. The lightning was all controlled by Aleam's magic anyway, and the old man wouldn't have let it strike a poor cat – especially a cute Bengal like me.

Olan woke first. She whipped out her head, and she turned her great eyes upon Aleam as if ready to flame him. But she settled down when she realised who had caused the racket. Aleam must have immediately told her about the issue at hand, because she roared, to ensure the other dragons were also awake. One by one, they joined in the angry chorus. Then they all lifted off into the sky, their heavy beating of wings pounding like drums in an orchestra

But if there were as many wargs as Go'na had claimed, we

wouldn't defeat them by dragon fire alone. Plus, there were all those golems to worry about, who were clearly part of the enemy's offensive strategy.

So, next came the time for setting traps. We probably had about ten minutes left. My ears perked up from my vantage point on the tree, and my hearing latched on to the gnashes and gnarls of approaching beasts. Their feral sounds told me they would take no prisoners on this charge. Ironically, the army that Astravar had created to take Cimlean city would also be destroyed by his creations.

Aleam was on the ground, rushing around giving orders. I'd heard when he'd served as one of the king's dark mages all that time ago, he'd also been one of the king's best military strategists. Right now, he seemed to suit the part.

"We shall dig a trench," he said. "A concealed one. That way, if we can stop the charge of as many wargs as possible, we'll stand a better chance."

"How can we do that quickly?" Driar Reslin asked.

"Glaciation," Aleam replied, and it really didn't take him long to explain the rest and set everyone into action.

It all started with Seramina. She used her staff to cast a beam of mind-magic – or dark magic if you wish to see it that way – straight at Rine's forehead. This was apparently to strengthen Rine's ice spells. Though he was a little slow taking his staff from his back, he seemed to speed up as soon as he cast the first jet of ice, as if the act of casting magic was cathartic to him.

Rine's enhanced stream became a massive wall of ice that seemed to span from one end of the forest to the other. But this wouldn't be enough to stop the golems, as they'd just smash holes in it, still allowing the wargs to stream through.

That's where Lars came in. After Rine's wall of ice was in place, Seramina cast her mind-magic at the high prefect's forehead. Lars then used his blue staff to cast shield magic. This time, though, he didn't cast the spell for protection. Rather, he cast this great shimmering sheet of energy – a long plane of it – designed to repel other magical energy. He brought this downwards, pressing the ice into the ground. There came a crunching and a creaking sound. The earth shook, and the soil parted to make way for the ice, which then compressed the soil on either side, creating a solid ditch.

In all honesty, I didn't have a clue what was going on. All the while, the gnashes and gnarls in the distance became louder, and I spotted the first signs of movement. Trails of dust kicked up by shadows. They would be here soon. Around me, from their perches in the trees, several Cat Sidhe yowled to communicate they'd seen the same.

Meanwhile, it was Bellari's and Asinda's turn to move. They had fire magic, and they cast intense gouts of it to melt the ice. Aleam and Reslin added their lightning to it, as Seramina augmented them with her magic at intervals to strengthen their spells. Bellari didn't look at Rine once during this time, but her magic seemed to flare sometimes as if bouts of anger inside her fed the fire.

After the ice had melted, the four magic users continued to heat it until it was boiling. Then the last part came down to Ange. She took her staff and closed her eyes as she squared her shoulders. She pointed the staff right at the stream, and then she made a humming sound from her lips as vines emerged from the glowing crystal on the staff. They crept across the ground so fast that I thought they belonged to those horrible Mandragoras that I'd fought when I'd first dealt with a Manipulator. The creepers found their way over the ditch full of boiling water, creating a carpet over it. But there were holes in that carpet I saw – holes that led into a ditch full of super-heated water.

"That should do it," Aleam said. "Perhaps we'll quarter their numbers."

"Well done," Reslin said. "You know, Driar Aleam, I'm sorry. I'm sorry to have doubted you, and it's great to work with the all-powerful Aleam." He flexed a bicep. "And Bellari, you did pretty well too. Looks like they've taught you at least something at Dragonsbond Academy."

"Why thank you, Daddy," she said, and she blushed. Then her face twisted into a scowl, which she directed at Rine.

"Oh, oh," Reslin said. "What did you do, Rine?"

"Nothing," he said, and he turned away.

"We've not got time for this," Aleam said, and he looked up over the ditch as a howling sound keened over it. More cries and wails came, sounding like a ferocious war cry.

Then came the wargs. They seemed to materialise out of the night, as if the darkness had created them, and they were charging towards us at breakneck speed.

37

CANNONADE

Where before the night had concealed the mist, now the mist seemed to push back against the night, much like we had pushed back against the dark smelly goo in the ghost realm. It glowed purple from behind the charging wargs, silhouetting their terrible hunched forms and bounding long legs that propelled them forwards. The air smelled of fear, and fury, and rotten vegetable juice.

Between the wargs and the mist, were the golems. There were the forest golems, in whirlwind form, seeming to whip the mist up into spirals. There were the clay golems, shifting and warping over the ground so fast that you only had to blink, and they'd have taken a different shape and position. There were the stone golems – massive blocks of moving rock that looked like they could crush the tallest of trees under their heaving weight. And there was something else – tiny forms that looked like shimmering candle flames, wavering as if upon invisible air currents.

"What in the Seventh Dimension?" Aleam said, peering out from underneath his hand.

"Fire golems," Prefect Lars said, alarm in his voice. He lifted his staff to the sky.

"Everyone to Lars. Now!" Aleam called, just as the burning fireballs launched towards us, as if fired by distant catapults.

I didn't hesitate. I sprinted right up to Lars' legs and huddled against them. Footsteps followed me, and then there came a flash of white from Lars' staff. The high prefect grunted and widened his legs as the shield dome spread out around him. Ta'ra was there next to me, growling, and many other Cat Sidhe had made it to the shield, as well as Reslin, Bellari, Seramina, Asinda, Ange, Rine, and Aleam. But many of the Cat Sidhe hadn't. We were huddled in so tight that I could feel the heat from the bodies around me. It smelled of sweat in here, and it was stuffy. I knew if we stayed in here for long, we'd run out of oxygen.

The flames came down from the surrounding sky. Then, with a gigantic crashing sound, explosions erupted across the terrain. High Prefect Lars widened his legs, and he grunted even louder; his face contorted. The shield flared out, together with the brilliance from the explosions outside, flooding the surrounding land with bright light.

I thought of all the Cat Sidhe who hadn't made it inside Lars' shield. They wouldn't stand a chance now. As the light continued to fade, Lars took a deep breath, and then the shield dome flickered out. I could breathe again, but the stench of everything outside assaulted me.

Flames spouted all around us, letting out a tremendous roar into the air. The heat raged so hot that it reminded me of that time I'd got trapped amongst lava in the Seventh Dimension. I longed once again to be in the ghost realm, as scary as that place was.

Fortunately, it seemed all the Cat Sidhe who'd been trapped outside the shield had transformed into their fairy form. Golden wisps darted around without purpose. They could use glamour magic, I guessed, but none of them would scare the wargs.

Rine shot large shards of ice at the flames. These hit right at the flames' sources, and then the melting ice suffocated the flames. Lars also started casting little shield bubbles across the landscape. These stayed in place for several seconds and then dissipated. Once gone, the flames underneath them would have also clearly drained of oxygen. Rine and Lars would need to do a lot more to completely quell the fire, and so they continued to work busily away, making a racket as they did so.

"What will those fire golems do, Aleam?" I asked. "Will they attack again?"

"No. They self-destruct as soon as they hit their target." And that was all Aleam said, as he was interrupted by another howling sound coming from in front of us.

The wargs had now stumbled into our trap, and they were stuck in the vines that Ange had woven. Soon, the dragons came down from above and they flamed the carpet of vines, so that the wargs fell in the water. The night filled with the yowls and whimpers of the dying beasts. I could only see their shadows and forms against the encroaching glow, but the sounds they made spoke of their torment.

As the dragons lifted back into the sky, more wargs flooded in, trampling over their dying brothers in the ditch. With angry red eyes, they scoured the terrain for something to attack. In front of them, golden wisps of fog emerged from the sky, and more Cat Sidhe were soon there, transformed back into their feline forms. Ta'ra led their charge into the fray, growing to the size of rhinoceroses as they went.

There were a good two dozen wargs, at least, for every Cat Sidhe. The wargs gnashed at their enemies, and then backed off when the Cat Sidhe lashed out with their claws. The wargs were too fast – much, much faster than the average cat. I wanted to join them in battle, and I felt the impulse to turn into a chimera. I summoned up the energy, and my muscles started to ache.

"*Don't do it, Bengie,*" Salanraja said, her voice stopping me in my tracks.

"What? Why?"

"I might need your magic up here. Olan might not think you're ready yet, but I do."

Whiskers, I had forgotten about the staff. The staff-bearer had been floating along behind me, out of view. Or perhaps it was invisible when I wasn't aware of it. I didn't know.

Behind the battle between the Cat Sidhe and wargs, the golems were marching even closer. The ground shook as they came. It pounded, in fact, like a thousand volcanoes were about to spring up around us and add an extra dimension to the battlefield. Those stone golems were massive – five times the size of fully expanded Cat Sidhe. They looked as if they could easily trample the battlefield down to flesh and bone.

"On your dragons!" Aleam called out. "Get ready."

The dragons were already swooping down towards us. Several wargs also approached us, their teeth bared, pink slaver dripping from their mouths. Aleam cast a yellow beam at them, and an orb of bolt-lightning shot out from where it hit at the centre of their formation. The wargs jerked to a halt, convulsing. One by one, their legs seemed to go weak as they collapsed to the ground, allowing room for the dragons to land.

Olan came first and touched down on the ground briefly enough for Aleam to clamber up into the saddle. The dragon roared and took off into the night. Ishtkar and Quarl came next. "Typical," Bellari said, and she glowered at Rine as he ran towards his dragon, aside Ange, who was also sprinting towards hers. They both vaulted onto their mounts. Hallinar landed next alongside Shadorow, allowing Seramina and Asinda to mount and then launch off into the air.

Next came the two yellows – Camillan and Pinacole. Before Lars and Bellari mounted, Bellari turned to Prefect Lars and gave him a wink. "Say," she said. "Maybe we should hang out sometime."

Lars scowled at her. "Focus on the mission, for demon's sake," he said, and he rushed off towards his dragon without another word. Bellari huffed, and then she followed. Immediately after they'd taken off, Reslin's royal blue and Salanraja scudded against the earth. I was immediately upon her and up into the air, with my staff-bearer close by my side.

38

FROM THE DEPTHS

The clouds seemed to gather around us as the golems watched us, waiting for us to charge. The dragons wheeled around above the golems, and the dragon riders studied them, searching for an opening. No one dared to attack yet, and strangely the golems didn't lash out at us either.

I called for my staff, and my staff-bearer closed in. Next thing I knew, the staff was in my mouth, the crystal glowing purple at the end. At that moment, I didn't care if anyone noticed. The world needed my magic now. It was as if I'd become possessed by a force greater than my mind. I was completely in control, and yet I didn't put conscious thought to any of my actions.

It was as if the very act of clenching down on the staff caused something to change within me. Like someone had flicked a switch in my brain and suddenly the lights had come on and made everything clear. I wasn't Bengie the Dragoncat anymore. Instead, I was Ben the warlock, consumer of dark magic. I knew exactly what I had to do.

At that moment, my mind belonged to nothing but the void.

"Bengie, what are you doing?" Salanraja asked.

"Don't worry, I've got this," I said.

"*Gracious demons... Not like this, you haven't... I know about the dark* magic, Bengie. Olan had warned me about it a long time ago. But don't use it now in front of everyone. There must be another way."

I wasn't listening to her. I had a different objective. In fact, every muscle in my body had a different objective. There was a pulsing sensation behind my forehead, directing my thoughts, telling me what my next move had to be and what spell I needed to cast.

The wind whipped past me as we flew, and that smell of rotten vegetable juice surrounded me. Yet I wasn't repulsed by it anymore. Rather, I felt like it was a part of me, and I drew it towards me. The mists formed tendrils that gently caressed me as I weaved the magic that would change the world for the better.

Meanwhile, the light at the end of my staff grew brighter and brighter still.

"Bengie, you're out of control," Salanraja said. "You don't know what you're doing."

"I know everything," I said, and it was as if something else was speaking through me. Another spirit. "I am, after all, the incarnation of the seven worlds."

"What are you—"

"Silence!" My voice shot out in my head, shutting off Salanraja's ramblings. I'd blocked her out again, and it felt good. Salanraja growled, and I could feel the rumbling in her belly underfoot. She careened as if she wanted to throw me off her. Wispy tendrils shot out of my staff, and they wrapped around Salanraja's waist, securing me in place. More mist crowded around us. It wasn't that I was attracting the mist, but it was growing out of me. I was all powerful, the greatest creature that had ever lived.

"You are fools to think you can challenge me." The voice came out of my mouth, but it wasn't me anymore. "Humans, dragons, and now cats… You have always been such fools. Now, I will show you the extent of my power. I will show you how puny you are compared to the force destined to govern all seven worlds."

I felt my body twist around – the muscles moving as if connected to strings dangling from the sky. I saw the golems again – a massive stone fist coming towards Salanraja, but she ducked out of the way. To my right, Ishtkar shot forward, Rine on top of her. She got knocked to the side by the fist of another stone golem. Quarl dove in from the other side to retaliate, but the stone golem also backhanded the sapphire dragon, swiping him away. Soon the mist clouded over again, and I saw nothing except the clouds rolling over each other to form something bigger, something terrifying.

Time seemed to slow as the clouds coalesced into the shape of a massive, bald, blue, male head. The features formed, displaying skin like a cracked eggshell, eyes burning like Seramina's tended to burn. The golems weren't moving, but the dragons were, darting in random directions in confusion. Wherever we flew, we couldn't reach that head. Astravar was always beyond us, watching us with his grey eyes from the clouds.

Soon, we all stopped to face him, all of us hovering in a loose formation. He cackled that horrible cackle that I'd heard so many times in my dreams.

"I hope you like the gift that your crystal gave you, Dragoncat. It's a great power, and now I shall use it for myself. It's time now for you to unlock some of the darkest magic imaginable. Soon, you shall behold the glory and the power of the fifth dimension."

Rine opened his mouth to shout something out, but his voice became lost to the void. Ange tried to cast some magic from her staff at the face, but the light just fizzled out at the top of it. Then, I was swinging around on Salanraja again, commanded by some substantial force.

Out of my staff came a gigantic bolt of white energy, shooting towards the ground. It hit the grass beneath us, where it spread out into a massive portal, lying horizontally. At first, it was pure light, which soon faded to reveal the gateway to another world. A world in rainbow colours, swirling around darkness, looking like a swirling pool of oil. A world where I couldn't even identify the forms that flashed around inside, they moved so fast.

"The thing that none of you ever did," Astravar said, "the claim that no mage ever claimed, was to unlock the secret of the uncharted dimensions. You see, there is a power running through all the dimensions even greater than magic. Once you know it – once you have touched it in every available world, then you can become it. That is the ultimate goal of a warlock. This is truly what it means to become whole."

That's when I noticed the golems were getting sucked towards the gaping hole. Their massive forms sliding towards it as if into quicksand. The portal swallowed the stone golems first, then the clay golems, then the forest golems whirled in last. After that came the wargs – hundreds of thousands of bodies now completely frozen in time like taxidermies. They glided towards the portal as if being dragged upon ice.

"Now, there are four warlocks present, I see," Astravar continued. "One fallen, two the relatives of warlocks, and then you, Dragoncat. According to the prophecies I've seen, you could have been the most powerful of all. Maybe one day I'll use you. If, that is, you can survive in the world I shall create. Oh, it shall be the most beautiful thing imaginable. You have no idea."

As I watched the wargs vanishing into the gaping magical hole in the ground, I realised what was happening. Any creature containing magic was getting sucked towards the vortex. Below, the Cat Sidhe started sliding towards the portal – slower than the wargs – and my heart skipped a beat. I also felt a slight tug against my fur – because I contained magic too.

There came a screeching sound from down beneath us. A sound so high in pitch it seemed to split the sky in two. Time had virtually stopped by this point. I couldn't move an inch. But my staff still fed that portal in the ground with massive energy as forms shot out of the ground. I recognised the creatures as soon as I saw them. They had the sharp beaks of buzzards, squat heads, and long necks leading to bat-like wings. They were larger than I remembered in the vision – around half the size of dragons, perhaps a little larger than that. They lifted into the sky, then whirled around in formation like a hungry flock of crows, ready to tear the world apart.

Meanwhile, Astravar's voice rumbled on. "You feared the demon dragon. But these creatures, are much, much, worse, and you know why? Because there's so many of them. They feed on magic, and the more magic they ingest the more powerful they become. All I need to do is give them a taste of how much of it has grown in this world. Then they'll come out to do my bidding. Together we shall destroy this world, and then we shall cross dimensions. Only a gift from a crystal can release them, Dragoncat. A measly mongrel like you, it seems, has been given the power."

Astravar's cackles filled the sky, and everything happened in slower and slower motion. This was really the end. The portal had now completely consumed the wargs, and I saw the Cat Sidhe edging closer and closer to the void. I recognised one of them – slightly larger than the rest, with bright green eyes that shone out even from this distance above her.

"Ta'ra," I screamed out. "No!"

The very act of seeing her being dragged towards her fate seemed to break the spell Astravar had on me. It was as if the strings tied to my paws, tail, and head suddenly loosened. I could move again, and the image of Astravar in the purple clouds was fading away – crumbling into tinier clouds.

"That is enough," he said, his voice getting fainter. "You haven't won. I finally have the power we need to destroy everything."

From below came a massive white flare. Then came a sound like the whole earth was shaking. Then came a shockwave pulsing out from the portal below, which converged quickly into a single glowing pinpoint, before guttering out.

My connection to Salanraja didn't return, and as I looked around, the eyes of the dragons had become pure white. Together, all the dragons crashed towards the ground, as the flock of bat-buzzard creatures that Astravar – that *I* had summoned – shot off towards the west.

They were heading straight towards Dragonsbond Academy.

39

BEATEN

I woke up in a puddle of rain, with a terrible headache. I was so thirsty that without even lifting myself, I lapped up some drops of water. It hurt to swallow.

There was a rough sandpaper feeling against my side, and I looked back to see Ta'ra – now normal cat size again – licking my fur. When she saw me stir, she ran forward to stand in front of me.

"Ben," she said, and she rubbed her wet nose against my face. "Ben, I thought I'd lost you."

"What happened?" I asked.

"I don't know… We were fighting thousands of wargs, when all you riders and dragons went up into the sky to fight the golems. There were so many wargs coming at us, trying to tear us apart. We thought we'd lost… But then…" She trailed off.

I stood up, every muscle in my body shaking. I turned to see Salanraja lying on the ground behind me. Her eyes were closed. I walked up to her, and pushed my head up to her chest, yearning for the warmth of dragonfire boiling within. She was stone cold, and I could detect no sense of her inside my mind, as if she'd blocked me off this time. Now I knew how it felt.

I let out a low and long growl, feeling absolutely terrible.

I'd done this. I'd let Astravar into my mind; I'd walked right into his trap. He'd been waiting until I got the staff, his magic within me probably building power during his period of silence in my mind and dreams. Then, when the moment arrived, he'd used me to unleash whatever terror those things were. Creatures from an unknown dimension. Creatures no one but Astravar – if his account was true – had encountered before.

It made me wonder about what I'd seen in the Ghost Realm. Aleam's ghost, Ta'ra's ghost, all those visions, my father… How much of it was real?

Whiskers, was that even my staff I saw floating nearby? The one my staff-bearer clutched just in front of me, as if it wanted to taunt me. The crystal on it was purple now – no one was making any attempt to hide it anymore. Maybe Astravar had created the staff-bearer and a second staff to trick me. It would have been the perfect way to manipulate destiny – for him to replace my staff with a device of his own that he could use to control me whenever he wished.

I tried swiping out at the hand with my paw, but it ducked away. It clenched its fist and punched the air in front of me as if to warn me off. I shrieked at it and swiped a couple more times until it backed away, keeping a safe distance.

"Ben," Aleam said from behind me, and he grunted as he hobbled over. Clearly, he was aching too. "Ben, you made it."

Even the act of turning towards Aleam sent pain shooting down my side. The other dragon riders stood behind him, looking at me warily. Across the field, I could see the fallen dragons and I couldn't detect any signs of life from them. Cat Sidhe also stalked the terrain, scouting around as if searching for an enemy. But there was no sign of any wargs anywhere.

"Aleam," I said. "I… I did this. Did you see what happened out there?"

"Astravar…" Aleam said, looking up at the clouds. "He must have been building power in that crystal inside you. But somehow, he didn't finish what he started, because he seemed to want to suck all of us into that place. Fortunately, something closed the portal just in time."

I looked up at the clouds where Astravar had been, but there was no sound of him now. "What happened to the wargs?" I asked.

"They all got sucked into the portal," Aleam said. "I'm guessing the stronger the magic inside the beast, the more powerful the pull. Whatever Astravar did, I've never seen anything like it."

"Those creatures… They came out of that portal. I summoned them, didn't I?"

"Yes, and I recognised them. They were the same as the ones as in your vision," Aleam said. "For a long time, I've been trying to work out what they are. No one, to my knowledge, has ever seen them before. Nor have I seen any mention of them in books."

"So, if we don't know what they are, how do we know if we can defeat them?"

"We don't," Aleam said. "It's very worrying indeed."

I bent down to lap up another gulp of water from a puddle. The air pressure was heavy on the sides of my head, and the clouds above were gravid. But it wasn't raining.

The water didn't go down well, and I felt suddenly nauseous. Then I was growling and writhing, as a sharp sensation shot through my head. It seemed to go downwards, past my nose and then towards the back of my throat, as if trying to escape from me.

I retched, and I thought for a moment I was going to suffocate. Was this Astravar's final move? Would he destroy me before I'd even had a chance to fight back? I fought in between retches to breathe, and then something came out of my throat into my mouth. I immediately spat it out.

A blue crystal lay on the floor. It had no light in it – depleted of all its magic. I touched it with my paw to discover it was cold and lifeless.

"What in the Seventh Dimension?" Aleam leaned over the crystal to study it. "Do you recognise this, Ben?" He lifted it up and wiped it against his tunic.

"It's… The golem crystal. The one I swallowed. Back when I first met my crystal."

Aleam stopped for a moment. He put his hand to his chin as if in thought. "So, you defeated it. You've defeated Astravar's control over you. You've finally got him out of your mind…"

"Have I?" I asked, and I looked again at my staff, wondering if it was more Astravar simply no longer needing the crystal inside of me anymore.

Aleam continued to study the crystal, turning it every possible angle and holding it up to the light. "It's completely dry. No magic left in there. Whatever magic Astravar had used on you, he'd finally used up all its power. You're free of him, Ben."

I should have felt a sense of relief at that. But I just felt burning guilt that I'd let Astravar take control of me. When I thought about it, I'd wanted that magic. I'd wanted to use it to beat those creatures, to show everyone what Ben the Bengal, descendant of the great Asian leopard cats and the mighty George could do. I was sure in my mind this was the reason Astravar had taken control of me. Because I wasn't confident about who I was. And because I didn't know, he had defined that image for me – he had used the dark magic inside me to mould me into what he wanted me to be.

"I still destroyed everything," I said. "Because of me, the dragons will die…"

Aleam shook his head. "Oh, don't worry about the dragons. They're magical creatures. A blast of magical energy will knock them out for a while. They shall recover soon."

"But you're not mad at me? You're not angry at what I did?"

Ta'ra came up to me, purring. "You might have released those creatures, but you also saved us. We wouldn't have survived those wargs otherwise. Even as fairies, we hadn't the magic to defeat them. Many of us would have been torn apart by those beasts. Because many Cat Sidhe here can't transform back into fairies – they'll never become fairies again, in fact."

"They won't?"

"Never," Ta'ra said. "Some of us were so dismayed by Ta'lon's lack of communication, that they decided they wanted to embrace the new life. So, they used up their remaining transformations voluntarily."

"And what about you?"

"I'm still holding on to mine. But I don't know for how long I will."

The thought that some of these fairies had chosen to be cats gave me courage. They had accepted who they had become, despite the circumstances handed down to them. I looked at my staff-bearer, and I wondered if I would have to do the same. Fate had changed me. It had wrenched me into an unfamiliar world. It had caused me to bond with a dragon, initiated me into Dragonsbond Academy, and now turned me into a warlock. But I would never win if I couldn't accept who I was.

"So, what now?" I asked, looking up at Aleam. My legs felt bandy beneath me, and I wanted to lie down. My eyelids felt so heavy that I had to blink hard to keep them open. Sleep would be upon me soon.

Aleam turned towards the place where the portal had been. In its place lay a deep crater, and smouldering piles of ash. The earth there was stripped bare, and the rock surface looked smooth, like a polished gemstone.

"We wait for the dragons to awake," Aleam said, "and then we get back to Dragonsbond Academy as soon as possible. Because we need to help them fight those things, whatever they are."

"And what must I do? Will I need to use my staff again?"

"You need to fulfil your prophecy. Embrace the thread of the future that the crystal has predicted. We have no way of knowing if the future where you defeat Astravar is the genuine prediction amongst all the possible threads. But we can only hope…"

"But my staff… Can I trust it? I mean, how do I know it's mine? How do I know it's not some kind of trick that Astravar pulled to help him destroy the world?"

Aleam smiled. "Oh, it's yours alright," he said, and he nodded at the staff-bearer. The conviction in his eyes told me he knew a lot more about this than I could possibly understand.

The exhaustion was really starting to overwhelm me. There was nothing more I could do for now. So, I lay down on the wet ground and I fell into a deep sleep.

40

FLIGHT

I awoke on a carpet of leathery skin, feeling slightly queasy. Heat seeped up from below, and something warm and furry was pressed against my tail. The light, and the heavy wind coming against my face forced my eyelids open. I must have slept through the night.

I was lying on Salanraja's back, flying high in the sky. Below me, fields whirred by – some of them golden, some of them green. Cows and sheep grazed in some fields. Others contained rows upon rows of wheat. The landscape was much more agricultural than the Caldmines Forest. We must have flown quite a way to get here.

A heavy layer of clouds filled the dark sky. It looked like it wanted to rain but hadn't quite got around to it yet, as if all the heavens needed was that one extra cloud to unleash their load.

I turned to see Ta'ra resting on my tail. She blinked at me, then yawned. My staff-bearer floated just above her, keeping pace despite the wind. It had two fingers and held my staff, pointing it towards the horizon. Probably doing this made it more streamlined for flight. That's what I guessed, anyway – it was going to take me a long time to understand the ways of my magical ally from the ghost realm.

It was such a strange thing to be saddled with. If you'd asked me days before, I'd never have said I'd spend the rest of my life accompanied by a floating human hand. But then, I'd never thought I'd bond with a dragon either, or make friends with a cat who was once a fairy.

"Ben," Ta'ra said. "You made it. I'm so glad to see you're okay. You must have slept for hours."

"How many hours?" I asked, mirroring Ta'ra's contagious yawn.

"I don't know. There's no sun to read the time of day. But I'd say you were out for the entire night and a good portion of the morning – if not some of the afternoon."

I studied Ta'ra. I didn't like the fact she was here. This wasn't part of the plan, or at least it shouldn't have been. It wasn't that I didn't appreciate her company. I just didn't want her to accidentally get zapped by a stray bolt of Astravar's magic.

"Why did you come, anyway, Ta'ra? It's too dangerous up here. You need to be somewhere safe…"

Ta'ra made a low rumbling sound that sounded like a human might sound if they tried to growl like a cat. As I said, she still had a lot to learn. "I came to look after you. We all decided you needed extra support just in case your magic went haywire again."

"But I got rid of the crystal that was controlling my mind. Aleam said that Astravar isn't inside my head anymore. I'm free of him."

"We're just being cautious. Besides, I decided I needed to know if something happened to you. I couldn't bear it if…" She trailed off and turned away to look back at the forest, now a thin line in the distance.

I tugged my tail out from underneath Ta'ra's weight, and I strolled over to Salanraja's neck so I could get a good view of the landscape below. I could see Dragonsbond Academy down there, looking kind of wispy through the layers of clouds. A massive blue magical dome of energy surrounded the fortress, with shimmering pulses of energy cascading over it – shield magic that would hopefully protect anyone within the fortress, because otherwise they wouldn't stand a chance.

The beasts I had released from the Fifth Dimension wheeled around the castle. They seemed attracted to it as a flock of crows would be to an abandoned meal. One beast broke away from its flock and charged straight at the shield. It hit its target, creating a sudden pulse of light. But it couldn't get in and bounced off like a rubber ball bounces off a table.

"It's almost time for me to fight Astravar…" I said "… to fulfil my destiny…" My mouth went dry at the thought. There was a bitter taste on my tongue as I thought about this.

"It's not time yet," Ta'ra called back. "Aleam sent word to Dragonsbond Academy through Olan. Once they knew a powerful force was coming their way, they erected the shield as an extra precaution. But, since I last heard, the warlocks haven't decided to charge yet."

"And how do you know this when you're up here stuck on Salanraja's back?"

"I can talk for real, you know," Salanraja said. I'd never heard her speak out loud while flying before, and her voice came out kind of muffled against the wind. But she was loud enough to be audible. "Just like you, I have sensitive enough hearing to understand when someone addresses me from my back."

Admittedly, it felt so good to hear her voice. Just before I'd passed out, I wondered if I'd ever speak to her again. "Salanraja," I said. "How the whiskers did you wake up faster than me?"

"Maybe because I'm hardier than you? I am, after all, a great mighty dragon." She crooned underfoot, almost as if she were purring. If I was getting more human, I would also say Salanraja was getting more feline day by day.

I took some time to look around us. To the sides of us, the dragons flew in a V formation with Olan at the centre, Aleam stooped over her neck. Ishtkar took one wing of the formation, Quarl the other. We were next to Quarl, with Hallinar between us and Olan. Shadorow and Camillan flew between Olan and Ishtkar.

"Wait," I said, elation rising in me as I realised who was missing. "Where's Bellari and Reslin? Have we lost them for good?"

"They stayed behind to look after the other Cat Sidhe," Ta'ra said. "They might need support from the air, as all of my brothers and sisters here are travelling across Illumine Kingdom to provide support at Dragonsbond Academy. We're going to need all the allies we can get for this battle."

I chirped in amusement. "Bellari is leading the cats into battle. She hates cats. Well, that's justice for you."

"You can be so cruel, Ben," Ta'ra replied. "Besides, Bellari won't have to deal with them if she's on her dragon, will she? I'm guessing she would rather be up there with her father than flying with Rine right now."

"Whatever…" I raised my head to study the horizon.

I could now hear those creatures that I'd summoned from the Fifth Dimension. Their shrill cries seemed to cut the air apart and make it shimmer a little. It hurt my ears so much when I was this far away from them that I couldn't imagine what it would be like facing them in battle. But I was meant to use my staff to knock hundreds of them out of the sky, or at least that's what I'd seen in the vision. I just hoped they didn't tear me to pieces first.

"So why aren't we going straight up against Astravar?" I asked Ta'ra. "I want this to be over with."

She might have answered me, she might not have. I can't remember, because I was interrupted by Salanraja laughing from beneath me. She continued to speak inside my mind, as if she didn't need to share her thoughts with Ta'ra anymore. "*Do you really think you're going to battle the warlocks without support?*"

"Why not? If our crystal's visions are to be believed, then I'll beat him whatever happens, won't I?"

"*Now you're thinking like that fool, Prince Arran. Don't forget you saw only one possible thread of the future. Our armies and the Dragon Corps are there to support each other. You may be destined to be our most powerful weapon – a fact that it's taken me a long time to accept, I might add. But powerful weapons are also prime targets. Trust me, we don't want to go out there alone.*"

"But we don't have any armies."

"*They're on their way. The White Mages have been marching from Cimlean for quite a while. They departed when Prince Arran did, didn't you hear him say? But armies move much slower than dragons, you know? Also, didn't Ta'ra just tell you that Reslin and Bellari were coming with the Cat Sidhe? That's two fronts already that we have for support.*"

"*I guess...*"

I had so many more questions, and I wished we had all the time in the world to discuss them. But a scream coming from nearby distracted me. It caused such pain in my ears that I flattened them against my head to protect them. I looked up to see the massive beak of a vulture heading towards us, propelled by bat-like wings. Its black feathered head led down to a neck made of brown, rough textured skin, which spanned out into a strong-looking body and massive wings, covered in fur that lacked shine. The thing seemed to suck some of the light away from the day, almost as if that black smelly goo from the ghost realm made up part of its composition.

"Watch out, Salanraja!" I called in my mind, and she swept down just in time.

The creature swooped right past us, then it turned as fast as a bat would, sending a massive gust of wind in our direction. The sun glinted off its open beak as it screeched again. The edges of it looked razor sharp, like it could slice through even dragon scales.

More shrieks came from the vicinity, and another four of those creatures swept into view. The dragons responded with a curt roar, including Salanraja, and they shot fire at the unidentified beasts. A jet of flame from Olan hit one on the wing. A shard of ice from Rine's staff hit another beast on the back. But both fire and ice seemed to bounce off from them, and our enemies continued onwards unscathed.

Aleam called out from his mount and gestured everyone inwards with a wide sweep of his arm. Our formation closed inwards. Seramina and Lars fell back a little so that they had a direct line to relay some magic. Seramina then shot a beam of white energy at Lars' forehead, and at the same time, he sent up a massive shield from his staff, surrounding us all in a protective bubble.

"What's happening, Salanraja?" I asked.

"*Do you have to ask so many questions? This is a time of crisis.*"

"But I need to know..."

"*Fine. We received word from the castle that they're invincible. The only* thing that can repel them is shield magic, and we're not sure how long that will last."

"And how do you know all this?"

"Because dragons can talk across great distances, remember. We discussed our options with the Council of Three's dragons while you were asleep."

"Then we need to get down to Dragonsbond Academy as soon as possible."

"You think I don't know that?"

Outside the shield, the hideous bat-buzzard creatures came in again. Each of them had a bulbous protrusion at the top of their beak, as if something was growing inside it. As we flew onwards, they kept charging at our protective barrier, seeming to want to break through using brute force. Their thick necks gave such strength to their black feathered heads that they looked like mallets banging away at the shield.

Fortunately, Dragonsbond Academy was in view. I could see the tall towers of the fortress, and the dragon riders who stood on top of them carrying glowing staffs that fed energy into the shield. *"How are we going to get through? Salanraja, we can't just fly straight at the thing."*

"Will you ever get any less annoying, Bengie? You slept through us working all this out, so please now let us get on with the plan."

I hissed at her, and Ta'ra came up to me and lay down close to me, as if to calm me down. From our side, Aleam raised his staff, and Lars cut off the shield for a moment. Aleam then cast a bolt of lightning that hit a point just above one tower. I recognised Prefect Calin standing on that tower, and he raised his hand as if to send a signal.

"Five," Salanraja said. We were heading straight at the shield, and we were going to hit it.

"What does that mean?"

"It's a matter of timing..."

"What?"

"One!"

Just before we made impact with the shield, it fizzled out for a split second to let us in. The dragons had arranged themselves perfectly, because as soon as they'd entered the shield wall it switched on again, the dragon riders on the towers sending up long beams of energy towards the centre of the shield. Just as it did, some of those bat-buzzards hit the wall, and they shrieked out in anger.

From the inside, the shield looked like the largest waterfall I'd ever seen, except with shimmering energy taking the place of water. I watched it for a while, so mesmerised that I failed to notice Salanraja land.

A sharp female voice calling out from the ground jerked me back to my senses. Driar Yila stepped over the cobblestones towards Olan as Aleam dismounted, and she looked worried.

41

COUNCIL ROOM

As soon as Salanraja had touched down on the ground of the bailey, I dashed down her tail and straight over to Driar Aleam and Driar Yila. I'd missed enough already when I was asleep, and I didn't want to miss any more. I was a big part of this thing, and it was about time that the humans let me in on their plans. It wasn't my fault that I, as a cat, needed a lot more sleep than they did.

Above, the shield added a sombre buzz to the entire tone here. Because of it, there was no wind. In fact, it was unnaturally hot, and I could smell sweat everywhere.

From behind Yila came the sound of clanging swords and students and other dragon riders shouting taunts at each other. The students had been arranged in pairs, sparring against their partner. Each face I saw in the chaos looked long, tired, and afraid of the future to come.

I could hear Driar Gallant, the academy swordmaster, gruffly screaming above all the others, screaming for students to get in line. He bawled out commands as he patrolled the courtyard, supervising the sparring. 'Attack'. 'Parry.' 'Lunge'. 'Thrust'. 'Block'.

"Aleam," Driar Yila said. She had a rather peculiar smile on her face – peculiar because that woman never smiled. "You made it through. I must admit I had my doubts."

"When, Yila, have I ever let you down?" Aleam asked.

Yila shook her head as she chuckled softly. Really, I'd never know her to act so out of character. It was as if the war had softened her a little.

"Come," she said. "Bring everyone to the Council Room. Driar Brigel and Driar Lonamm are there already."

She turned on her heel and marched off. Aleam waited for Lars, Asinda, Ange, and Rine to dismount before he led us after her. I had to weave my way through masses of feet darting forwards, and then retreating in random patterns. I'm surprised, in all honesty, I didn't get kicked.

Fortunately, the Council Courtyard wasn't jam-packed like the bailey. It was empty, in fact. We crossed the lawn, and stepped up onto the dais, passing underneath the ceiling-mounted crystal the Driars often used to augment their magic. It looked cracked and lifeless, as if it hadn't been used for a long time. Or perhaps the Driars had needed to use it so much that they'd broken it. Either way, I didn't want to know.

The double doors of the keep led into a foyer with a mezzanine, underneath which I had once seen Rine and Bellari kissing. We passed through this and then into the meeting room itself.

The first thing I noticed in this next room was how tidy the desks were. Gone were the papers and ornaments that had littered the desks last time I was in here. It was a shame – they had looked like they'd be such fun to knock off their perches.

The only remaining item was on Driar Lonamm's desk – a large parchment that I assumed to be a map. Driar Yila, Driar Lonamm, and Driar Brigel stood stooped over it. Driar Brigel was pointing to something on the map as we walked over, my staff-bearer hovering behind us.

"Let me up," I said. "Someone pick me up. I can't see anything."

Ange did the honours, cuddling me in her warm embrace. She clucked softly as she stroked me under the chin, causing me to purr.

"Me too," Ta'ra said from beneath me, and she sounded just a bit jealous. "I'm a part of this too."

Rine sighed and picked her up. I looked at her, blinked, and then I turned back to the desk.

The map displayed an overhead view of Dragonsbond Academy and the surrounding lands. The thing had been painted ornately. It wasn't one of those weird human maps that looked nothing like the landscape. In fact, this was like an aerial picture of how the terrain looked when I viewed it from Salanraja in the air. I tried to imagine a student sitting on top of their dragon with an easel and a paintbrush, studying the landscape below as they worked out every single intricate detail. But the thought made me queasy.

"The warlocks have set up camp, thirty miles west of here," Driar Lonamm said, pointing to where an ornate red wooden pin with a dragon carved into the top of it lay on the map. "They're stationed under a reinforced shield, but it doesn't matter anyway, because we can't send anyone out with those beasts flying around like they are."

"After we'd set up the shield," Driar Yila said, "we sent three of Arran's dragon riders to fight some of those creatures from the Fifth Dimension. We sent a lightning mage, a fire mage, and an ice mage – a classic elemental trio. But they didn't return." She looked up at the doorway. "I watched the three of them from the towers, being ripped to shreds."

"So basically, we're under siege," Aleam said, and he tugged at the wattle on his neck.

"I wish there was a better way of saying it," Brigel said. "But yes. We have two options: we either fly out and fight, or we stay here and starve."

I shuddered. Since they had started rationing, there really wasn't any food here suitable for cats. I hadn't seen any cats in the bailey or courtyard when we arrived, and I imagined my poor brothers and sisters stuck in the cattery, meowing because they hadn't eaten for days. It made me so sad, really. Given us cats couldn't eat yucky vegetables, we would be the first to die. Of course, it would be this great and mighty Bengal who would save them, and I'd make sure they remembered that for years to come.

Prefect Asinda broke the silence with a heavy sigh. Up to this point, she'd been silent. But I guess being Driar Yila's niece made her feel like she should also take part. "So, what can we do?" she asked, looking at Driar Yila with her cornflower eyes. Driar Yila took a deep breath, and she glanced up at Driar Brigel, as if she was out of options.

"I don't know," Driar Brigel said, and he scratched his massive bald head. "I'm going to be honest with you. None of us know what to do. It seems we have two options, to charge and get destroyed, or to wither under the siege. But I don't know which of those two evils is the lesser one."

"But you have me," I pointed out. "You saw me defeating those things in the visions. I shot purple tentacles out of my staff."

"Yes…" Driar Lonamm said. "But not everything the crystal shows is necessarily true in this thread of the future. You have a mind-magic staff, after all, do you not? It doesn't matter, anyway, because no magic works against those things. We've sent out volleys from the towers, cutting off the shield for very short spurts. Nothing we use can touch them. We're powerless against then."

"Actually, there is a way to defeat them." The pompous voice came from the doorway. Everyone turned towards it, clearly surprised. Because Prince Arran strolled towards us, with Captain Onus and another couple of armoured guards trailing behind.

42

AN UNWELCOME VISITOR

Arran's hands were tied at his front with what looked like some kind of silk, as if not to hurt him. He also didn't have his staff with him.

As he approached, Yila gave Captain Onus a hard stare. I also bristled as I saw Prince Arran, and I was ready to leap right out of Ange's arms and hide in a corner. Or maybe, if he provoked me enough, I might even try scratching him in the face.

"I thought we ordered him locked up?" Driar Yila said.

"You did," Captain Onus said, and he scratched his big, squashed nose. "But Prince Arran insisted he had important information for you. Information, he said, that could save the kingdom."

Yila turned her icy stare on the prince. "Explain?"

Arran scowled at her. "Might I remind you who your commander-in-chief is? Once this is over, the three of you will be court-martialled, believe you me. As well as you, Aleam."

"I think all of us are much more concerned with the matter at hand," Aleam snapped. "What do you know, Arran?"

"I know the shield won't hold forever. And I know what magic you need to defeat those creatures."

"Go on..." Driar Yila said.

Prince Arran turned towards the fireplace. I noticed then that a white staff was leaning against the marble mantlepiece. Arran's staff... He turned to look at me. I didn't particularly take to being stared at by people I didn't like, and so I growled back at him, perhaps with a little hiss in it too.

The prince didn't seem to notice. Instead, his gaze roved even further towards my staff-bearer, which floated behind me. Arran walked up to it and studied the crystal on the staff with intent.

"This crystal is glamoured," he said.

"What?" Aleam said, and he let out a faint cough. "Preposterous."

"I know glamour magic when I see it. This isn't a staff of mind magic."

"What is the point of this, Prince Arran?" Driar Brigel said.

"Yes, you are wasting a lot of time here." Driar Lonamm said.

"Didn't you see the vision in the cat's and his dragon's crystal?" Arran said. "Were any of you paying attention? The cat used dark magic against the flying creatures. He summoned purple tentacles out of his staff to bring the creatures down. These beasts are called *aeriosaurs*, by the way, and do you know how I know that? Because they're recorded in the only account of the Fifth Dimension and Sixth Dimension in the king's inventory. A book kept only for his most trusted advisors, locked deep within his treasury. It's one of his most valuable and most dangerous assets. Because these dimensions are the most dangerous of them all. Anyone who learns of either of them can release terror upon our world."

"But Ben doesn't have a dark magic staff," Driar Yila said. "I can see that."

"As I said," Arran said. "It's glamoured. And *I* would know."

Aleam scratched his chin. "We saw a vision of Astravar when the aeriosaurs were released into this world. He said that he'd explored the Fifth Dimension, and by the sounds of it, the sixth one too."

"And now the force that controls these beasts also controls Astravar," Prince Arran snapped back. "There's a reason he's more powerful than all the other warlocks. That man doesn't have a mind anymore. He has completely lost himself to the darkness, and these beasts are just like Astravar – completely controlled by the dark magic. Now, only the same dark magic can defeat him and these creatures. Nothing else will work."

"So, it's down to the cat?" Driar Yila said. "He'll have to take all those beasts out, and then he'll take out Astravar, and we must support him. Thank you, Prince Arran. Your information has been invaluable. Captain Onus, you may return him to his cell."

"No," Prince Arran said. "He shall have more support than that. Captain Onus, can you hand me my staff please?"

"Err…" Captain Onus said, and he looked askew at the members of the Council of Three in turn.

"Do it," Driar Brigel said. "We have enough of us here to overpower him if he tries something foolish. Cut his ties first, of course."

Captain Onus nodded, then took a dagger from his hip and released Prince Arran from his bonds. He turned towards the fireplace, but Arran raised a hand to stop him. "I'll get it myself. This matter must be handled delicately. I'm sure you understand."

The captain clenched a gauntleted fist by his side, but he said nothing. Meanwhile, the prince strolled over to the staff and clutched it in both of his hands. He closed his eyes and mumbled something under his breath. The crystal on his staff glowed white for a moment, and this light faded to reveal a purple crystal. "This is why the king entrusted me with this role. Because I am now the only user of dark magic still in control of my mind, and we need dark magic so that we can win."

The three members of the Council of Three studied Arran underneath furrowed eyebrows. But they said nothing. Meanwhile, Ange and Rine were looking at each other, both biting their lips. Rine sneaked a glance at Seramina, and then probably realised that he might give too much away and instead lowered his head.

It was Aleam who stepped forward, also clutching his staff. "So, you and the cat want to go in alone?"

"Of course," Arran said. "And everyone else will provide support. It is crucial that I don't die. You realise I could have defeated Astravar without the cat? That is what *I* was destined to do. We didn't need any of this debacle that involved locking me up in a room not even half fit for a prince. This could have all been over by now."

"Except there's one thing you're overlooking," Aleam said, and he raised his staff above his head. This time there came a yellow flash before Aleam broke the glamour on his staff. Now, he had a purple staff as well. "There are more of us than you realise. It's good that you chose to come out of hiding. Because this has been going on for too long."

Arran stared at the tip of Aleam's staff in astonishment. "This—"

"Seramina, Asinda," Aleam said, interrupting Arran. "I think it's time."

Seramina looked at Asinda, who nodded and reached out to hold her hand. Together, they both raised their staffs, Asinda's red, and Seramina's white like Arran's. In a single moment, and behind two bright flashes, they had broken their glamours in much the same way. Prefect Lars looked at Asinda in shock, his face blanched of colour.

The only other person in the room who seemed surprised was Arran...

"I think it will be I who leads this battle," Aleam said. "Talking of experience and all that."

Arran rubbed his brow. "This can't be... The stories say that it was your bond with Olan that completely wiped out your ability to use dark magic. You were too far gone over to the other side. The magic had consumed you – everyone in the royal palace read the reports. If you've been a warlock all along, then... Did you ever change?"

He looked around as if trying to find his guards – or at least someone he could entrust to arrest Aleam. But I also had had my staff-bearer nearby, and if Arran tried anything on Aleam, I would be the first to use my dark magic against him. I'd cover him in a sea of salmon from the North Atlantic so thick that he'd drown. Then we wouldn't need to worry about this idiot anymore. Plus, all the cats would have plenty to eat and the best food they've ever tasted at that.

Alas, I didn't need to do any of that, because Aleam had this well-handled.

"That's where you're wrong," the old man said. "It's sad that no one's been around to teach you the true history, Prince Arran, for you must be descended from a dark magic user yourself.

"Olan bonded with me because she believed she could save me from the dark magic. Then, once King Garmin saw what a dragon could do, he chose to tell the people that I'd been cleansed of dark magic. It was a lie to protect me and others who had once used dark magic in the kingdom. Given how the magic had corrupted us, the crimes we had done, the public couldn't believe there was any turning back. They wanted to see all warlocks – and all dark magic users – as monsters. For them to think I still had access to that power would have caused great civil unrest.

"But with Olan's help – what she taught me all these years ago – I learned to push the dark magic away. It became less like a curse, and more like a resource that I could call on whenever I needed, so long as I was aware how dangerous it is. It's like alteration magic – if we use it too much then we become it. I vouched I would only use it on the rarest occasions, and I'd only use it when there was no other option and I knew it was for the greater good. Dark magic – or whatever force it is that runs across all dimensions – is natural and can be used for good or evil. This is what I've been teaching Seramina and Asinda how to do all this time in private – how to respect such power. Now, it looks like I'll also need to mentor Ben."

Prince Arran's mouth had gone wide, and his face white. He twisted his staff around in his hand as he studied Aleam. Then he looked at Seramina, then at Asinda, and then at me, shaking his head as he did so. The shrieks of those aeriosaurs – as Arran had called them – punctuated the silence, and we could still hear swords clanging outside. Every so often, I heard a loud crashing sound, and a flash of light came from the window as one of the beasts tried to break the shield. I curled up in Ange's arms, appreciative of the warmth, because I knew that this comfort wouldn't last forever.

Out there, one of us could die.

"Might I suggest," Driar Brigel said. "That we work all this out after the battle. We now have those beasts we need to contend with."

"Yes," Arran said. "And yes, Aleam, you should lead this battle. But if anything happens to you, command transfers to me. Is that understood?"

"I understand," Aleam said, his head lowered.

Driar Yila stepped forward. "Captain Onus, order the buglers to call an assembly. It's time to go to war."

43

SPEECHES

The only residents of Dragonsbond Academy who didn't attend the assembly were the shield mages responsible for feeding the massive dome that protected us. The towers those shield mages stood on housed the dragons, and I could only imagine the anticipation of the great beasts. Though Salanraja was silent in my mind, I could sense her need to fight. She didn't seem scared so much but, like me, she seemed to just want to get this over with.

Once we defeated the aeriosaurs, we could vanquish the warlocks once and for all. I would shoot Astravar out of the sky, just as I was destined to do. Then, either I got to retire or perhaps someone would finally offer to open a portal for me to return home. Now, with Ta'ra, Rine, Ange, Seramina, and Aleam in my life, I would much prefer to stay here. But I still craved a life of comfort. Cats should enjoy nothing but lives of comfort.

I stood on the dais behind the three lecterns as I gazed at the mesmerising effect of the buzzing, glowing beams of ozone cast by the shield mages into the sky. Seramina and Asinda stood close to me, and my staff-bearer hovered right in front of me, holding the staff erect as if it was proud of it. For now, mine and Seramina's staffs were white, and Asinda's staff was red, all three looking like they normally did.

Prince Arran and Aleam stood at the centre of the dais, in front of the lecterns. Both men's staffs also had their glamours on them – Arran's white and Aleam's his characteristic yellow. The three Driars of the Council of Three stood just behind Aleam and Arran, as if ready to provide support if needed.

But the prince and the old man were to run the show.

On the lawn below us, stood the members of Prince Arran's Dragon Corps, the Driars behind them, then the Prefects, then the Initiates, then the support staff and guards at the back. I could smell tension everywhere, and the students murmured in funereal tones. I didn't hear anyone laughing from the crowd. Nor did I see anyone jostling their friends, or playing games, or behaving like teenage dragon riders like to behave.

Because everyone here knew what that final call of the bugle had meant. There were no pretences anymore.

"Silence!" Driar Yila's voice cut through the noise, and it hung there for a moment as the surrounding voices faded to emptiness. Driar Lonamm let out a loud cough to help still the noise, and Driar Brigel put out his hand, palm down, pressing against the air.

This gave Arran room to deliver his speech.

"The king has appointed you to—" he said. Yada, yada, yada. I just couldn't listen to that stupid, pompous voice without yawning. He might have accepted us now as dark mages who would fight alongside him. But still, he had one of the most uninspiring voices I'd ever heard. I caught snippets, of course.

"By law, everyone over the age of sixteen must fight..." Which meant everyone here, except Seramina and me, and we had to fight, anyway.

"Your deeds will be remembered and go down in history. Your names will be carved on tablets in King Garmin's hallways. Whatever the outcome today, you will go down in history as heroes." Now I was there thinking, is that what people here really wanted? If so, they were crazy. I certainly didn't get into this dragon rider business to have my name carved on a tablet. Besides, if someone scribed my name there, it would be a name that humans had chosen for me. My feline name, and the name that really mattered to me, couldn't be represented by any symbols from the human languages.

Arran then described the plan. Of course, he had to show off as he did so. As he was speaking, and without even telling anyone he was going to do so, he raised his staff and with a flash of light, erased the glamour from it. The white glow faded, to be replaced by a purple one that Arran held there for a moment.

A murmur erupted from the crowd again. Then, as if they were being pushed by a powerful ocean wave, they backed away from the dais.

"Do not be scared," Aleam called out. He raised his staff next. One moment it looked like he was about to cast his lightning magic over the entire crowd, the next he also stood with a glowing purple crystal.

Then, Seramina and Asinda raised their staffs above their heads and removed the glamours on them, and I also commanded my staff to do the same. The three of us, and my staff-bearer stepped forward, as the Council of Three parted to make way for us. We stood together, our staffs high above our heads as mumblings of terror and consternation enveloped the crowd.

"Silence!" Driar Yila called out again with her cutting voice, even louder than before. This time, it completely stunned the crowd into submission.

"Oh, for demon's sake." Prince Arran mumbled.

"At least we now have their attention," Aleam pointed out.

"We do..." Arran said softly, and then he raised his voice to address the assembly once again. "I am only choosing to reveal this to you, because dark magic is the only way to conquer the beasts called aeriosaurs that fly around this castle, as well as Astravar himself. Now, we five are your unexpected allies, as well as an army of Cat Sidhe that is approaching from the east."

More angry murmurs came from the crowd. Prince Arran turned to Aleam and shrugged his shoulders. From the side, I could see his raised eyebrows, and his expression told me he wanted Aleam to take control. Aleam smiled at Arran and gave him a conciliatory nod. Arran took a step back, and Aleam took a step forward. About time, I thought. Aleam would know what to do.

"I said, silence!" Driar Yila screamed. Her cry didn't do much this time, though. Everyone was too scared.

Arran turned to Aleam. "I've had enough. You handle this, Aleam."

Aleam let out a cough, and he raised his hand. Then, with his voice at a volume that belied his age, he continued the speech. He didn't even need to tell the crowd to shut up. His voice commanded such power that all heads eventually turned up to him. The assembly watched him in awe as if they were studying fish in a tank.

"I know you're all afraid," Aleam said. "And I don't blame you, because I would also be afraid in your shoes. But I have lived for eighty good years plus some, and all those years I've had to deal with a lot of change. I saw dark magic being used in its very infancy, and through all this time I've learned that it isn't the dark magic that's bad. It's the greed that causes people to consume and hoard until they forget the value of what they're consuming and hoarding.

"I was once a man with too much of that pride, and I wanted far more of it. Until I met Olan, my dragon, who I'm sure you all know well, and she taught me the value of humility. She is a far wiser soul than I can ever be, and she taught me that I didn't need the dark magic. So, instead I learned how to use the lightning magic that my crystal gifted me with when I bonded with Olan. Through Olan's guidance, I resisted using the dark magic that always remained available to me, and eventually the spell it had on me went away.

"All this time, the stories you've heard about me are true. King Garmin never lied about me, and I never lied either. Olan cured me during those three years I spent in the crystal mountains, learning the ways of the dragons, and at the same time learning what it truly means to be alive. She taught me how to be complete. She taught me, how to be more human.

"Remember, the warlocks were once just men and women like us. We are not fighting these warlocks – we are fighting the forces that seek to destroy us. Day by day, we fight such forces, and as we grow, we learn better to overcome them.

"So do not be afraid of us who need to use dark magic to vanquish the warlocks, because we will only do so when we absolutely have to. Also, do not be afraid of the warlocks. Be afraid instead of what might happen if we let these dark forces consume our kingdom.

"At the end of the day, it does not matter whose name is written on the tablet. What truly matters is how we fought. Because do you want to live in a world where we are scared of who we are? Such worlds spawn the type of false pride we need to be wary of.

"So go out and fight the battle you must fight. Be true to yourself and what you believe in deep inside, and we shall prevail. Because that's the grandest lesson that Olan has taught me – truth always wins in the end."

Aleam stopped speaking with his head held high, and his staff raised even higher above his head, the crystal a dull purple. Beneath him, everyone listened in deferential silence, allowing him to speak. I could see his long grey hair falling behind his shoulders, and he didn't look like stooped old Aleam from this angle. He looked like a leader. Someone you want to follow. Someone you could trust to look after your dinner while you go and do your business.

"So will you fight with us, despite our choice of magic?" he shouted.

"Yes!" the crowd roared back.

"Will you fight for your kingdom?"

"Always!"

"And will you fight for your true selves?"

"Forever!"

"Then let's go out and conquer, because this day will be remembered forever."

A roar came back from the crowd, growing in intensity as they raised their arms and chanted, "For the kingdom! For the kingdom!" I didn't like loud noises, and I wanted to shrink into a corner somewhere with my ears flattened against my head until it was over.

Soon, the dragons joined in the chorus, making this cacophony even louder. But then there came another roar of voices from the crowd, and I don't know who started it. Rine, perhaps. Yeah, it was probably Rine.

"For Ben," they said. "For Ben! For Ben! For Ben!" Because everyone here by now, even if they hadn't seen the vision, knew what I had to do.

I stepped to the front of the dais, and I stalked across the edge with the perfect grace of a cat. I could swear someone even threw rose petals over me and I basked in the adulation for as long as I could before the battle commenced.

44

AERIOSAURS

The shield mages needed to work even harder to expand the shield so that the dragons could emerge from their towers. A few of the senior dragons – namely Driar Yila's ruby dragon, Farago, Driar Lonamm's sapphire dragon, Flue, Driar Brigel's emerald dragon Plishk, and Olan – flew around the inside wall of the shield to supervise the operation. The other dragons came out of their towers in twos, and soon hundreds of dragons were arranged on the cobblestones of the bailey, ready to launch into the air.

Those that had to stay in the academy did so behind locked doors, barred tightly shut from the other side. This included the support staff, the guards, and anyone who hadn't been trained to ride a dragon. Also, many of the shield mages weren't going to come with us – even if their dragons would join the battle unmanned. These dragon riders needed to stay behind to keep up the shield. If the warlocks got into Dragonsbond Academy, then most thought we wouldn't have a chance of getting it back. The land around would become the new Darklands – the territory of the warlocks – and our enemy would continue to expand their dominion, using Dragonsbond Academy as a strategic point, until there was no non-magical life left in this kingdom.

Despite my erratic path, my staff-bearer stayed close. Whenever a dragon lurched into position, almost blocking its path, it twisted skilfully in the air as if it was a martial artist trained in the use of the quarterstaff.

"*Salanraja, where are you?*" I asked in my mind as I weaved my way between two scaly legs, each as wide as tree stumps. "*There are too many dragons. How am I meant to find you in this mess?*"

"*I thought you could navigate by smell,*" Salanraja said, her tone of voice amused.

"*I can when there aren't so many conflicting smells. But what do you expect in this heat? It's suffocating. I can't wait to get out of the shield.*"

"*Well, you'll have to wait until we're in formation. We can't hurry these things, you know. Meanwhile, navigate using your mind. You should instinctively know how to find me by now.*"

I growled. I was so tired from my adventures that I couldn't bear to do this 'navigating with my mind' stuff. It took concentration. Fortunately, I didn't need to, because I ducked around another dragon leg, almost getting trampled, and I saw Salanraja, or rather I saw her peculiar arrangement of spikes. Once upon a time, the dragons used to mock her because these spikes prevented her from bearing a saddle. Now, with her being bonded to the famous descendant of the great Asian leopard cat, they apparently all respected her.

"*Very good, Bengie,*" Salanraja said in my mind.

"*When are you going to stop calling me that?*"

"*Never. It's a fine and mighty name.*"

"*Whatever.*"

Just as I reached Salanraja's tail and was ready to leap up onto her back, I heard a meowing sound from nearby. Ta'ra had found her way towards me, and she looked at me with angry eyes. "Please don't tell me you were thinking of leaving without me, Ben," she said.

"Didn't I tell you once? It's too dangerous up there."

"You tried to tell me, yes, but I didn't listen. You need someone to keep you in check. Salanraja can't be watching your every move when she's focusing on navigating through the clouds."

"I'm bonded to Salanraja. She knows exactly what I'm thinking at any point, and she'll notice at the first sign of trouble. Our bond is designed to protect me."

"That didn't stop you doing what you did last time, Ben. I'm coming with you and that's the end of it."

I growled at her, but I couldn't be bothered arguing anymore. Salanraja didn't seem to object, either. For all I knew, it could have been my dragon's idea.

Soon, I was on Salanraja's back, and Ta'ra wasn't far behind me. "If anything happens to you," I said to her, "then I can't be held responsible."

"I'll take responsibility for my own life, thank you very much. Besides, if I'm falling through the clouds, I can always become a fairy. I have one transformation left, remember?"

"So, you take responsibility for my life, but you don't let me take responsibility for yours?"

"It's not like that," Ta'ra said.

"Really, then how is it?"

"Oh, why do you have to be so…"

"So, what?"

"So… I don't know, irascible? You've got a lot on your shoulders right now, and surely it's better to have someone to help you through this."

"Fine," I said, and I didn't have the time to object any more, because a bugle sounded, and Salanraja immediately lifted off. Once she got high enough, I could feel the shield pulling on my hair as if someone had blown up and charged a massive balloon with static electricity up there.

There were so many flying dragons, that at first it was hard to recognise my friends. But after a moment of searching, I spotted Rine sitting upon his great emerald, Ishtkar and Ange upon her sapphire, Quarl. They were flying not far from each other, gazing into each other's eyes, sharing some kind of moment. Things really were going well between them. So long as we got through this, everything was going according to plan.

I found Arran, standing upon the weirdly shiny, jet black dragon

Corralsa. No dragon I'd ever seen looked like that. I saw Shadorow with Asinda and Camillan with Lars, slowly hovering around each other in circles. Then there was Seramina aboard Shadorow, and Aleam on Olan – both of whom had their staffs clutched in their hands, their purple crystal in full view for everyone to see.

From up here, I could see the camp of the warlocks below. They had already drained the land of life, and the terrain surrounding them looked purple, windswept, and dry. They had a shield dome over their white tents, which must have been even larger than ours. A ring of Manipulators fed this shield, sending white beams into it. They stood on the outside of the camp, with bone dragons lying dormant nearby.

All manner of magical creatures waited outside the shield. I noticed the different types of golems that I'd seen outside the Caldmines Forest – except maybe around ten times the amount of them. At the back of the formation, stone golems towered so high they looked like they could knock down the walls of Dragonsbond Academy and reduce it to rubble. Clay golems morphed across the ground near the front, and in front of them too stood a line of fully formed forest golems. I had to squint to see them, but I also saw flames on the horizon – no doubt those dangerous fire golems.

One thing was for sure. If we lost that shield, then Dragonsbond Academy was doomed.

Meanwhile, the aeriosaurs plugged away at the shield. They were relentless – not seeming to injure or tire, as if they thought they could break their way in. I had a feeling they'd manage if they tried for long enough. More and more sparks lashed out of the shield, each time making almighty bangs that were even louder than fireworks. My ears were in so much pain.

We waited until all the dragons were aloft – still protected by the shield. Then, we slowly filtered outwards, facing the shield, leaving Corralsa and Olan at the centre. The bugles called out again from below.

"*This is going to be a delicate operation,*" Salanraja told me. She was flapping her wings slowly, to keep herself aloft. "*Hold on to your horses —or should I say dragon...*"

"I have no intention ever to ride a horse..." I couldn't think of anything more ridiculous.

"Must you be so literal? Now call your staff-bearer. We need you and Seramina to take out the aeriosaurs."

I did exactly what she suggested, knowing that if I didn't, the aeriosaurs would tear Salanraja and me to shreds pretty quickly. I reached out in my mind, and my staff-bearer swung forward so fast I thought it would club me off Salanraja. But it slowed just at the last moment and placed my staff gently in my mouth.

Suddenly, a different kind of sensation washed over me.

The muscles all over my body hummed, and power surged through me. I felt strong, and I felt complete. But this time, I would not let the magic consume me. I could see the aeriosaurs in slow motion, swooping by at the speed that feathers swoop when caught upon the wind. I wasn't Ben the Bengal anymore; I was a Dragoncat – a powerful mage.

The bugles cried out again, and the shield fizzled out. Salanraja charged so fast that I felt myself sliding down her back. But I was in complete control, and I quickly dug my claws into her scales to secure myself in place.

I looked over my shoulder to check Ta'ra was okay. She'd grown in size a little, and she'd secured herself by sticking one strong paw between two of Salanraja's spikes. Behind her, the shield had released a wave of dragons – everyone except Olan and Corralsa.

The shield turned back on immediately, letting only several aeriosaurs inside the perimeter. But Aleam and Arran were already there to attack them with beams of dark magic. They reduced the aeriosaurs to dust, and then they flew out towards the shield wall.

I turned back to the matter at hand. We were out into the open, and the aeriosaurs swooped in – coming at me in slow motion. Or at least that's how it appeared from my magically augmented perspective. I summoned up the energy inside me, putting all my focus into the staff. It warmed up in my mouth, and out of the crystal came thousands of tentacles. They whipped at the aeriosaurs, just as I'd seen in the vision, soon lashing across their bodies and cutting them in two like a chef chopping fruit. As each tentacle hit the enemy, the creature flashed purple and then crumbled to dust.

Meanwhile, other dragons flew around me, their riders casting all manner of spells. These hit the aeriosaurs, not seeming to scathe them, but still distracting and confusing them.

It was chaos. Yet I was completely in control, as Salanraja flew across the sky, and I eliminated anything that crossed my path. I felt all powerful – as if I could conquer anything Astravar might throw at me.

But a roar ten times louder than thunder coming from the distance brought me back to reality. I recognised that sound, and that recognition jerked me out of my trance and set a shudder down my spine. Underlying this noise came gnashes and yowls and yaps from the horizon, getting louder fast.

I saw the wargs first, charging towards the shield that would keep Dragonsbond Academy safe. But not for long, because something even more terrifying came through the sky. A dragon ten times the size of Olan, with skin like rock, rents within it leading to pools of burning magma.

I'd fought one of these creatures a while ago and sent it back to the Seventh Dimension through language alone.

But now I had no chance of controlling it. Because Astravar piloted this demon dragon, his staff in his hand. Before we could react, he flew right at Dragonsbond Academy. Then the demon dragon opened its mouth and let out a roar so powerful that through demon magic alone it destroyed the shield. This opened up the castle for the wargs to flood in, an army of golems trailing in their wake.

45

TENTACLES

I watched the demon dragon in shock as it turned away from where the shield had once been over Dragonsbond Academy. For a moment, the sky smelled less of rotten vegetable juice and more of sulphur. It smelled as if the world beneath was about to erupt, bathing the ground in magma and leaving no place left to land.

This wasn't how it was meant to be. The crystal had never shown us fighting a demon dragon in the visions. Astravar was always on top of a bone dragon and me on top of Salanraja. But then, I'd never seen Ta'ra in any of those visions of the ultimate battle either.

Beneath us, the shield mages had retreated into the towers, and the wargs hungrily stalked the bailey and the Council Courtyard, looking for prey. Fortunately, the support staff and the castle guards remained safely inside, while the shield mages had also found their way back into the towers. They would be defenceless, standing out in the open against an army of hungry, oversized wolves. If we had the dragons, we could wipe the bailey and courtyard clean, but all the dragons were up here fighting the aeriosaurs.

Arrows sailed out of the embrasures near the bottom of the towers. Some of these hit wargs, battering them down to the ground. Meanwhile, other wargs flooded towards the doorways. They took it in turns to charge at the doors with all their strength, trying to ram them to splinters as they tore at loose pieces of wood with their mighty jaws.

If we didn't do something about them soon, then Dragonsbond Academy wouldn't survive – especially after the stone and forest golems had charged in and knocked down the walls with their mighty strength. Those golems were moving slowly but surely. Meanwhile, the clay golems moved much faster, morphing along the ground in their characteristic way. Only the fire golems stayed behind as if waiting for a target to catapult their kamikaze fireballs at.

But we still had thousands of aeriosaurs to deal with up the air, and that wasn't all. The shield blinked out above the warlocks' camp, just long enough for the Manipulators and bone dragons to flood out. The bone dragons joined the swarm of aeriosaurs, sailing every which way through the sky, whilst the Manipulators fed them with magical energy from the ground.

Astravar sat atop his demon dragon as he searched the sky for a target. Waves of aeriosaurs and bone dragons wheeled close to him, blocking our own dragons from getting near him. He had his staff raised up high above his head, and the crystal on it was glowing bright purple. He seemed to spot me, and the demon dragon bucked in the air and turned towards me. I called energy to my staff, the magic coursing through my veins, my muscles thrumming as before.

"*It's show time,*" I said to Salanraja. "*Charge!*"

"*Wait,*" she replied.

"*What for? This is our moment. This'll be even bigger than winning the dragon egg-and-spoon.*"

"*Look behind you. We're a team, remember.*"

I checked over my shoulder. Ta'ra was already near the base of Salanraja's tail, staring out into the distance. Behind her, Olan, Corralsa, Hallinar, and Shadorow approached in formation, with their riders on board. They were much closer to us than the demon dragon was. Within seconds they had arranged themselves to either side of me – Arran and Asinda on one side, Aleam and Seramina on the other. Aleam put his hand on his head in salute. I raised a paw to salute back.

Then, there came another mighty roar from the sky, and Astravar was amongst us.

He charged right at me first. As the demon dragon came, it opened its great gaping mouth and let out a vortex of energy. Last time this had happened, it had almost knocked Salanraja out of the sky. But this time, I was ready for it, or at least my instinct knew what to do. My throat tasted dry, and my tongue had a slightly metallic tang on it.

I summoned energy to my staff and out came what looked like a ball of bolt lightning. This travelled through the air and met the vortex head on. Both flashed together, and the ball shrank to the size of a ping pong ball, encasing the vortex within its folds. Together, both magical spells dissipated into nothing.

Unfortunately, this didn't stop the demon dragon in its tracks. Still, it barrelled right at us, and Salanraja had to veer sharply to dive out of its way. The demon beast overshot its target and let out a mighty roar that not only would have shaken the ground, but also seemed to try to shake every single dragon out of the sky. Astravar's manic laughter pealed through the air as he turned to face us, and we turned around to face him too. It wasn't just his staff that glowed purple, but his eyes did, too. They cut through the gathering purple mist around him, which also gathered around me and the other dark mages.

I expected to hear Astravar in my mind then, or to see his face upon the clouds or something. But his golem's crystal was no longer lodged in my brain, so he couldn't control me. His demon dragon hovered a safe distance from us as his staff gained power. The crystal on it glowed brighter and brighter, the colour now verging towards white.

Our dragons fanned out around us as more aeriosaurs flooded in. I pushed power to my staff again, whipping our enemies out of the sky with another load of tentacles. They didn't just shoot out of my staff, but Aleam's, Seramina's, Asinda's, and Arran's too. I hadn't been trained to use this magic, and I guessed Seramina and Asinda had never handled such power before, either. But the magic seemed to just fill me with knowledge as if as soon as I'd picked up that staff, I'd automatically memorised an entire grimoire of spells.

Thousands of aeriosaurs got cut out of the sky. Then a good swarm of bone dragons charged in, and the magic took them out too. Bone dragons might have been invincible to normal magic, but it seemed dark magic could still destroy them. The white energy that the Manipulators fed them with meant nothing against our flashing purple tentacles.

As one bone dragon crumbled into bone dust, I saw Quarl and Ishtkar flash past. Rine shot down a bolt of ice at a Manipulator on the ground, then Ange used some vines to whip up the crystal into the air and then another tangle of vines to crush it into shards.

But I couldn't focus on the battle for too long, because Astravar's magic was now ready. He shot a red beam out from his staff, and I responded in kind by shooting a blue beam from mine.

46

BEAMS

This was the moment I'd been waiting for all this time – happening just as my crystal had foreseen. Two beams of magic meeting straight on – Astravar's red, mine blue. They fused in the middle, in a display of bright purple light, with that terrible mist gathering around it. If that light hit me, then I knew I'd die. If that light hit Astravar, then he would die.

It was a game governed by simple rules – a battle of two beams. I could swear that I'd seen something similar on television – in those cartoons the mistress' and master's son liked to watch.

But Astravar was too strong for me. I might have had a magical staff, but I wasn't practised in battling the most powerful warlock of all time. Slowly, that purple light crept towards me, and even with all the concentration in the world, I couldn't keep it away. Sweat welled from the glands in my paws, and my fur itched. I put even more mental power into it, but no matter how much I tried, the light crept ever closer. Powerful static tugged on every single strand of fur in my body, causing intense pain.

I hadn't a chance in the world. The game would soon be over, and I would die.

Fortunately, I wasn't fighting Astravar alone. After Aleam had wiped away another wave of incoming aeriosaurs, he turned Olan to face Astravar. From a pouch on his hip, he took into his hand a fist-sized crystal. It was purple, and almost as shiny as a diamond. He threw this right at the beam, and it latched on inside the magic and held in place. It hovered just in front of where the purple fusion of light crept towards me. Astravar's red beam thus split in several directions, sending out searing jets of energy into the clouds.

Aleam flew into the path of one of these jets and met it with a beam from his staff, which he directed towards the crystal. Arran flew into another beam, and he also cast some energy at the crystal from his staff. Seramina latched on to another beam and Asinda another. Once all the dragons were in place, five of us fed energy into the crystal, pushing it back towards Astravar. His expression had gone from one of arrogance to abject fear, and his face twisted as he pushed more and more magic into the spell.

Yet we continued to push the crystal back, our strength combined. Astravar might have stood a chance against any of us alone, maybe even two of us. But now the crystal gained speed, and soon it was shooting towards Astravar.

Just before it hit him, his demon dragon roared again, sounding like the crack of ten thunderbolts in unison. Astravar also bellowed out something at the top of his voice. He had such power in his lungs, probably through years of being augmented by magic. Then, there came a blinding flash of light from his staff, and the crystal shattered.

For a moment I only saw spots, and things moving in the spaces between those spots. Behind it all, more aeriosaurs flooded in, and it took all my concentration to track their motion. More tentacles whipped out around us, and we became surrounded in purple mist.

Once I could see clearly again, Astravar had vanished.

"Ben, behind you!" Ta'ra shouted out.

But she didn't need to, because soon Astravar's crazy laughter resounded from behind us, and I spun around sharply to see him on our tail. Except there wasn't one Astravar this time. There were five of him, each of them sitting on top of a demon dragon.

"Gracious demons," Salanraja said. *"He's split."*

"Is it a glamour?" I asked.

"Neither Aleam nor Arran think so... There are five Astravars. What kind of sorcery is this?"

Each version of Astravar shot out a red beam at each of us. I didn't see what the other dragons were up to before Salanraja swooped downwards, then entered a loop-the-loop. It made my stomach churn, but I tried not to let it get to me. I also I hoped Salanraja's crazy flying tactics wouldn't throw Ta'ra off her back. She wasn't as acquainted with her aerobatics as I was.

Once we reached the top of her trajectory, Salanraja corrected herself with a half barrel roll, so we were facing towards Astravar's red beam. It swept up towards us, and I immediately hit it with a beam of my own – a brilliant blue one full of dragon fire or something. The purple fusion of light danced at the centre of our two beams once again. In my peripheral vision, I could see the other beams searing through the air, met by beams from my allies' staffs. But I knew it wouldn't be wise to check to see which of them were winning.

Instead, I applied all my concentration towards that focal point where the two beams met. Not only did I need to will as much magic as possible from my staff to counter Astravar's, but I also needed to focus on this image or doppelganger or whatever it was, reading its every move so it didn't cut around my beam. It wasn't just a matter of watching it. I could feel the movements, great swings in the field of magical energy that I had to adjust to, using micro-movements in the muscles in my neck and mouth.

It was like that elaborate sport that the humans in my world called fencing. Except the length of the swords seemed to stretch out to infinity, and they were constructed from pure energy.

I'd hoped that Astravar, having split his form, would have significantly weakened his strength. Yet he seemed even stronger than before, fuelled either by rage or abject fear. Again, the white light that separated the two beams was getting ever closer to me. In a matter of seconds, it would fry me to a crisp.

I had lost...

"Ben," Ta'ra said from behind me. "I'm sorry. We don't have a choice Ben..."

"Ta'ra, what are you—"

"Don't say anything. Just remember. I love you."

"What?" But I couldn't put many more words to thought, nor did I dare turn around to see what she was talking about. Yet this soon became obvious, because a golden wisp floated out underneath the beam, heading straight at Astravar.

Whiskers, she'd used her last transformation. But I couldn't worry about it. I couldn't worry about her. I needed to focus on keeping that light away from me. I willed as much energy as I could into the staff as I clenched my jaws tight around it. My muscles hummed like I was sitting on a washing machine at the peak of its cycle. The light between mine and Astravar's staff grew so bright it almost blinded.

Meanwhile, I could see that golden glow getting ever fainter as it flew towards Astravar. The warlock didn't even seem to notice. Out of everything he was fighting today, he probably had never thought his greatest threat would be a stray fairy.

The golden glow that was Ta'ra got in front of Astravar, and she swept upwards into Astravar's beam in one swift motion that caused my heart to lurch in my chest. Whatever she did there was powerful enough to cut off Astravar's beam, and I felt my beam being released from Astravar's grasp. My magic hit Astravar in the chest.

Then, there came a flash of brilliance, accompanied by a tremendous bang. A bright golden flare filled the sky. As the light faded, it left behind a glowing cloud – also golden. From it, I noticed a tiny golden flake fluttering towards the ground, shimmering in a thin beam of sunlight that had just emerged from the clouds.

I saw everything else in slow motion. Astravar had completely vanished. No sign of him or the demon dragon was to be seen. Instead, around the golden glow, four fist-sized obsidian-coloured crystals seemed to hover in the air, as if someone had thrown them straight up and they'd just reached their apex. Meanwhile, a stone golem had just rammed its fist through the West Tower of Dragonsbond Academy.

Time seemed to return to normal as simultaneously the four crystals and the rubble from the top of the tower plummeted to the ground.

47

VANQUISHED

I didn't know what to feel. One moment Astravar had been there on his demon dragon, and then both had vanished into whiskers knows what dimension. One moment, Ta'ra had been sitting behind me, providing that 'support' that she'd said she'd provide. Then she'd exploded into a golden flash of light.

She had been lying to me all along. She hadn't come along to support me at all. She'd known this was going to happen. Everyone must have discussed this when I'd been asleep.

She couldn't be dead, could she? Somehow, I doubted she could have downed both Astravar and a demon dragon with whatever fairy magic she used and survived.

Had one of the crystals shown her something that I didn't know? Had this been part of the plan? My dark magic – everything I had fought for all this time – was always going to end like this. No matter how much I tried, I couldn't convince myself otherwise.

Whiskers, I felt like such a fool.

But it didn't matter anyway, because Ta'ra was gone…

Even the last golden flake that I assumed was once part of fairy Ta'ra had vanished from the sky. There was no trace of her left to be seen. It felt so cold now, up here against the icy wind. As we flew, more and more purple mist developed around us – and it now seemed to be becoming part of the clouds.

We were still losing. The six warlocks stood safely behind their shield, watching from afar, not even having to cast any magic. Despite Astravar having been defeated, those infernal aeriosaurs still flocked around us. They seemed to come in from all directions at once, and I felt rage surge to me whenever any of them got close. Out of my staff came great flashes of purple light, creating a display like fireworks that would have made the humans back home proud.

The Manipulators below floated across the purple land, feeding more bone dragons with energy. From there, great crashing sounds seemed to split the clouds apart. Stone tumbled down from the towers that had once been vast. They fell like that game my mistress and master liked to play when they invited friends around – the one where you only needed to remove a single block, and everything would collapse. More wargs came from behind the warlocks' shield in the meantime – filling up the courtyard now like water fills up a dammed lake. Meanwhile, the fire golems launched themselves at the high towers. They hit their targets bathing the parapets in flame. In time, those fires would roast the people and cats inside and force them out into the open. They didn't stand a chance.

Above it all, the sky was filled with the shrieks and cries of beasts, and no matter how we tried, our enemy wouldn't let us anywhere near Dragonsbond Academy to save them from their fate.

Now, Ta'ra was dead, and soon we all would die.

"Come on, Bengie," Salanraja said. "Pull yourself together."

She said this just as more aeriosaurs flooded in, and I let out my rage at them, whipping them out of the sky with my magic.

"It's okay for you to say. You haven't lost your..." My voice trailed off inside my mind. What *had* Ta'ra been to me? Really, I didn't want to think about that now.

"It's hard, I know," Salanraja said. "I've lost loved ones in my life too. But dwell later. Now, you need to fight."

She swooped down underneath a bone dragon coming from her tail, and I shot out a beam of energy at the Manipulator that fed energy into it, sending its crystal spinning across the ground. Salanraja caught up with the bone dragon and flamed it to bonemeal as it shrieked out its dying call.

I watched it wither underneath Salanraja's searing flame, and I stopped feeling the will to fight. It didn't matter anymore. I'd done my duty here. I'd defeated Astravar, and I'd fulfilled my destiny, just as my crystal had foreseen it. I didn't want to live through to see the end of all of this. I just couldn't…

I called my staff-bearer onwards in my mind, ready to return my staff. I wanted no more to do it. I wanted to die a cat, not a dark mage. Hovering several metres away, it clenched a fist at me, but I gave it a mental nudge to tell it that it didn't have a choice. It pushed forward, slowly, just as Salanraja dived out of its way.

"Knock it off, Bengie," she said. "*More aeriosaurs inbound.*"

I couldn't stop myself. The will to destroy was too strong. More tentacles whipped out, disintegrating the vile beasts into purple dust. One moment there were thousands; then there were none.

But I didn't want such power anymore. So, my jaw went slack, and the staff fell out of it and spun towards the ground.

"Bengie," Salanraja said. "*You moron! Stop this. We cannot lose.*"

She went after the staff, the staff-bearer charging alongside her. She accelerated at such a pace that she got underneath the staff. She tossed it upwards with her head, and the staff-bearer caught it in a tight grip. Olan, Corralsa, Hallinar, and Shadorow meanwhile streaked across the sky in random motions, as the four allied dark mages knocked more aeriosaurs out of the sky.

Nevertheless, we wouldn't stand a chance against those golems. Around us, everyone looked beaten. The dragons' wings beat slower than normal, and the riders atop them swung their staffs with far less vigour. Meanwhile Dragonsbond Academy was crumbling like Welsh cheese – it was beginning to look like that ruined castle I liked to explore on the hill in South Wales. It wouldn't be long until the wargs flooded into the corridors and tore the place apart.

I stared out at the clouds, at the ever-thickening purple mist, as I remembered that flash of light – Ta'ra sacrificing herself, but for what? But then, a voice came in my head. Her own words. "I love you, Ben," she'd said. As I remembered, I felt a little strength surge up in me. I turned towards to my staff-bearer, reconsidering…

Suddenly, a call of bugles came out from Dragonsbond Academy. The dragons responded with an almighty roar, and the dragon riders cheered out a triumphant cry that for a moment silenced the shrieks of any aeriosaurs or bone dragons left in the sky.

"Gracious demons," Salanraja said. *"Take hold of your staff now, Ben, and fight. Our reinforcements have arrived."*

"What? Who?"

She didn't need to answer that, because coming from the east I saw a massive gathering dust mound. A yellow and a royal blue dragon came out of the clouds, with presumably Bellari and Reslin mounted on top of them. Next came the Cat Sidhe – giant beasts charging with purpose, as if they knew about the death of their beloved leader.

But they weren't the only reinforcements, because from the north came the sound of thousands of whickering horses and trampling hooves. The great white horses that emerged seemed to shimmer with a radiant glow, as if each of them had burning stars inside their hearts that pumped light through their veins. Mages in white cloaks with white staffs rode on top of these – and by white, I mean both the crystal and staff shone like glowing diamonds. But what seemed most unusual, as the horses came closer, was that each of them had a horn on its head.

"What the whiskers are they?" I asked Salanraja, forgetting the whole situation with Ta'ra for a moment.

"*King Garmin's White Mages,*" Salanraja said. "*Help at last has come.*"

"No, I mean the horses. Why do they have massive horns on their heads?"

"*Because they're magical. They're called unicorns… I can't believe you don't know that. They are to the White Mages what dragons are to dragon riders.*"

"How weird…"

"*More aeriosaurs inbound, Bengie.*"

I didn't hesitate to call my staff back to me. The new arrival had seeded an inkling of hope that was quickly growing in power. As I summoned more tentacles, using my staff, I put all my will into the fight. I fought for my owners back in South Wales that had looked after me. I fought for Aleam, and Seramina, and Rine, and Ange, all of whom had the kindness to guide me through this world, despite its prejudices. I fought for all the dragon riders, and the kingdom, and most of all, I fought for Ta'ra, because she'd almost certainly wanted me to live.

After I'd lashed those beasts down, no more remained in the sky. There were no more bone dragons, either. I could see now, with the vast numbers of Cat Sidhe and unicorns and White Mages that cascaded across the fields, the warlocks didn't stand a chance.

More creatures came from behind these unicorns. Magnificent birds as big as dragons, with massive beaks and their huge wings which were covered in fire. Wispy looking dragons that soared through the sky – their bodies so long that they almost looked like serpents and their bodies seeming to be formed of clouds. And chimera – an entire regiment of them. This time, fortunately, they weren't demon chimera, but valiant looking creatures, with impressive manes that waved in the wind as they charged.

Some wargs had, in the meantime, ripped open the double doors of the Dragonsbond Academy keep, and it looked like they were about to flood inside. But out charged a large charcoal dragon, blocking the wargs' path. I recognised the rider – Prefect Calin, who carried a sword in one hand and a glowing yellow staff in the other. That meant the charging dragon must have been his injured dragon, Galludo.

We had won; I realised that now. The warlocks also seemed to realise it, because the warlocks' shield went down and out of it six birds emerged into the sky. I couldn't see what type of birds they were from here, but they all looked like birds of prey, or some kind of carrion eaters at least. They retreated towards the purple mist that still lingered on the horizon – back towards the Darklands, where the warlocks belonged.

48

TRANSFORMATION

After we'd defeated the last of the wargs and golems, I asked Salanraja to deposit me down on the ground. I didn't want to face anyone yet, nor did I want to return to Dragonsbond Academy. I needed to find her – or at least I needed to try. Whether she had fallen as a Cat Sidhe or fairy, I needed to at least see her with my own eyes. Otherwise, I'd never be able to believe.

Salanraja deposited me by a massive husk of smouldering rock on the ground. It smelled of sulphur, and after a brief inspection, I saw the great teeth and the closed stone eyelid. This had been the demon dragon – the invincible creature that we could never defeat. Yet we had.

Some purple clouds remained in the sky, but they slowly dissipated, and the sun's rays filtered through them, making everything look magical. Dandelion seeds and motes of dust danced around, and sometimes with the way they reflected the light, I could almost imagine them to be fairies. Perhaps Ta'ra waltzed amongst them. But who was I kidding?

My staff-bearer hovered nearby. It moved in front of me, and bowed with its staff, as if wanting to offer sympathy. But it just reminded me of the version of Ta'ra in the ghost realm who had led me to the staff. I didn't want to remember her in that form.

"Just go away," I said, and I willed as much with my mind. To my surprise, the staff-bearer immediately vanished. I didn't need to have it follow me around, I realised. It was a ghost, after all. I could summon it when needed, and then command it to hide when not.

Two more dragons came down from the sky and landed close to me. They were Ishtkar and Quarl. Rine and Ange hopped off their mounts, and Rine stepped towards Ange, looking at her with intent. But Ange turned her head and saw me.

I turned away.

"Rine, wait," Ange said. "Just a moment." I heard her scuffle towards me through the long, dry grass. Then she reached down and stroked me on the neck. I flinched, and I backed away. I really didn't want to be comforted now.

"Wait, Ben," Ange said. "Where's Ta'ra? She went up with you, didn't she?"

I growled deeply. "Gone... She killed Astravar, and she..." I couldn't finish it. I just didn't want to say it. Not until I saw it.

"Are you sure?"

"I'm going to find her. I need to know..."

Ange nodded. Rine walked up behind her, looking kind of pleased with himself. But his expression fell when he turned to Ange, and he noticed her concerned expression. Tears had welled at the bottom of her eyes as if she was about to cry. If only I could cry like she could. Humans often told me it made them feel so much better.

I turned, and I searched for her scent. She smelled so often of lavender as a cat, because of those weird baths she used to take. Still there was that lingering miasma of rotten vegetable juice, but this was fading with each minute, and instead, many distinct aromas of pollen floated upon the breeze.

It wasn't the scent of lavender that I latched on to first, but a flash of white. It seemed as if one of the sun's rays coming down through the sky had focused on it – a beam highlighting where I was meant to go. I rushed towards it, as the clouds broke even more, letting an even thicker beam onto this target. It filled the land with warmth, pushing the last vestiges of purple mist away.

Then, I caught the scent of lavender, and once I found it, I scouted her out pretty fast. She lay in the grass, tinier than I ever remembered her. She was so small that I had to push away blades of grass with my nose to see her in full.

She had dark skin and straight raven hair whisked up like foamy water around her cheeks. Her dress was pure white and short enough to accentuate her slender thighs and calves. Her eyes were still green, but behind them, there wasn't any life left them. I couldn't bear to look at them, and so I tried to close her eyelids with my nose. But she was far too small, and they seemed so delicate I thought I might damage them. So, I decided to leave them alone.

The sunlight coming down from the sky seemed to be getting warmer – almost searing, in fact. It felt as if the sun was concentrating its energy on this one spot. But it had to be an illusion, surely. I'd been freezing cold up there, which is why down here the sun felt unnaturally warm.

I took one last look at Ta'ra, sad I'd not seen her in cat form. Then I turned away. I didn't want to go to Rine and Ange. I didn't want to go to Salanraja, or Dragonsbond Academy, for that matter. I turned towards the purple mist, wanting nothing but a good long walk.

It was as if the magic happened when I wasn't looking. As if the sun filled her with new life, healing her as might one of Aleam's cures. Her voice came from behind me, stopping me in my tracks for a moment. "You know, I always heard it said that cats have nine lives."

It was Ta'ra's voice. It couldn't have been anything else. Yet I had to be hallucinating, surely. I was hearing what I wanted to hear. I growled and continued on my way.

"For whisker's sake, Ben, look at me when I'm talking to you."

I wasn't going to listen to the delusions. So, I didn't turn around.

"Dearie me. Must I do everything myself?" A scuffling sound came from behind me, and I knew it to be Ta'ra before she even bounded in front of me. I stopped, and I looked at her, and I blinked the dust out of my eyes.

It couldn't be, surely. "Ta'ra... How?"

"I don't know," Ta'ra said, examining herself. "I thought I was using my last transformation, but I guess my last was always going to be turning back into a cat. I must have still had that one last life left." She cocked her head. "It makes sense, right?"

"No..." I really wasn't sure it did. It didn't matter, I guess, because either this was all a dream, or I was experiencing a miracle. I didn't know what else to say. I was just so happy to see her. I sprung up to her and rubbed my nose against hers.

"Oh, Ben, you..." She lowered herself on her haunches and pounced. She landed over me, and we played swiping at each other – without claws of course – tumbling over each other. Being the stronger and greater of the species, I ended up on top of her.

Ange's voice floated over from the other side of the meadow. "Look Rine... It's Ta'ra. She survived. Will you look at that?"

I looked up, purring, as the familiar smell of Ta'ra's breath washed over me. Ange had a wide smile on her face, and Rine's eyes seemed to glisten in the light. Then, as if to celebrate, he took hold of Ange's hand – exactly as I'd told him to do so, all this time.

EPILOGUE

Respect is why the warlocks had chosen me to sign the treaty. That is why I came to the palace today.

I stood in the king's throne room. King Garmin sat on the throne a safe distance away from I, the revered Lasinta. It didn't matter, anyway. I'd left my staff behind to come here, and they'd searched me from wrinkled head to toe for any rogue crystals.

The king wore his celebratory red silk robe. Over his well-groomed blonde hair sat a diamond crown that I would one day knock off his head and claim as my own. But that would take time, because the only way to gain respect is through unerring patience. I had lived many years, and I had many more to come.

That was Astravar's undoing – he didn't have that patience and he certainly didn't have that respect. He'd tried to take over the world alone, rather than attempting to commandeer the service of loyal allies and subjects. Which was why we warlocks had watched him fly to his fate from our safehold in our protective shield as he foolishly tried to change the tides of destiny.

We'd waited, happily. Then we'd retreated, happily. It was all a part of the plan.

The king had two guards posted by the doors to the throne room and two guards posted by his throne, each of them wielding halberds that rested on their shoulder nearest to the door or throne. The only other person in the room was the king's trusted nephew – Prince Arran – commander of their Dragon Corps. I knew him well, and he knew me well, but no one else in the palace knew that. He was just one of many in my web of influence.

Of course, everyone in this palace knows my name – Lasinta, the great condor, the queen of the skies, the warlock who the other five remaining look up to the most. Age is a great asset, you see. It's one of the most powerful catalysts for respect. That's why I never tell anyone my true age, not just because I don't want them to take advantage, but because none of them would believe me.

A cooling draught filtered through the palace, coming from the open windows and gently caressing the red curtains. The sun shone through one window, but not a speck of dust was to be seen dancing in its rays. Marble arches spanned across either side of the throne room, adding to the cooling effect, much appreciated on this warm spring day.

In front of me stood a reading lectern with a leather-bound black book placed on it. Right now, it was closed, and the title shone out at me in gilt letters. "Treaty between the Warlocks and the Kingdom of Illumine." Next to this lay a spoon containing sealing wax and a lit candle in a holder.

Once my seal was placed, there would be a time of peace between the kingdoms. A time for the king's people to feel a sense of security. A time for us warlocks to weave through the kingdom, recruiting allies, plotting our way to usurp the throne.

Astravar never understood this, you see. Treaties and times of peace can be incredibly useful things.

I flicked through the pages of the book, every one of them crisp, the ink neatly pressed into them. I scanned the text for any warning signs, but the king wouldn't be foolish enough to include laws that we would likely break. I found the last page of the book, and I ran my

EPILOGUE

finger over the king's seal – the unicorn and dragon imprinted in the puddle of dried wax.

I took the ring from my finger. I also took hold of the spoon and rested it over the candle. An aroma of fresh pine and cinnamon wafted upwards from the sealing wax – all a part of the ceremony handed down across ages of kings.

Once ready, I dripped the hot wax from the spoon, and I printed my seal, leaving an impression of a condor in mid-flight, its broad wings stretched out from tip to tip. I raised my head and spoke to the king.

"It is done," I said.

He nodded but said nothing. Too much blood had been shed in the names of the warlocks, and I would never gain his respect. But I did have the respect of Prince Arran, who stepped forward with his two hands wrapped around a scroll. "Here is the deed of treaty. You can sign it when you return home."

"Thank you, Prince Arran," I said out loud for everyone to hear, and I studied his grey eyes to check that his respect was still there, and that it hadn't dwindled - because if it had we might need to send an assassin in the night.

It was there, all right. He lowered his head and spoke under his breath so that only I could hear. "No, thank you, Grandmother. We shall all be together, eventually."

"That we shall," I whispered as I took the deed out of his hand. Then, without another word, I turned on my heel and strode out of the throne room, my work here complete.

Once outside, I ignored the guards staring at me and transformed into a condor underneath a plume of glorious purple smoke. I sailed over the fields – the lands that were part of the Kingdom of Illumine. Farmers in those fields would gaze up in the sky and watch in awe at the great condor, the largest bird in the realm. That was how it should be, because one day Illumine would be mine.

It was only a matter of patience, because I had all the time in the world.

THE END

But not forever. Ben will be back for more adventures in a new trilogy coming soon...

AFTERWORD

If you liked the Dragoncat trilogy, you might enjoy the Secicao Blight series, also by Chris Behrsin.

You can get the first three books in the series in a boxset edition called Dragonseers and Airships for a reduced price on Amazon.

ACKNOWLEDGMENTS

Well, it's been a journey, but now the first Dragoncat trilogy is complete. It's been said many times, but it's well worth repeating – no book is written alone.

Many have helped with this book and the others in this series to come to fruition, and I would like to extend my gratitude to everyone who has helped me every step of the way.

In particular, I'd like to thank my editor Wayne M. Scace, for his patient and thorough editing work. I'd also like to thank Carol Brandon for providing extra proofreading and editing. Both of you helped immensely, not just in getting rid of the typos, but also in identifying the plot holes in what proved to be a tricky exercise in world-building.

I'd also like to thank my friends and family, particularly to my parents and my brother and sister for their continuing support during my career.

I wish I could say thank you also to all the cats who helped inspire this book – some of them still amongst us, some of them long passed. This includes my old childhood friends, Raffles and Mitzi, Lion who saw me through my stay in Vietnam, Raffy and Taffy, my brother's cross-bred Savannah cats, and also the cats of the Alhambra – I'll write a story about you one day.

I'd also like to give a special thank you to my wife Ola. Thank you for sticking with me through the whole process, and all the hard work that you've put in to getting this work as good as it can be.

Also thank you to everyone on my ARC team, for all the feedback and support you've given me through this series and my other books.

Last but not least, thank you to all readers of my works. I appreciate everything that you do for indie authors.

ABOUT THE AUTHOR

When Chris Behrsin isn't out exploring the world, he's behind a keyboard writing tales of dragons and magical lands. He was born into the genre through a steady diet of Terry Pratchett. His fiction fuses a love for fantasy and whimsical plots with philosophy and voyages into the worlds of dreams.

 facebook.com/chrisbehrsin
 twitter.com/chrisbehrsin
 instagram.com/chrisbehrsin